# Five Questions

# Five Questions

## KITTY BURNS FLOREY

For information address iPublish.com, 135 West 50th Street, New York, NY 10020.

An AOL Time Warner Company

ISBN 0-7595-5020-4

First edition: July 2001

Visit our Web site at www.iPublish.com

# Acknowledgments

My thanks to:

Mary Alice Kier and Anna Cottle, agents from heaven with the patience of saints; Ron Savage, for all our after-dinner talks; Katherine Florey, for her witty insights; Jude Balsamo, for inspiration and support; Karen Kleinerman, for her brilliant e-mails; and Bob Flavell, for the fish.

# Prologue

Please?"

We are sitting on the roof terrace on a September evening. The roses are in full bloom, and beyond them, over the river, the sky is aflame: vermilion, peach, fuschia, livid pink.

"Well?"

I can't answer yet.

"Please? As a favor to me?"

"Does the world really need another memoir?"

"It's not for the world." There is a long pause, then, finally: "It's for me. Because I want to understand. I want answers. Why you were who you were. Why you did what you did."

I can't stop looking west. I can't resist these sunsets, no matter how many I see, how many I have painted. Each one is different. The pinks blaze against deep blue; the Hudson gleams pewter with jolts of silver. Across the river, the lights begin to blink on.

"Or think of it this way. It's for posterity."

I turn away from the view then. Our eyes meet, and we look

steadily at each other. Far below us, a car alarm goes off and halts midscream. "Okay."

"You'll do it?"

"I'll do it."

"You will?"

"I will."

I don't say that the prospect of writing it all down both terrifies and excites me. Like flying over the ocean. Like an empty canvas. Like childbirth.

"Promise?"

I look out over the river. The sky is already different, darkness overtaking the highest shreds of cloud.

"Promise?"

Fasten the seat belt. Pick up the brush. Breathe deeply.

"Yes. I promise."

# *Question One*

# Who Were You Then?

Oddly, when I look back on that time, the Edna Quinlan Home is the first thing I see—not my own face, or Suzanne's, or even my mother's with its disappointed frown, but the melancholy brick house on Beacon Street. I still dream about that place. I was there less than four months, but in those dreams it's vivid, solid, stored securely in my memory all these years. I'm going up the stone steps and through the ponderous door into the hall (warped mirror, scuffed bench, tangle of galoshes), I'm climbing the wide oak staircase to the second floor, I'm opening the last door on the left, the one with what looks like the mark of a hatchet blade dug deeply into the wood. . . .

My room contained two lumpy beds with stained greenish bedspreads that roughly matched the faded drapes. The two windows looked out on the backyard. I arrived in late December, and by April I was gone, so all I ever saw out those windows was snow, a wire fence, the back wall of the market around the corner, the peeling clapboards of the garage next door—a winter scene as relentlessly gray and white and black as one of my mother's photographs but, except for a few mornings of slanting sunlight after a snowfall, much less pleasing to the eye.

There were twelve of us. I roomed with Suzanne Lombard from Vermont. She was just my age, with a round face and long black hair, and she was enormous.

"They think it's twins," she said. She told me that the day I met her, and her eyes were perfectly expressionless. A week later, when we had become friends, she said it again, and this time she broke down and sobbed. "Twins!" she said. "Twins! It's so *special* to have twins! What am I doing, giving them away? I must be crazy! Oh God, I don't know what to do!"

I loved Suzanne because she said what was in my mind, and she listened to me. The fact that I was carrying a real live individual in my big belly—the most important thing about being pregnant, it seemed to me—was something I hadn't been able to discuss with anyone else, not with my friend Marietta, not with the social worker—and especially not with my mother. The staff at Edna Quinlan concentrated mainly on our day-to-day health; my mother on life after pregnancy.

When I met Suzanne, she was seven months along, and tormented by the kicking of her twins. We both slept badly. Once in our beds, we would turn out the light and whisper. We speculated about what our babies would look like. We shared what we knew about adoption, pro and con. We talked about how we felt when we found out we were pregnant, about the babies' fathers, about what we hoped for someday when we would become mothers for real. Sometimes we cried together, and sometimes we would reach across the space between our two beds and grip each other's hands, but there was no comfort for us.

Suzanne had brought with her a copy of a book containing photographs of the fetus at different stages. Such things were discouraged at the Edna Quinlan Home, where pregnancy was treated like a bad case of flu, something to be gotten over. But Suzanne and I studied the pictures compulsively, furtively, as if they were pornography. I was terrified by those wet, serene fetuses with their huge closed eyes, their fingers spread, their vague sex organs. They were so horribly real. They made me profoundly miserable. And yet I looked at them all the time.

Suzanne was gone by the end of February. She began having labor pains in the middle of dinner one night, and toward midnight they took her to the hospital in a blizzard. We weren't allowed to visit each other, and I didn't see her again until she came back to Edna Quinlan to get her things. Her mother was with her, a nervously smiling woman in a hurry. Suzanne's big stomach had disappeared, but she looked puffy and unhealthy.

"How was it?" I asked her.

That blank look was in her eyes. "How the hell do you think it was?" she asked. "It was exactly how I thought it would be, only worse."

Her mother, from across the room, said, "Suzanne."

"I heard it really was twins."

"Boys," she said. Her voice was belligerent. "Two boys. Identical."

I put a hand on her arm. "Suze—"

She turned away. "I've got to pack and get out of here," she said.

Time crawled by those last two months. The Edna Quinlan Home worked hard at keeping us busy: That had been one of its attractions for my mother. "They don't give you time to mope," she had said. This wasn't true, of course. I could always find time; I could mope anywhere. But Miss Parnell, the impatient, disappointed-looking woman who ran the place, posted a formidable schedule of activities on the bulletin board every week. We did school assignments. We went to art classes and learned to use a sewing machine. We listened to lectures on birth control and did exercises so we'd get our figures back. We learned the Lamaze method. We took field trips to museums and walked the Boston Freedom Trail in stared-at groups of six. We helped with the cooking, and after dinner at night we played Twenty Questions and watched our allotted two hours of television. Sometimes we were shown educational movies on Australian aborigines or the Nova Scotia fishing industry.

In between, and during, and afterward, and lying in bed at night, I moped. We all moped. There were times when the stench of misery at the Edna Quinlan Home was as inescapable as the pine-scented air freshener in the bathrooms.

After Suzanne, my new roommate was a silent black girl named Darcy who would sit in bed in her underwear making tiny slits in her arms with a razor blade, then pressing a tissue to the cuts until the blood stopped, staring dreamily into space and rocking back and forth. The first time she did it I stared at her in horror, but all she said to me was, "Don't tell."

I had no intention of telling, but I tried to talk to Darcy—not about her cuts but about anything: the weather, sewing class. I missed Suzanne desperately, and I needed a friend, and Darcy, God knows, obviously needed something. But she was locked in her own world, and after lights out I lay awake alone, listening to Darcy's asthmatic breathing, feeling the baby kick, getting up every couple of hours to empty my bladder. I spent long hours alone in my room with the fetus book—Suzanne had left it behind—looking at the pictures, or staring out the window at the dirty snow, or reading long novels about other troubles than my own.

I went into labor on a Sunday night in April. I was in my room, reading *War and Peace*. I was at the part where Natasha goes to the ball in her white muslin dress with the pink ribbons—her first long dress—and dances the mazurka with Denisov.

My due date was a week away, and I was exhausted, morose, sick to death of my monstrous belly. Natasha, to my relief, refused Denisov's proposal of marriage, but said she hoped they could still be friends. I had just reached the end of Book One when the first stab came: a knife in my stomach, then a rush of such panic that I almost cried out, though not from pain. And along with the panic, what I can only call exhilaration: It was true then, this was what it was about, this sharp urgency was what my body had been heading toward.

I put down my book and lay back on the bed, sweating, my heart racing. We had been instructed to get Miss Parnell or the assistant matron, Mrs. Glover, the minute we felt a twinge. *Sometimes these things happen fast, girls,* they said, *and we are not equipped for emergencies.* It always seemed to me that it was *babies* they weren't equipped for: pregnancy, yes, but its logical product was outside their scope.

For a while I did nothing. Perversely, I wanted to keep it to myself. I didn't want to face Miss Parnell's cold efficiency or Mrs. Glover with her saccharine concern. Long minutes went by, half an hour, an hour. From downstairs, I could hear the noise of the TV. The phone rang. Someone laughed; then a voice was raised in anger. Everything was unreal but the pains. I waited for each one impatiently, my hands trembling. After a few minutes: yes, again, the knife, exactly like what a shallow cut must feel like, I thought, the thrust of a blade—worse than a cramp, keener, more immediate. Then gone, completely, as if I'd dreamed it. I thought of Natasha, that foolish girl. I wondered what would happen to her in Book Two, and then the pain returned again, and again, at long intervals that I realized eventually were getting shorter. I tried to breathe deeply, as I had been taught in childbirth classes. I tried to keep track of the intervals. The pains were every five minutes, then three. I lost track. The knife went in deeper, and I screamed.

Lucy, from next door, stuck her head in. "Wynn? What?"

"Lucy! Help me! Get someone!" I was crying, ashamed of myself. In that instant, everything was gone—exhilaration, dignity, even the pain itself. All that was left was fear. I stood up, and the knife struck again, and my water broke.

Miss Parnell called an ambulance. She had no sympathy for me. "I told you not to wait until the last minute," she kept saying, tapping her foot angrily while I sat doubled over on the bench in the hallway, bundled into my coat, shivering with terror, the pains coming fast. When we finally heard the siren and I was hustled out, the girls drew back and didn't say a word to me, as if I were contagious. In the narrow shelter of the ambulance it was better. "Don't cry now," the paramedic kept saying. He put his hand on my shoulder, smoothed back my hair. The siren wailed. "You're going to be okay. We can deliver that baby right here if we need to, don't worry about a thing." I swallowed a Demerol, and things got hazy. They must have wheeled me directly into the delivery room—the night air was frigid, I do remember that, vaguely: the cold like distant music—and the next thing I knew was a headache and my mother.

She was sitting by my bed in the recovery room, and tears were running down her cheeks. "It was a girl," she said. She turned away and hid her face in a wad of tissues. "She looks exactly like you looked. Exactly."

• • •

I wouldn't have been at the Edna Quinlan Home if it hadn't been for a party at Deirdre Coyle's house. Her parties were famous. I had never been to one. Deirdre and I, to say the least, moved in different circles at Dunster High. But my friend Marietta was going, and she asked me to come along, and so I went. I can look back now and see how absurd it was, and yet somehow inevitable. All the clichés of adolescence in the sixties were in place: oversexed teenagers, pint bottles of cheap booze, the humid air of a July night, the irresistible beat of the music we loved. It was all so commonplace. It changed my life forever.

But I suppose the story doesn't really begin there. There were sixteen years before that party at Deirdre's, before I became an inmate at Edna Quinlan, and when I look back on them now, it seems as if everything, every event, every noon and morning, every birthday and milestone and decision, led up to that July night and what came after it.

I'll start over. My name is Wynn Tynan. My father, James, was New England Yankee and Italian; my mother, Molly, was Irish and Welsh. Wynn was her maiden name. I was an only child, long awaited. Before me, there had been two miscarriages. As long as I knew her, even when she was an old woman, my mother still became quiet and depressed twice a year on their anniversaries. It was my father who explained this to me, on a morning when I came downstairs to find my mother sitting at the kitchen table in tears. I had never seen her cry before—my strong-willed, dignified mother. I'm not sure I was aware that grown-ups *could* cry. It shocked me, and I started to cry myself.

My mother raised her head and said one word: "James." My father scooped me up and took me out to the back steps. Jo-Jo the cat came with us and rubbed his head on my bare knees. My father was a reticent man, awkward with words, and a long moment passed before he could think what to say. I sat beside him, afraid to speak, my fingers in Jo-Jo's fur, wondering if the world had come to an end.

"You should have had two older brothers," he said at last. I stared up at him. I was perhaps six. He put his arm around me. "But they died before they were born."

I had only recently begun to understand what it meant to die, and so the tears ran down my cheeks. But the grief I felt for these dead brothers was tinged with a kind of thrill: they died before they were born. It sounded like a riddle—*How can you die before you're born?*—and I wondered if maybe the answer to the riddle was that they would somehow get another chance. I thought about having two older brothers, like Marietta did.

"What are their names?"

My father frowned down at me. His brown eyes were melancholy; his whole face drooped. I could see the long furrows in his cheeks, the three level lines across his forehead. "*Were,*" he said gently. "Kevin and Jeremy. Those *were* their names, Wynn."

There was a long silence. It was summer: Both my mother's miscarriages had happened in hot weather. I can remember Jo-Jo's burning fur, the exuberant pole beans climbing their wooden supports, my father's large warm presence, and then my mother, bright-eyed, in the doorway behind us. "Who'd like some blueberry pancakes for breakfast?" And the quick, reprieved joy in my father's face.

• • •

I grew up in the town of West Dunster, in southern Maine, about thirty miles from Portland. The town was tiny, an adjunct of the more bustling town of Dunster where my friends and I went to school. West Dunster lay tucked in a hollow between two low hills like a jewel held in a cupped palm. The hill to the west, rather grandly known as Burbank Mountain, was dense with fir trees. We could see it from our kitchen window: arrows of black rising up against the sky. The other hill was crowned with a house that everyone called the Castle—a vast stone pile belonging to the Erlings, of the Erling Paper Mills.

We lived on Brewster Road at the very edge of the town, in a drafty farmhouse with a small barn out back where my father had his workshop. Everything was tidy and tended; my parents believed in beauty—they were nutty on the subject—and their concept of beauty demanded rigorous neatness. They were exacting about it, as if they were Shakers. The grass was always mown, the front walk swept, the leaves raked, the bushes pruned. The Maine weather was hard on perfectionists. Every few years, my father had to repaint the house and the barn: the barn a dusky red, the house a deep forest green trimmed in white. These were unvarying, but my mother changed the color of our front door from time to time: turquoise, crimson, screaming yellow—whatever took her fancy. (I remember a short-lived shocking pink that I particularly loved.) My little bedroom at the end of the hall was painted stark white, and decorated only with art posters my parents chose from museum catalogs; I grew up under the eyes of Van Gogh's postman and Renoir's jolly boating party. My father constructed my high-backed, high-sided bed from tiger maple, and on it was a crazy quilt my mother stitched one winter out of random scraps of my old blouses and overalls and pajamas: a history of my life that kept me warm at night. I made up my bed neatly every morning, first thing when I awoke: one of the inflexible rules my mother laid down, and something I did well into adulthood without even thinking about it.

My father was a gentle, inward man—a carpenter who scraped out a meager living remodeling people's kitchens, occasionally making a piece of furniture or a wooden toy. Both my parents were determined bohemians who believed in supporting themselves by doing what they loved and would have considered steady jobs a curse. I was only vaguely aware of how hard up we were, but I recall intense discussions about whether it would be cheaper to put up our own vegetables for the winter or to buy frozen ones, and the crisis when my father's truck needed a new transmission and he had to ask my Uncle Henry for a loan.

Then, when I was ten, the toys my father had always made for fun, as presents for me, and that he sometimes sold at a shop in our small Maine town, were suddenly discovered—featured in magazines, sought out by stores in Portland and Boston and New York. Those beautifully simple wooden boats and cars and rocking horses, with their bright-painted wheels and knobs and pegs, that began to be made later in the sixties by woodworkers all over New England: my father's were the first of them. A sign went up on our barn—West Dunster Toy Works—and we became, rather suddenly, prosperous. Neither of my parents had a head for business, so we were never wealthy, but the anguished financial discussions came to an end. We actually paid someone to paint the barn, my father bought a bright red Ford pickup, and my mother acquired not only the 5 x 7 Rolleiflex she had been craving but a new Nikon with all the gadgets.

My mother was a photographer. She produced artful black-and-white images for Haskell Graphics, a small Boston card company, driving all over Maine in her ancient Volkswagen Beetle—gone for two or three days at a time while my father and I tried to pretend we didn't absurdly, desperately miss her—looking for what she always called "pretty pitchers," returning home with stories of terrible back roads, a flock of wild turkeys, a motel keeper who was a dead ringer for Norman Bates. She refused to take her work seriously. The truth was she had started out as a painter, and she had failed. I can barely remember her paintings—mostly quiet watercolor still lifes, I think. She didn't talk about them, but I was aware that she had destroyed everything after a show at a gallery in Portland that had been a disaster in some way I was never clear about. What I remember is that her determined cheerfulness was dimmed for a while, and that one night I was shocked from sleep by what sounded like hysterical laughter from my parents' bedroom down the hall, but which, as I listened in puzzlement, I recognized as sobbing.

But it was not like either of my parents to give in to disappointment. I don't think my mother ever got over the wreck of her artistic ambitions, but she set herself briskly to the task of becoming a photographer, and her photographs were extraordinary. *Pretty* is the wrong word for them: they were stern, witty, elegant, controlled—a lot like my mother herself. When she began, we probably just plain needed the money: photography paid, painting didn't. In the end, I know she grew to love what she did, though it was hard to get her to admit it.

I grew up living with those two artists, my father working in maple and birch, my mother in silver nitrate and acetate. How could I help but become an artist myself? I was to be a *real* artist—a painter. Not a Sunday painter, not an illustrator, not a teacher or someone who painted just for fun, but a serious professional who was represented by a good gallery, whose work was collected and bought by museums, who was given solo shows and retrospectives. My parents looked at me—at seven, at twelve, certainly at sixteen—and that was what they saw.

• • •

When I surfaced again, I was still in the recovery room, and my mother was still there. She was smiling; her eyes weren't even red. Had I dreamed her tears? "You came through beautifully, Wynn," she said, squeezing my hand. "You'll be up and about in no time." She kissed my cheek. "I'll be back in an hour. I'm going down to get some coffee."

"What time is it?"

"Just after sunrise," she said. "A beautiful, sunny morning."

I was wheeled into the private room my parents had paid for. My head pounded. I sucked down a glass of ginger ale through a straw, and took aspirin. A nurse came in and gave me a sponge bath and helped me put on my nightgown—a new, pretty one my mother had brought for me. I realized I was bleeding, hooked up to thick sanitary napkins. I had had stitches, and they hurt. When the nurse helped me out of bed and to the bathroom, I cried from the pain. "You're all right, honey," she said. "This too will pass."

The effort of emptying my bladder wore me out, and I dozed off again. When I awoke my mother was back, and there was breakfast on a tray. I ate a bite of cold toast, took a sip of tea. My mother bustled around the room, doing God knows what. I saw a pile of magazines, a vase of white roses.

"How's the food?"

"I don't want it," I said, and my mother obligingly pushed the tray out of the way.

"How are you feeling?" she patted my arm. "Still a little dopey? It will wear off. You'll be back to normal by morning. I've brought you some reading matter, and tomorrow I'll bring you some real food. How would that be?"

"Great."

"You should be able to leave the day after tomorrow, or the day after that. Depending. They'll want you to get out of bed tomorrow, walk around. That will help you feel better, too—more like yourself."

She chattered on. I didn't listen. I had never been in a hospital before. Lying in the metal bed, drugged and achy, with the blood leaking from between my legs, was even more disorienting than being pregnant. I had wanted to experience it—*something*—and all I could remember clearly was Natasha and that awful Denisov, then the quick knife in my gut. The rest was a far-off dream: the ambulance, the cold air, the anesthesiologist making me count backwards from twenty, the bright lights. I lay there dozing, waking up to my mother's hovering presence, the chatter of voices in the hall, the occasional pinging of a bell, the loose skin of my belly under the new nightgown. Where was it all? What had happened? Who was I?

• • •

Thinking back now on my childhood, I can see how strange it was—how what I took for granted was in reality very unusual, the kind of upbringing that's usually given to athletes or dancers. With me, it was art. Art was what my I did, talked, breathed, dreamed. It was what was expected of me: I would win the contests, get the prizes, go away some day to a good art school, become famous. The space behind the kitchen at our house, an airy sunroom, was officially designated my studio—mine to do with whatever I liked, as long as I kept the place neat and organized. "You are an artist, Wynn," became my parents' mantra, beginning when I was very young. "And an artist can't work in chaos." It took me years to learn that chaos can be the artist's oxygen.

I'm not sure how my parents would have coped with a child who didn't spend long hours absorbed at her easel. What of Kevin and Jeremy, I wondered when I got older: what if either or both of those phantom brothers had loved only biology, or been color-blind, or thought putting colors on canvas was a silly waste of time? It was a question I never thought to ask my parents. And I had another one: Which came first, my talent or their hopes? I won an art contest when I was five: The local drugstore presented me with a ten-dollar bill and a box of chocolates for the best drawing of a Christmas tree in the five-to-eight age group. I still have a finger painting of our cat Snarly dating from soon after my third birthday that perfectly captures his odd little face and oversize ears—obviously a fluke, but there's no denying it's a fresh and funny image, one of the few of my own creations that I've kept through the years. I can imagine my father seeing it, projecting a proud future for me, and my mother sensing that she had produced a true artist, one who would succeed where she had failed.

• • •

My mother supplied me with light reading matter while I was at Edna Quinlan—in case the classes and activities and long gloomy novels didn't quite do the trick. She would bring me murder mysteries, and *The New Yorker* and *Glamour*, a magazine she normally disapproved of as frivolous but now thought would do me good. "Life after pregnancy!" she said—her theme song—opening it to a picture of a hollow-stomached girl in a bikini. Or she'd hold up a *New Yorker* cartoon. "That's a good one, isn't it?" she'd ask, peering at me hopefully. If she got me to laugh, it made her day. I knew this, and so I tried to laugh as little as possible. It wasn't difficult.

She had a gift for providing me with exactly the wrong thing. Once, she brought a folder of paintings by Millet—at the time my favorite artist—and, from behind her back, presented them to me as if they were a magic charm. "I know how much you love these," she said, her eyes shining. "So I went over to the museum and found this for you." Then she set the folder on my lap, smiling her wise-mother smile. I looked down at it dumbly, not touching it. Her smile faded only slightly. "I think you'll enjoy looking at it later," she said. "If you should get bored."

When she was gone, I opened the folder, and the paintings leapt out at me. At first they gave me comfort, those badly reproduced but still powerful images of noble French peasants idealized in golden fields. They were so familiar, so beloved. But the longer I looked at them, the worse I felt. Life wasn't noble, or simple. The paintings made me think of my childhood, a bygone world that seemed as distant as the world in the Millets, when happiness was as natural to me as my frizzy hair.

I had discovered Millet in the days when my mother and I used to drive to Boston, and she would drop me off at the museum—the only place she considered safe—while she did business with Haskell Graphics on Marlborough Street. I remember how long those afternoons seemed, how I would wander around the museum in a fog, overwhelmed at first, confused, bored, before I found the Millet room and settled on a bench in the middle as if I'd reached home at the end of a journey. I would look at the paintings, drinking in the gentle light, the muted colors, the emotion. I couldn't have explained why I liked those little landscapes, the peasants in the fields bending to their work, and why I sat there at times in a state of barely suppressed excitement. To me, those work-roughened faces were beautiful, like the faces of people I knew. They were company. Then my mother would pick me up, and on the way home I'd describe to her what I had seen. This was a ritual, part of my relentless artistic education: *What did you like and why did you like it? What were the colors? Describe to me what it looked like.*

There in the Edna Quinlan Home, in another part of Boston, in another world, those innocent little paintings of honest country people were a joke. I leafed through them once, until sadness overwhelmed me, and then I put them away.

• • •

My parents were in their mid-forties by the time I was born. I know I was spoiled—they even admitted it, with a kind of pride: *Our spoiled only child,* they called me with a smile. But my mother always added that I wasn't "spoiled rotten," a subtle distinction that apparently meant I wasn't a hopeless brat. All my life people have told me I'm like my mother, Molly Tynan, not only in looks but in manner. I know I inherited her coloring, her triangular face, her pouty lips and stubborn chin and her wild mop of dark, frizzy hair. I know our voices and our laughs were eerily similar; people were always telling us that. As for the rest of it, even after all these years, I can't really judge. Certainly, parts of my mother live on in me—maybe not the best parts. Isn't our whole life an attempt to find out who we are? And in the end doesn't the self that emerges often turn out to be all too familiar? Aside from her formidable chic, her fashionably toned body, my friend Marietta in middle age is a recognizable version of her mother, right down to her contempt for politics and her forthright laugh and her melodramatic way of sneezing.

Marietta had been my best friend since we were toddlers. She and her family lived down the road in a rambling ranch house full of children, dogs, a ne'er-do-well uncle, and what I saw as devilish, fascinating untidiness. At my house, Marietta and I would sit together reading on the long modern sofa my father had built, feet to feet, with the sweet, docile cats curled up on our laps. Or we'd head for my father's workshop and build imaginary villages out of scrap wood and shavings. He always listened to a classical music station from Boston, whistling along softly through his teeth as he worked. He taught us, patiently, to play chess and to use the lathe. My mother would bring us just-baked cookies and mugs of cocoa.

At Marietta's we fought over Barbies with her sisters Carrie and Pat, listened to tales of Uncle Al's buddies at the unemployment office, gobbled down potato chips and Oreos and endless pitchers of Kool-Aid, played softball in the scruffy backyard, wrestled with their mutts Bruno and Bessie. Marietta's father taught math at the high school, and he graded papers at the kitchen table, yelling at us from time to time to shut the hell up so he could hear himself think. Her mother was a skinny, red-haired dynamo, opinionated, intrusive, full of jokes, unrattled by the demands of five children. A household more different from mine was hard to imagine, and yet I was at their house almost as often as I was home, and my parents and Marietta's were old friends.

From the time I was eleven or twelve, I had adored Marietta's older brother David. He was a tall, serious boy, freckled and red-haired like all the Donnellys—and, to me, devastatingly handsome. For a while, the summer I was fifteen and he was seventeen, he used to take me to movies and afterwards, in the front seat of his old Valiant, he taught me how to French kiss. In the fall, he went away to the state college, and it was abruptly over. I wrote him long reckless letters that he wisely didn't answer. By Thanksgiving I heard he had a new girlfriend. My heart was officially broken, though I think what I minded most was the end of the cozy fantasies I had spun with Marietta, of being sisters-in-law, of our children being cousins, of living on the same street forever and ever.

I loved West Dunster. Despite the fact that, eventually, I thought only of escaping it, part of me, even now, is really content only when I'm in Maine, in the midst of those vast pine forests and the endless frigid winters. The place is in my blood, like it or not. But from the time I was little, the biggest treat in my life was to be taken to a city, any city, but if possible to New York, where my only surviving grandparent, my father's mother, lived in Greenwich Village. I adored New York, revered it, thrilled to the color, the glitter, the noisy uncertainty of the crowded streets. It had everything our Maine town lacked.

We never stayed in hotels, of course; we squeezed in with my grandmother at her tiny apartment on Cornelia Street. Her name was Anna Rosario Tynan, and I called her Anna Rosa. She had been widowed for many years; I never knew my Grandfather Tynan, who had married Anna Rosario, a smart young immigrant girl working as a tailor at a shop in Portland, where he was carrying on the family hardware business. My grandmother must have been an exotic addition to the stolid, old–New England Tynan family, bringing not only homemade gnocchi and a tomato sauce that started with beef knuckles roasting in the oven, but a wild, gutsy glamour. I saw pictures of her when she was young—short and plump and pretty, vivid in a picture hat and a coat with a fox collar, or in a sundress holding my Uncle Henry on one hip, my father on the other, her head thrown back in laughter. There's one great shot of her wearing a low-cut gypsy blouse standing beside my gaunt, bearded grandfather against the backdrop of Tynan & Sons hardware store on Main Street. She looks like someone who has been cut out and pasted in.

When her husband died and her sons were grown, Anna Rosa surprised everyone by moving to New York, where, until her eyes began to fail, she supported herself again as a tailor—she loved the work—for a shop on the Upper East Side. She used to make dresses for me when I was small, beautifully smocked, silky things that in rural Maine I had no occasion to wear. My mother folded them away in white tissue paper in a dresser in the attic. I used to beg to be allowed to put them on, and once or twice my mother let me dress up in one so she could take my picture: a little barefoot princess—barefoot because I had no shoes that matched the elegance of those dresses. Then they went back into the drawer, while I sulked and, one horrible afternoon, threw myself down on the attic floor in a full-fledged tantrum that my parents still talked about with awe when I was in my teens.

It was a tight fit for all of us at Anna Rosa's apartment, but I would have been as upset as my grandmother if we had stayed at a hotel. Incredibly—she was well into her seventies—she lived in a fourth-floor walk-up. Her back windows looked out on the garden of a restaurant around the corner on Bleecker Street. She liked the romance of that: she used to take me out with her to sit on the fire escape where we could gaze down on the red umbrellas and white tables while the laughter and chatter of the diners floated up to us. There was a dry cleaner on the first floor, and the steamy smell of perchlorethylene used to make its way upstairs, especially in the summer. I can't pass a dry cleaner now without a vivid memory of my grandmother's firmly permanented gray hair, her closet with its bright dresses, her tiny refrigerator crammed with food.

When we visited, my parents slept on the pull-out sofa in the living room. I slept with Anna Rosa in her lumpy iron bed, and she would talk to me until I fell asleep—rambling, half-whispered tales of her girlhood in Naples, her life back in Maine, her job at the tailor shop. She had a gentleman friend named Roy, a shy, pudgy, retired butcher with a thin gray mustache, who lived on the third floor. He had a passion for musicals, and when Anna Rosa and I sat on the fire escape we could hear his hi-fi downstairs playing *Oklahoma!* and *Guys and Dolls*. For my fifth birthday, he treated us all to a matinee of *My Fair Lady*. Sometimes he took us to dinner; he always wanted to go to the restaurant around the corner, the one with the garden, but Anna Rosa refused to eat there: She said it would spoil it.

We spent nearly every Christmas in New York, and always went uptown on the subway to High Mass at St. Patrick's Cathedral, where the color and the lights, the incense, the Latin, and the choir all exhilarated me. Once I became so excited it made me ill. I turned green and broke out in a cold sweat; my grandmother saw it coming and, for some reason, grabbed her handbag and held it open: I threw up directly into it, an event that Anna Rosa recalled for years afterward with helpless laughter.

When I was seven my parents took me for the first time to the Museum of Modern Art. I vaguely recall my first sight of those big strange Picassos and some of the more tender Impressionists, but what I remember most clearly was eating ice cream in the café afterward while my parents quizzed me about what I had liked best. I liked the gift shop best, with its racks of postcards, though I knew enough not to tell them that. I said "Mondrian," the first painter that came into my head, and basked in their approving astonishment. When I finished my ice cream we walked up Fifth Avenue to Central Park; I remember holding both their hands while they talked about the hawks that lived in the park. I even recall what I was wearing: pink-and-blue striped tights, a short red skirt, and my white fur earmuffs. That day lingers in my memory, but there were plenty of others like it: My parents had a gift for happiness.

Many years later, in London, I told this to a friend, and she raised an eyebrow. "For whose happiness, Wynn?"—one of those casual remarks that opens up a whole new world, or closes up an old one.

So I will say as a child that I found happiness in my parents' satisfaction with their lives—that for years, until the longing for my own happiness became unbearable, I subsisted on theirs.

• • •

Marietta and I weren't the type to go to Deirdre's loud, wild, drunken parties—the kind of parties where the police were sometimes called to break things up. Our own parties were quiet, dark, pot-smoking affairs, with Dave Van Ronk and Jack Elliott on the stereo, where people got into intense, indignant discussions about the war. We called movies *films*. We thought Paul was a drip, adored John. Bob Dylan could do no wrong. We would rather have died than go to a football game. Our crowd was arty, hippie, peacenik—a small but not insignificant slice of the student population. We were the ones who played guitar, who wrote poetry, who dressed like gypsies and wore our hair long and marched in antiwar demonstrations carrying candles.

I was a founder and editor of *Dead Duck: A Journal of the Arts*. Deirdre Coyle was a cheerleader. I suppose that pretty much sums it up.

I had no real desire to go to Deirdre's party. But Marietta was in love with a football player named Spencer Lewis, and she wanted to see him. "I just want him to *notice* me, damn it!" Her jaw was set; her green eyes blazed with determination and lust. "Just *look* at me, that's all. I'm not even saying he's got to dance with me. Just tell me he likes my earrings or something. *Anything*." Her face softened. "I'm pathetic—right? Going after that jock playboy animal. Like I've really got a chance."

"You've got a chance," I said loyally. "Remember I told you how he was staring at you that time in geometry class."

She feasted on such crumbs. We all did. Our sparse romantic lives were mosaics of such tiny triumphs: a glance, a few words, a smile, a rumor. Marietta pleaded with me to go to the party with her for moral support. It was a hot, boring Saturday night, and I had nothing else to do, so I went.

Deirdre lived in Dunster. Marietta and I got a ride to the party with the Hausers—Terri and Neil—stocky blond twins who lived near us. Neil drove. He was already a bit drunk, sipping from a quart-size beer bottle in a paper bag. "Deirdre's folks are in Europe," Terri said as we pulled up to the Coyles' front door. "This party could go on for a *week*!"

Marietta had had her hair cut: a mistake. She usually wore it long and loose, but now it was hacked into a jagged, severe cut that made her pretty face look too thin. She caught sight of herself in a mirror in the front hall and let out a little scream. "I look horrible! Horrible! I look scalped!" She was right; I didn't know what to say, except that it would grow out. Small consolation. Marietta took one last, despairing look and announced, "I'm going to get shitfaced. It's all I can do. If Spencer paid any attention to me, he'd have to be nuts."

It was a discouragingly underpopulated party. Deirdre barely spoke to us; she was in black bell bottoms and a tank top, her hair was teased into a beehive, and she was visibly unhappy. She kept making phone calls, frantically trying to get more people to come over. "This party is *dead*," I heard her say into the phone. "It's full of *losers*." As the evening went on, everyone began to get very drunk, especially Marietta, who swallowed enough rum and Coke to remove all her inhibitions. She kicked off her sandals and retied her gauzy white blouse high under her breasts. Her hair became tousled and lost its prim, gamine look. She danced alone in the middle of the floor—all tight jeans and bare midriff—and everyone watched her. Spencer Lewis came in just then with his friend Mark Erling. Marietta went up to Spencer and asked him to dance, and they did what passed for dancing at a drunken party: rocked slowly together in a dark corner, his cheek against her hair, her arms around his neck. "Goin' Out of My Head" was on the stereo. "Light My Fire." "Never My Love." "A Whiter Shade of Pale." I danced with Neil. I danced with a boy I hardly knew named John Hannigan, who held me much too close and kept trying to slide his hand under my T-shirt. I danced with Neil again. Finally I escaped upstairs to one of the bedrooms and shared a joint with Janet Luther and Chuckie Garrone, who were in my American history class. Then I fell asleep for a while.

When I went back downstairs, it wasn't very late—not even midnight—but the party was breaking up. Deirdre was sitting cross-legged on the kitchen floor, drinking whiskey from a bottle. Marietta hung on Spencer, who was holding her up. John Hannigan leaned against the wall as if he might fall down without it. Mark Erling stood by, looking uncomfortable, jingling his car keys in his pocket.

"Who's driving you guys home?" Mark asked me.

"Terri and Neil, I guess."

"Well, Terri just left with Chuck, and Neil went home half an hour ago."

After a lot of conversation, it was finally decided that Mark would drive Spencer and John Hannigan and Marietta and me home. Deirdre looked up briefly as we left. She had combed out her hair, and it hung on her shoulders, lifeless and ratty. "Hey," she said. "It's been real. Stay loose, guys."

"Yeah, right," Mark said. He didn't seem thrilled about chauffeuring everyone, but we piled into his car anyway—a baby-blue Oldsmobile Cutlass convertible. I was just sober enough to refuse to get in the backseat with John and his roving hands. So Marietta and

Spencer and John got in back—Marietta flopped across Spencer's lap in a stupor—and Mark and I sat in front. We drove down Main Street in a comfortable haze of music and alcohol and heat. The radio played Dylan, Judy Collins, Simon and Garfunkel; hesitantly, Mark and I softly sang along. He reached across to the glove compartment, took out a pint bottle of vodka, and offered it to me.

We dropped John off in town, and then headed out Route 8 to West Dunster. Marietta and Spencer were very quiet in the backseat. When I turned to look at them, I saw that they had recovered enough to be frantically necking; when I looked again a minute later, Marietta was asleep, her mouth slack, her blouse undone, Spencer's arm around her.

Mark and I passed the vodka back and forth. I had never talked to Mark Erling before. He was the rich kid who lived in the big ugly stone castle on the hill. I was dimly aware that he played some sport—basketball?—and wasn't exactly a dedicated student. He was widely believed to do drugs more serious than pot and acid. I knew he had once gotten into a fight with George Fisher, a boy in the class ahead of ours, and George had ended up in the hospital. That was the extent of my knowledge of Mark Erling, except that he was tall and good-looking in a movie-star kind of way, with lots of wavy blond hair he was always brushing out of his face. I can't say that, aside from his bland gorgeousness, he impressed me much. And I was quite sure he had never noticed me before.

"Not much of a party," he said.

"Where was everybody?"

Mark shrugged. "Deirdre's parties are getting kind of lame." He glanced over at me, his hair whipping back in the breeze. The side-burns that grew down his cheeks looked soft, pleasantly furry. "I haven't seen you around much."

"I try to keep a low profile," I said. This amused him. He passed the bottle, and then he put his arm across the back of the seat, and I slid closer. Before I knew it, I was snuggled against his shoulder, and when we stopped at a red light he leaned down and kissed me.

We pulled up in front of Marietta's house, and I got out and made her sit up in the backseat. I buttoned her blouse and shook her until she opened her eyes. Spencer woke up briefly; he and Marietta exchanged a long kiss. Then Mark and I helped Marietta up the front walk. She was humming to herself and smiling. Her sister Pat came to the door in a nightgown with a Dunster High T-shirt over it, her hair up in rollers. "Oh Christ," Pat said. "She's fried."

Gladly, we turned Marietta over to Pat and went back to the car. Spencer lived half a mile down the road in a housing development; we dropped him off and watched him weave unsteadily to his door. A light went on in an upstairs room. Then Mark turned to me and smiled. "What time do you have to be home?"

I shrugged. "It doesn't really matter."

This was a lie; I had a one o'clock curfew. But I can remember, all these years later, the odd mood of recklessness I was in, how the vodka had pushed me over some edge into that agreeable state where I was still functioning normally but everything was different, heightened. I didn't care if I got home late, angered my parents, did something stupid. I liked kissing Mark. I liked being a girl who rode around in a convertible with her hair flying, singing along with the radio.

Mark pulled away from the curb and said, "Let's go down to the lake."

I hesitated demurely. "Well, just for a little while."

Mark pulled me over to him again. "Half an hour." He winked. "Just long enough to see the submarine races." Ha ha.

Osmar Lake was big, clear, cold—beautiful on a summer day, romantic on a summer night. Mark parked in the lot, and we went down to the beach. He tossed the empty vodka bottle far out into the water, then took my hand, and we walked along on the pebbled sand. I can still see the shiny-black water, with the moonlight spilling across it and vibrating on the moving surface. I remember the moon, and the lake, and something else: the way desire rose up between us, desire as solid and inescapable as the beach under our feet. We didn't even get as far as the woods before Mark stopped, pulled me close, and began kissing me again.

He was a good kisser, and he was handsome in the moonlight. And he was sweet. I had never expected to even like Mark Erling; if anyone had asked me, I would have insisted scornfully that he wasn't my type. And there I was kissing him with more passion than I'd ever felt with David Donnelly. And then I was lying down on the sand with him. My clothes came off and were bunched up beneath us—my long purple skirt, my blue tie-dyed T-shirt—and he was on top of me, and—well, et cetera.

I was sixteen. A virgin. Drunk, on a soft summer night in 1968. Stung, maybe, by Deirdre's scorn. And in love, for that half hour, with Mark Erling. I decided I'd been a virgin long enough. It hurt, too, but I didn't care. By the time he collapsed on me with a groan, I had almost started to enjoy what he was doing, or at least to have a sense that it might, in some other circumstances, be enjoyable. Then he kissed me, whispered my name, helped me to my feet, hugged me against him. "You were great, baby," he whispered. "You were fantastic."

I believed it. I put my clothes back on and we drove to my house. "I'll call you," he said at the door, and kissed me again. I believed that, too. I went inside and opened the refrigerator and drank half a quart of orange juice straight from the carton. Then I leaned my head against the cold white porcelain. There was sand in my shoes, sand between my legs, down my neck, in my hair. I felt dizzy, elated, drunk as a skunk. I wanted to call Marietta and tell her what I'd done, tell her what a great guy Mark was, and how come we'd never known him better, and just because a person lived for sports and got C's in English and drove a big glitzy car, it didn't mean he wasn't a nice person.

What I did do, though, was go upstairs to my room, trying not to stumble into walls. My parents were sitting up in bed reading.

"Congratulations on getting home at a decent hour," my father said as I went by their door.

"How was the party?" my mother asked.

I didn't stop. "Fine," I said, trying to sound normal. "But I'm exhausted, I'm going straight to bed."

Unbelievably, the clock on my bookcase said it was only ten minutes to one. Hours and hours seemed to have passed since Mark and I got out of the car at the beach. I stood in front of the mirror with my eyes closed. *July seventh, 1968,* I said in a whisper. I opened my eyes and looked. My hair, of course, was beyond description. Otherwise I looked no different on the seventh than I had on the sixth. And yet everything was transformed.

I dragged myself into the bathroom and wiped the blood off my thighs and washed out my underpants, then crawled into bed and was out until noon the next day when Marietta called to compare hangovers.

I had thought, vaguely, if I had thought anything, that it was a safe time for me. But I knew within a couple of weeks of Deirdre's party that I was pregnant. During that time, everything had clarified itself perfectly. Mark Erling and I were not in love with each other. He wasn't going to call me. I didn't want him to call me. We'd gotten drunk and done it. I'd thrown away my virginity with some guy I barely knew. And then I didn't get my period. I was as regular as moonrise, and on the fifteenth nothing happened. Or the sixteenth. Or the twentieth. Or the thirtieth.

On the last day of July, I went to a doctor in Dunster for a pregnancy test, and on the fifth of August I got the results. I called Mark that evening when my parents were out. He had his own listing in the phone book, under his father's name. My hands were shaking as I dialed.

"Erling here," he said when he picked up.

"Mark, this is Wynn."

He paused for only a split second before he said, "Wynn! Hey! I've been meaning to call you. How are you, anyway? What have you been up to?"

It was worse than I expected: the insincerity, the absolute cool. *Erling here.* Oh God. "I'm pregnant," I said.

"Come on," he said with a little laugh. "You're kidding."

"No. I'm pregnant."

There was a pause. Then, to my horror, I heard Mark Erling begin to cry. "Oh Jesus," he said. "Oh Jesus fucking Christ."

I lay awake all night, weeping, shaking, trying to think it through in a sensible way. It was a hot night, but I was chilled, and I pulled the old, soft quilt up around my neck. I thought about abortion. It was the era of coat hangers, desperate jumps down flights of stairs, scalding baths, strange chemical concoctions, evil doctors who would butcher you and leave you for dead. A girl from our school had gone to Puerto Rico for an abortion, and I had defended her to David Donnelly, who called her an unnatural monster. I knew I could find out where to go, whom to see. There was a notorious Dr. Finster in Boston, expensive but supposed to be trustworthy. There was a Penobscot Indian woman in Portland who accomplished things with herbs.

But I rejected the idea, surprising myself. I didn't know why I couldn't do it, I just couldn't. I considered the ludicrous scenario of marrying Mark and moving into the Castle, the two of us starting junior year wearing wedding rings. I thought seriously about running away, taking the bus to New York, where the baby and I would live with Anna Rosa; it would grow up eating gnocchi and cannoli, I would wheel it in a stroller around the Village, I would get a job waitressing at the Café Figaro. . . .

I tossed and turned until the sun came up. A baby was growing inside me, its cells multiplying and dividing even as I lay there, even as I cried and shivered and huddled under my quilt. There was no way I could stop that life from continuing. I didn't know what to do. But I was pretty sure my own life was over.

Later that morning, I broke it to my parents. My father sat in silence, looking down at his hands. My mother raked her fingers through her hair and asked me how, *how*, I could have been so stupid. She didn't seem to require an answer. She fished around in her pocket for a tissue and blew her nose and groaned, "Oh God, oh God."

We were out in the barn, in my father's workshop. Suddenly it seemed to me a paradise, that big, bright, wood-smelling room. It held so many of the blissful hours of my childhood. The floor was scattered with wood shavings, dusty sunlight beamed through the window, the cats were entwined on a chair. I looked at these things instead of at my parents: the elements of a paradise that was now lost.

"This boy," someone said. My father, I think.

"He's no one," I said quickly. "I mean—it was an accident. We didn't—" I stopped and burst into tears, something I swore I would not do. "I hardly know him," I said. "He's just a boy from school that I got drunk with at Deirdre's party."

"Oh God, Wynn," my mother groaned again. My father turned away. It was inconceivable that this conversation was actually taking place at our house. My mother stowed her tissue back in her pocket and looked at me, shaking her head. I wanted to turn and walk out of there, go back to the house and pack a bag and thumb a ride to somewhere, anywhere. My mother had never looked at me in quite that way before, and my only thought was to escape it.

I did nothing, of course. I stood there crying quietly, absorbing my mother's disappointment, my father's appalled silence. Finally, my mother said, "Well, we could probably find a doctor."

My father raised his head.

"No," I said.

I could see the relief in my mother's eyes—I knew she was thinking about my two lost brothers—but my father said, "Then—Molly—Wynn—what on earth—?"

We both looked at him. In his faded blue overalls, he was picturesquely handsome, like the lovable, fatherly carpenter in a children's book, but the look on his face was both impatient and frightened. I knew he wanted only for it all to go away, to be left in peace in his sunny workshop. I remembered the day I first got my period, when my mother had sent me out there to tell my father. "He'll want to know," she insisted. After I blurted it out, he stared at me and blushed, and for a moment I thought he might cry. He shook my hand and said, formally, "Congratulations, my dear," as if I had won a spelling bee, and then, slowly, the awkwardness left him, a smile spread across his face, and he said, "Well, I'll be damned, Wynn. I'll be damned," and we both stood there and laughed.

Now he looked at my mother, and she said, "I'll figure something out, James."

My father's face unknotted a little. He stood up and patted my back. "Right," he said. "Okay, then. Don't worry, Wynn. About anything. It's not the end of the world."

I didn't want to contradict him. I nodded, trying to smile, and my mother and I went back to the house and left him to his work.

I could sense her wheels spinning already. My mother's way of coping with disasters was always to take action and get things under control—maybe it was to keep herself too busy to think, but I believe also that in some way she almost enjoyed this kind of dilemma, she liked calling on her creativity, she saw it as a challenge. She spent two days making phone calls. We were having a heat wave, and I sat for long hours in the tub staring at the pattern on the shower curtain, using the toes on my left foot to let in more cold water, the toes on my right to open and close the drain. I looked down at my reasonably flat stomach, my small breasts. By Thanksgiving, I would be fat and ugly, with swollen ankles and morning sickness. At school, everyone would either hate me or pity me. I could imagine the gossip. *Did you hear about Wynn Tynan? She got knocked up. That whore. What an idiot. How could anyone be so stupid?* My own mother had said it.

Late in the afternoon of the second day she called me to come downstairs. She was sitting by the kitchen phone, frowning, drumming her fingernails on the table. When I came in, she looked up and said, "I've found a place you can go."

"What do you mean?" I don't think I'd realized until then that I would be going anywhere.

"It's the Edna Quinlan Home for Girls," she said, reading from a piece of paper. Her voice was neutral. "It's in Boston. They have an opening. It's nondenominational, which believe me is not that easy to find. It sounds like a decent place." She smiled unhappily. "The woman I spoke to says they keep the girls nice and busy. I guess that's good."

"Um—I don't really understand." I felt my face getting hot. For a moment, I thought she was talking about a reform school. "You mean, this is a place where—?"

My mother's voice was brisk. "You go there, you have the baby, and they find some nice people to adopt it."

"Oh." The baby. There would be a baby. Of course. I knew that. There would be a person, a human being, a little Kevin or Jeremy who would be adopted by nice people.

"There's really no other choice," my mother said.

She clicked her pen and made another note, then sat back and looked at me with satisfaction, her slight smile still in place. Suddenly I hated my mother's efficiency, her competence. I was a problem, the baby was a problem, the problems were solved, that was that.

"I can't believe this is happening to me," I burst out. "Why are you treating me this way? Like I'm some kind of inconvenient object that has to be moved around!"

My mother never answered this kind of outburst. Her smile retreated; she sighed heavily. Then she stood up and went to the stove, put on a kettle of water, got out her old brown teapot and the tin of Darjeeling. I watched this ritual with resentment and disbelief. My life was over; my mother made tea. I wanted to smash the venerable brown pot, dump the tea on the floor.

"This is all so unreal," I said. "I don't want any tea! I want you to listen to me. I can't do this!"

My mother came across the room and stood in front of me. Her eyes were cold. "What do you mean, you can't do this?"

"I mean that I can't! I don't want to do it this way."

"How do you want to do it?"

"I don't know. I haven't had a chance to think."

"You're not being reasonable."

"I don't want to be reasonable! I want you to listen to me!"

I couldn't get up and leave the room. I would have had to push past her, and in that moment I hated my mother absolutely: If I touched her I knew I would strike out at her. I stared straight ahead, at the waistband of her old denim skirt, the buckle of the worn leather belt she'd had for as long as I could remember. Why couldn't she wear a cheap, colorful polyester sundress once in a while? Why did we have to torture the lawn into submission every two weeks? Why couldn't I cut my hair and wear it in an unbecoming honky Afro? Why did everything have to be so deliberate, so worthy, so fixed up until it was perfect? Where did that leave my flawed self and the poor baby growing in my uterus?

My mother said, "Wynn," but I wouldn't look at her. I stared at her stupid belt buckle. "You're being ridiculous," she said. "Of course I'll listen to you. You know I always listen to you. What kind of mother do you think I am? But first you listen to me. You did something very, very stupid—you and that boy." She said *boy* as if what she really meant was *pervert* or *animal*. "You created a problem—a huge, horrible, upsetting problem for all of us. That's the situation. Let's not sit around crying over it. When you have a problem, you solve it, Wynn. It may seem abrupt and coldhearted, but it's the only way to deal with it." Her voice became gentler. She said, "Honey, we have to be realistic. We can't reverse what happened—though I know you would like to."

*No, I wouldn't!* I wanted to say. *I fucked my brains out and I loved it and I'd do the same thing again!* But of course that wasn't even the truth. My mother was right, as she was always right: If I could have rolled the film back to Deirdre's kitchen, I would have said, *No, thanks, I'll walk home, I'll hitchhike, I'll stay here and sleep in the bathtub, I'll do anything, just please don't let this happen.*

"I've made these arrangements for *you*, Wynn—because it's the best course of action for you," my mother finished up. "I hope you understand that. It's you I'm thinking of." We were silent a moment, and then the kettle whistled and she went to make tea. From the stove, she said, "Now tell me what you wanted to say. Believe me, if you have another idea, I'm listening."

She put in exactly three tablespoons of tea, filled the pot with boiling water, took the old knitted tea cozy from the drawer and covered the pot with it, set it down on the table in front of me, brought over two mugs, and poured milk into a pitcher. This familiar sequence of actions revolted me. I squeezed my eyes shut.

"Wynn?"

"I don't want to give the baby away."

I heard my mother sit down across from me. I didn't look at her, but I knew exactly what kind of frown she was frowning, what look of concern she was directing at my bent head, what complex of thoughts was raging through her brain. "Wynn—"

"I don't want to hear it," I said. "The eight reasons why there's no other choice."

But she surprised me. "It's not a decision you have to make now," she said. "I mean, it's not as if you have to sign a surrender form to get into this place. I'm sure some girls keep their babies. You can leave it open for now, and see what you think when the time comes."

I looked up at her. "I can?"

"Of course."

"Do you really mean that?"

"For heaven's sake, Wynn. I'm not a tyrant! It's your decision."

I sank to the floor before her and hugged her around the middle. Her belt buckle dug into my cheek. I didn't care. She pressed her palms to my temples and gently massaged them. It's what she used to do when I was little, and it always calmed me down. "It's going to be okay," she said. "It is, sweetie. Wait and see. Everything will be fine."

Her voice was calm and confident. Maybe it was true. And of course I would go away; it was the only thing to do. I leaned against my mother, the sweat trickling down my back. She kept rubbing my temples and after a minute she began to hum softly, an off-key

"Eleanor Rigby." I leaned against her and closed my eyes. I could have stayed there forever.

But under my jeans there was the baby: Its toes and ears and liver and lungs were creating themselves. I couldn't feel it happening, but I was intensely conscious of it. So, apparently, was my mother. "Time's a-wasting," she said. She pushed me away, patted my shoulder, and reached for the teapot. "We need to talk about what to do next."

What we did next, two days later, was meet with Mark's parents up at the Castle. Mark wasn't present; my parents and I were ushered in by a woman I assumed was Mrs. Erling but who turned out to be a servant of some kind. She showed us into a living room as big as our barn and frigidly air-conditioned. A pitcher of iced tea sweated on a tray, but no one touched it. I sat alone on a stiff brocade sofa, shivering. The parents sat on chairs that flanked the fireplace. There was an idyllic oil painting of two golden-haired toddlers over the mantel; about halfway through our visit I realized they must be Mark and his brother.

The Erlings were remote but cooperative—obviously relieved that I wasn't making any embarrassing claims on their son. When my name came up, they glanced vaguely in my direction; they never once met my eyes. Mrs. Erling was willowy and glamorous, with short white-blond hair and a black sheath dress. Mr. Erling wore a seersucker suit and a tie. He asked my father to spell *Quinlan,* and wrote down the name and address of the home in a pigskin notebook. "It will probably be best just to have the bills sent to my accountant," he said, as if to himself, and made a note. "I'll take care of that."

My father's face turned red. "That's not necessary."

"To us it is," Mr. Erling said shortly.

My father was stubborn. "I would like to share the expenses."

Mr. Erling produced a tight smile, showing perfect teeth like

Mark's. "We'd prefer to do it this way." My mother gave my father a look, and he subsided.

"Thank you," I said when we left to no one in particular, and no one answered. The fathers shook hands. The mothers got teary and looked as if they thought they should embrace, but didn't. I hated Mark for getting out of it.

In the car, my mother said, "Did you get the impression that this isn't the first time one of their boys has gotten into trouble?"

Very few people knew about my predicament. My parents didn't tell Anna Rosa; somehow they managed to avoid going to New York for Christmas. My teachers had to be in on it and agreed to send me assignments so I could keep up with my class. Miss Morgan, my English teacher, gave me *War and Peace* to read while I was away; she said it would take my mind off things. Mrs. Diamond, my art teacher, hugged me and said, "Artists are born to suffer, Wynn. It's the way of the world."

And I told Marietta. By the time I did, she was well over her crush on Spencer and was absorbed in a boy named Keith Emery who was new at our school that fall and who had shoulder-length hair and a thin beard. She was so happy that I kept putting off telling her, and when I did she wept and said, "That rotten scum rich kid, that son of a bitch."

"It was my fault as much as his," I pointed out.

She turned on me fiercely. "It's *never* the girl's fault as much as the boy's!" Marietta was discovering the women's movement. "*He* stuck it in *you*—right? And *he's* not going to have to be in labor for long horrible hours and hours."

I preferred not to think about being in labor. I did my best not to think at all, and I took care not to look at my naked self in the mirror—my rounding belly and alarming breasts. Clothed, I didn't look particularly pregnant. I was a tall, chunky girl, and I hid things successfully under the big sweaters and full skirts that we all wore. Marietta advised me to deflect attention from my thickening waist by wearing plenty of beads and earrings and letting my hair out of its braid to fly around my head. I don't know if any of this worked or not. I avoided people as much as possible: I resigned from *Dead Duck* and stopped going to parties. Neil Hauser kept asking me out, and I finally told him I had a boyfriend who was away at college. Princeton, I said. Neil seemed impressed. I threw myself into my schoolwork. When I left for Boston just after Christmas, five and a half months pregnant, my grades were better than they had been in my entire life.

It was Marietta who concocted my story. A rich great-aunt of mine needed a companion while she recovered from a serious operation and had asked my parents if I could come and stay with her. It was pretty lame, and I wasn't sure how many people it fooled, but my parents seized upon it with relief, and Marietta fabricated letters I wrote from Aunt Sarah's townhouse on Beacon Hill and quoted from them to the kids at school. Aunt Sarah was rather dotty, she wandered around Boston singing to herself, wearing sandals and ragged blue jeans with her mink, but she had taken a fancy to me, she was sure to leave me everything in her will.

Mark Erling wrote me one letter at the Edna Quinlan Home for Girls just after New Year's, telling me that if I needed or wanted anything, anything at all, please to let him know, and he would get it for me, no matter what it was. I was surprised at Mark's unexpected torment—his tears on the phone, his guilt—and I tried to imagine what expiatory quest I could send him off on, what outrageous item I could ask him for: an original Picasso? a date with John Lennon? The last sentence of his letter was, "Please forgive me for this, Wynn." I ripped it up and didn't reply. Then he sent me an irritatingly silly Valentine's Day card with a note: "Please let me know what happens." I didn't.

At first, my parents drove down to Boston to visit me every week. My father was almost ludicrously distressed at seeing me pregnant. His eyes burned into mine when we talked, and I realized it was so that he wouldn't have to look at my stomach. My mother tried so hard to be sympathetic but cheerful that she always left with a headache. Finally I told them they didn't have to come, a weekly phone call would be just as good. My father sent me books and art supplies and wrote me letters that were meant to be light and funny. My mother kept coming anyway, every Saturday. She always took me out for lunch. She would order coffee and a bagel for herself, and a large, wholesome meal for me: a glass of milk, a grilled cheese sandwich, a green salad, oatmeal cookies—pretty much what I would have had back at Edna Quinlan. We would sit in the restaurant while she talked and talked, about anything, everything, Nixon's inauguration, the new Beatles album, a quilt she was making, the cats, an antiwar rally at Dunster High, Marietta's father's gall bladder operation.

I didn't have much to say myself, so I was grateful for her flow of conversation, but I couldn't help feeling that it was a diversionary tactic, as if she knew that the one thing I did want to say was exactly what she didn't want to hear.

My mother was always upbeat, but at the first signs of spring, she became aggressively so. On a sunny March Saturday, we walked slowly back to Beacon Street in the chilly air. She hugged me hard, my monstrous stomach against her flat one. Her car was parked at the curb, and she got into it and grinned at me through the window. "It won't be long now!" she trilled, as if I were having a show of my paintings instead of giving birth.

After she drove off, I went inside and placed a collect call to my father. He accepted the charges, then asked, "What's up, darlin'?" in the hearty new voice he used now for talking to me. "Is your mother still there?"

"She just left, Dad. That's why I called. I wanted to talk to you."

"Uh-*huh*," he said, and after a pause, "Well. What about, then, Wynn?"

"I want you to help me."

"Help you? Help you what?"

The phone at the Edna Quinlan Home was in a tiny closet on the first floor under the stairs. The closet didn't have a door; it obviously had at one time, you could see where the hinges had been removed, but secrets weren't encouraged at Edna Quinlan—clandestine calls to inconvenient boyfriends, demoralizing weeping sessions with parents or friends. I kept my voice low.

"I want you to help me convince Mom that I shouldn't give up the baby for adoption."

"Oh, Wynn, honey—"

My father's voice was weary, as if he'd heard this too many times already, and I knew my mother had told him how I felt, they had discussed it, they had agreed not to encourage me. I went on quickly. "Just listen to me, Daddy, please. I don't want to give it away. I don't! It doesn't seem right!" I heard my voice getting louder, and I knew it must be carrying out to the living room where a crowd of girls was playing some game, even down to the kitchen where the evening meal was being prepared. I expected any minute to be interrupted by one of the matrons or the social worker, so I calmed down and went on, as softly as I could. "Daddy, I can't talk about this with Mom, I don't know why, I just know she doesn't want to hear it, and I don't understand that, she was always so upset about the two babies that she lost, you know how she cries every year, it meant so much to her, why can't she see that this means something to me? She said I could make my own decision, but I know what she wants me to do, we never talk about it, I know she wouldn't listen to me."

I stopped, sensing the approach of a wave of hysteria that would have felt so good I could hardly keep from giving in to it, and yet I sensed that if anything could convince my father it was quiet rational argument. I had rehearsed this conversation for days; bringing up my mother's miscarriages had been, I thought, an inspired move.

"Please talk to her, Daddy," I said. "Please try to convince her. She'll listen to you."

My father said, gently, "Wynn."

I pressed my hand to my hot forehead, I switched the phone to my other ear, I tried to stay calm. "What?"

He didn't answer right away, he gave a soft sigh, and I had a quick, crazy moment of hope. I pictured him sitting at the kitchen table, his brow furrowed, weighing what I had said. I felt his love for me through the phone wires like an electric current, and I relaxed, resting a hand on my big belly. I knew exactly what the baby looked like now, I knew that it could hear, its lungs and heart and brain were fully developed, if it were born tomorrow, a month early, it could survive. It kicked against my hand; I could feel my stomach distend. A tiny foot, an elbow. This always made me smile. *Baby,* I thought absently. *Baby baby little baby.*

"Wynn, you've got to be sensible," my father said finally. "Your mother knows what's best for you. You have to believe that. When the time comes, you'll decide. But I think it's the only thing you can do."

"What?" I asked. I gripped the receiver with both hands. "What is, Daddy?" I wanted to make him say it. "*What* is the only thing I can do?"

He hesitated.

*"What?"*

"Give it up," he said. "Like all the other girls, Wynn. Just try to accept it, and when it's all over you'll get on with things and it will be as if this never happened."

"Daddy."

"We've talked about it enough," he said. "I'm not going against your mother, and that's final."

From the living room I heard a scream of victory, then laughter. The smell of frying onions came up from the kitchen. My father and I sat listening to each other breathe for another minute or so, and then I hung up the phone.

• • •

In the evening of my second day in the hospital, I was dozing, my mother was leafing through a magazine, and the nurse stuck her head in and asked me if I was feeling well enough to see the baby. My mother raised her head in alarm, but I said, quickly, that I did, and painfully hoisted myself up against the pillows. The nurse wheeled in a tiny plastic crib and, smiling, placed the baby in my arms.

She was wrapped tightly in pink, asleep and unexpectedly heavy, a sturdy girl with a full head of dark hair. The baby I had imagined, the unimaginable baby: eight pounds, thirteen ounces, twenty-one inches long. A perfect little human. Dark eyelashes against her rosy cheek. Double chin. Fingernails like fragile bits of shell. A Cupid's-bow mouth, red-lipped, drooling.

I couldn't stop looking at her. I kissed her soft cheek, I rubbed my face against her fuzzy hair, wiped away the drool with a corner of the sheet, unwound the blanket and squeezed her tiny feet. My heart unlocked. *Baby, baby.* I forgot the nurse was there, and my mother, until she said, very gently, "You know—this is going to be all right, Wynn. Really. It is."

Just then the baby opened her mouth and let out a sudden little contradictory cry that frightened me. The nurse reached out for her with a chuckle. "Sounds like feeding time," she said, and wheeled the baby out the door in her cart.

When her cries died away, the room was full of an eerie silence.

Out the window, the early spring darkness was falling. I saw lights go on in a building across the way.

"That was a mistake," my mother said after a minute. "I don't think that nurse could have known your situation."

I sat without speaking, propped against the pillows. The baby's reality had exhausted me: the smell of her, her tiny ragged nails, the fretful cry like some strange bird. But without her the room was empty. I stared out at the lights until I fell back to sleep.

The next day I signed some papers and filled out the form for the birth certificate. I named the baby Molly, after my mother. I couldn't give her anything else; at least I could give her a name. Maybe her new parents would keep it. The nurse brought the baby in again, and I fed her with a bottle, but she dropped off to sleep almost immediately. *I'm your mother,* I whispered to her. She didn't wake. *My name is Wynn Tynan. I'm your mother. Remember me. Remember me.* Looking at her, red and blank and helpless in my arms, I felt nothing but despair—that and the disquieting sensation that I had become someone else: literally, I was not Wynn Tynan any more.

My breasts were sore and swollen, bursting, but I was not allowed to nurse the baby. I was given a drug to suppress the milk. Mrs. Del Banco, the social worker from the Edna Quinlan Home, came to see me. The baby had just been brought in; she was sleeping in my arms.

Mrs. Del Banco said, "When you're giving up your baby, Wynn, we find it's better not to have too much contact with her. You've seen her, that's enough." She smiled at me sadly. "You have to let her go."

"Suppose I want to keep her."

The baby was hustled back to the nursery, and Mrs. Del Banco, my mother, and the social worker from the hospital assembled around my bed. "You're sixteen years old, you have your whole life ahead of you, you've already signed the preliminary papers," they said. None of these seemed like reason enough to give that baby to someone else, to let the milk in my breasts dry up, to go back to Dunster High as if nothing had happened.

Finally, the others left, and my mother and I were alone. "I don't think I can do it," I said. The sound of my voice surprised me: It was mechanical and sullen. I sounded like Suzanne. I couldn't remember ever talking to my mother in quite that way. My stitches throbbed, my chest felt tight, my stomach knotted. "I don't think I want to do it."

It took my mother a minute to respond. She was standing at the window; her profile was stern and preoccupied. *Please,* I wanted to say. But I wasn't sure what I was asking for. "I just don't think it's right," I said when she didn't speak. Was she listening? "It's not right," I said again. "It feels wrong to me."

My mother turned her head in my direction. Her blue eyes were steady, and when she spoke her voice was very quiet and precise. "Daddy and I don't want to hear this."

"I named her after you," I said.

She just looked at me. "Wynn." She closed her eyes for a moment, shaking her head. "We've been through this."

"You said I could decide."

"You know this is the only possible choice."

"But *why*?"

"Do you mean aside from the fact that you're sixteen years old and a junior in high school?" She looked very tall against the window. Her voice rose. "That the idea of raising a child at your age is complete madness? You have no idea what that entails!" She came over to the bed and sat down on a chair beside me. "Wynn, your whole life is ahead of you. You'll have more children someday, when you're ready. But for now—think of all the things you want to do! One more year and you'll be in art school, you'll be having such wonderful times, you'll be learning so much. You're an artist, Wynn. That's so important—you know it is. I hope you haven't forgotten how much you want that, how much you want to be a painter."

No, I hadn't forgotten. Nobody ever let me forget. In fact, a week or so before the baby was born I'd had a notification from the Maine Artists' Association that two of my paintings would be included in their annual spring show; my art teacher at the high school had called to congratulate me. But an odd thing had happened while I was at Edna Quinlan. I stopped painting. I had brought paints and canvas, but, for some reason, when I picked up the brush, my mind refused to focus. What was there to paint? Why would anyone want to *paint*, of all things? I seemed unable to be pregnant and paint at the same time. In art class, while the other girls produced pale, drippy, dutiful watercolors from photographs, I ripped up paper and made collages. I took a fierce pleasure in their construction, tearing images from a stack of old magazines and pasting them to the posterboard my parents sent me—jagged hunks of paper in violent bursts of black and purple and red that produced dark, tangled designs pleasing to no one but me.

"Nothing has changed," my mother said. "You're still an artist. You're a painter before anything else. Think about what that means."

"I do think about it, I think about it all the time, and the whole thing just seems stupid and wrong," I said again, stubbornly.

"Then you're not really thinking," my mother said. "About what your life is about, what you want to do with it. You're so young, Wynn—I know it's hard for you to see it, but the decision you make today will color your whole life." She stood up, leaned over and kissed my cheek. Then she patted it twice, as if I were asleep and it was time to wake up. "*Listen to me.* This is a serious moment. Don't throw your life away. It's the only one you get. I want you to promise me you'll think this through—*really* think." Her eyes were hard, glowing, her cheeks pink with conviction. Just looking at her made me tired. "Okay?" she asked. "Wynn?"

"Yeah, okay," I said, and turned my head away.

After she left, I lay there in my bed, my mother's voice echoing in my head as the sleeping pill took hold. The television on the wall was mute, a gray blur of heads with moving mouths. *You're an artist, Wynn. You're a painter.* Words I had heard all my life. I don't deny that they were powerful words, as much a part of my life as the cats and the Van Gogh posters and my father's overalls. I fell asleep and dreamt that I was preparing a canvas for painting: stretching it, stapling, covering it with gesso. But I didn't paint anything on it. In my dream, the canvas stayed white, pristine, empty.

When I woke early the next morning to the sound of babies crying in the nursery down the hall, it was clear to me that the battle was lost. The thin, helpless wails of all those hungry infants made me profoundly depressed. One of them was mine: what could I do for her? I was sixteen years old. I knew nothing. My baby deserved better. They were right. What I wanted was absurd.

When the social worker came in, I signed the final papers, not letting myself think about anything but going home, seeing Marietta, applying to art schools, wearing normal clothes. My mother hugged me, beaming—triumphant—her face full of love and approval. The next day I was presented with a brief "non-identifying profile" of the adoptive parents—blue-collar, Midwestern, decent—and then I drove home with my mother.

"Look! It's spring!" she said as we drove up Route 95. She pointed out the window. "You know how you love spring. The snow is practically gone. And look at the trees." Dutifully, I looked. The dark branches were blurred with a fuzz of yellow-green. Snow lurked in hard brown piles along the roadside, but the pavement was black where it was melting. The sky threatened rain. "Isn't it wonderful, sweetie? Life does go on, you know."

"I can't talk about it, Mom," I said. I kept my voice even, I didn't cry.

"Wynn—"

"I don't want to talk."

"You know it was the only possible decision."

I said, "There's a difference between that and the right decision."

"Wynn—"

*"I don't want to talk about it!"*

My mother gave a small, angry sigh and tapped her fingers on the steering wheel. I turned on the radio and thought about my baby, wrapped in her pink blanket, driving away in a car with people I would never know or see. I kept that image in my mind, my baby daughter on the lap of some strange thrilled woman, sitting beside a man who kept looking at them, smiling, full of the new joy of parenthood.

All the way home, I cut myself with that picture the way Darcy cut herself with her little blade.

## *Question Two*

# What Made You Happy?

I didn't get to know Patrick Foss until I had been in art school for almost two semesters. But I was aware of him—a tall, haunted-looking boy, always in a hurry. I remember how he used to stride down the halls of the school as if they were country roads, his hair falling on his forehead and the sleeves of his ancient black sweater so short that a couple of inches of bony wrist protruded. And I remember once, when I happened to be in an elevator with him, how startling his eyes were: light golden brown, intense and preoccupied beneath his heavy dark brows. Our eyes met, but he didn't seem to see me; he looked as if he were engaged in some fierce internal struggle, some life-or-death dilemma that rendered virtually invisible the shabby old elevator and the tall, awkward girl leaning against the wall opposite him.

I didn't know then that Patrick Foss was what I was searching for. But right from the beginning, I knew he was important.

• • •

I had returned to Dunster High after Easter, just in time for the Junior Prom. *You've made the right decision.* Everyone said it, kept saying it. My parents, and Mrs. Diamond my art teacher, and Miss Morgan my English teacher, who made me do a report on *War and Peace*. And Marietta, who was horrified that I'd even considered keeping the baby. "Are you crazy?" she said. "You're a kid! You can't be somebody's mother!"

My parents were convinced that time would work its magic and my unfortunate trauma would be smoothed over, and they were always looking for signs that this was happening. "You really should go to the prom," my mother said. "It would do you good to get out and have some fun." The prom rapidly became a symbol: If I went, it would be a sign that I was my old self.

Unexpectedly, Mark Erling followed me to my locker one day and asked me to be his date for the prom. The sight of his blond hair and conciliatory smile sickened me. Barely civil, I said no thanks.

Marietta was going with Keith, who offered to get me a date, but I was in no mood for a dance. Dunster High was an alien planet. I would have rather put on a hair shirt than a prom gown.

My mother ran into Neil's mother in the supermarket, and Mrs. Hauser told her that Neil wanted to ask me. I told her that there was no one I could stand to go with, certainly not Neil Hauser who had long, greasy hair and drank too much. I said I was still too fat and wouldn't be caught dead in a prom gown. I said I felt overwhelmed in Spanish and Intermediate Algebra and I needed to spend the time studying. My mother had an answer for everything: You look great, Neil is sweet, you're doing fine, blah blah. I tried a joke. "Don't you know that proms are decadent and evil? Symbols of the outmoded and destructive patriarchal values to which our corrupt society is irrevocably wedded?" My father chuckled nervously. My mother laughed, then pursed her lips and frowned, but she finally dropped the subject.

Home, unpregnant, I had begun painting again; it was what I was used to, what I did. There was my studio, my easel, the painting I'd been working on when I left for Great-Aunt Sarah's. Putting paint on canvas gave me something to think about. When I showed Mrs. Diamond my first painting, a portrait of Marietta I did from a photograph, she was silent a moment. Then she put her arm around my shoulders. "There's no doubt you've lost something, Wynn," she said. "But maybe you've gained something as well."

"What?" I asked her, my heart in my throat.

She considered for a moment, squinting at Marietta's red hair and green sweater. "Hmm," she said. "I'm not sure what to call it. A kind of detachment, maybe. A stepping back from your subject."

"Is that good?"

Mrs. Diamond smiled. "Up to a point," she said. "It's okay. Before, you were too close sometimes, too involved. Just don't let it get out of control."

I became obsessed with people's faces. I took my sketch pad everywhere, drawing them on the school bus, in the library, in class and then, back in my studio, putting their faces into paintings. For a long time it was only people, as I looked at their faces and transferred what I saw to canvas, who could bring me back from the dark place I had been, and make me feel connected to the world again.

• • •

It was hard for me to be at home with my parents, and I sometimes got off the school bus in the middle of town and sat in a booth at the West Dunster Diner, drinking coffee and doing my homework or drawing. I became friendly with Tina, the waitress; I made a pencil portrait of her and she bought it for ten dollars and a piece of banana cream pie. I used to sit there until I knew I'd better get home for dinner or my father would come out in his truck looking for me.

Everything was turned upside down. I hated the walk down Brewster Road, the walk I'd loved all my life, and the smug coziness of the little house at the end of it, as colorful and neat as an illustration in a children's book—and as unreal. My parents were always waiting—anxiously, I could tell. They greeted me with a kind of rehearsed joviality, encouraging me to talk about my day, trying urgently, pathetically, to hang on to the old way of life, clinging to the old jokes and rituals.

When I was in a good mood, I knew that they were decent but fallible people who loved me, and who had done their best. But most of the time that spring and summer I felt I had never really seen my parents before, as if my pregnancy and its aftermath had removed from my consciousness some protective coating that had been there since my childhood. Now I could step back and, with my new, raw vision, watch my mother and my father as if they were people in a play, a sour satire of the American family. Cast of characters: the ambitious, dominating woman, her weak and worshipful husband, the child they valued because she fulfilled their dreams. By the end of the last act, all their filthy secrets are exposed, their ignorance and their blind spots, and the cruelties they perpetrated in the name of love and kindness.

My aloofness wasn't something we discussed, any more than we'd discussed how I felt about the baby. Once my mother asked me if I was okay, was there anything bothering me, and it was all I could do not to run screaming to my room and slam the door. Instead I said, with a civilized little smile, "The famous pressures of junior year, Mom," and she smiled back as I knew she would—a smile that said: *I know perfectly well how angry and resentful you are, but thank you for not talking about it, and one of these days you'll get over it and everything will be just fine.*

I escaped to Marietta's house as often as I could. We studied together, played intense games of Scrabble, watched TV. There were plenty of times when she deserted Keith so she could be with me, and I was grateful to her. If it weren't for Marietta, I never would have survived the end of junior year at Dunster High. She had fielded awkward inquiries during my absence and helped cover for me when I returned chubby and morose. She spread the word around school that I was pining for my Princeton boyfriend, that things weren't going well with him, that I was depressed about it and mad at the world and everybody should leave me alone and respect my bad mood.

I went over to her house the day before the prom to see her gown and discuss possible hairdos. Her hair was almost shoulder length by then, and we decided finally that she should just curl the ends and wear it loose.

"You ought to wear my silver and jade barrette," I said.

Her eyes lit up. "Could I? Oh God, that would be so great with this dress."

I ran home and got the barrette, one of my prized possessions. Marietta clasped it in her hair. "What do you think? Too much?"

"Nope," I said. "Perfect." We stood in front of her mirror and stared at our reflections. We had done this for years, enjoying the contrast in our looks, Marietta with her straight red hair and pale skin, me with my high color and dark, frizzy mop. "It looks incredible. Red hair, green eyes, jade barrette, pale green dress. Keith is going to die."

Marietta tilted her head, sucked in her cheeks, struck an exaggerated fashion-model pose. "I am actually quite gorgeous, aren't I?" She grinned. "Thank you, thank you, thank you, Wynn! I promise I'll take good care of it."

"I want you to keep it."

"What? The barrette? Are you kidding?"

"It looks much better on you than it does on me."

Marietta shook her head. "I can't. It's too expensive."

My affection for her overwhelmed me. I thought of Natasha at the ball. Marietta did look beautiful, and she had been my friend forever, and she was going to the prom with the boy she was in love with. I couldn't have expressed it then, but I was aware that, for all her sophistication, there was an innocence about Marietta that was gone from me forever. At that moment, I wished I were Marietta, I wanted to be in love and normal and looking forward to something. But, failing that, I wanted her to have something of mine. I had a confused idea that it would be a good omen.

"What?" she asked, seeing my face.

"I owe you everything, Marietta."

"Give me a break."

"I do. I couldn't have gotten through this without you. Please take it. I want so much for you to have it."

"You're a dope," she said.

We put our arms around each other, and I cried on her shoulder. "Oh Marietta, I wish everything was different. I wish I hadn't screwed up my life."

"You didn't, Wynn," she said. "Just a little piece of it. You're going to be okay. We're both going to get out of this hick town and do something great."

"We are?"

She found a tissue and wiped my eyes. "Yeah, we are. All this is going to be over soon. Summer's coming. We'll get great jobs and make tons of money and have a million laughs and everybody will fall in love with us, and one more year and we're out of here and we're famous and beautiful and rich and we'll never look back and everything is going to be completely fabulous."

By then, we were both laughing. "It will? We are? We won't?"

"Silly girl. How can you doubt me when I'm always right?" She kissed my cheek. "Thanks for the barrette, dollink. You know I love you, you wacko."

The night of the prom I was reading *Great Expectations* for English class. My parents went out to a movie. I took a break to get myself a snack, and as I was spreading peanut butter on a cracker the phone rang. It was Mark Erling. He wanted to come over. I told him he couldn't. I asked him what he wanted.

"I want you to tell me about it," he said. There was a catch in his voice. "I don't know anything! Don't I have some kind of right?"

I stood there silently for a full minute, thinking. He didn't say a word. He waited. I remembered lying under him on the sand. He hadn't forced me. I remembered what it felt like: the quick pain, then, gradually, something resembling pleasure. It occurred to me suddenly that Mark Erling was a human being. This may seem obvious, but it was actually a revelation: that this wasn't just a druggy, basketball-playing rich kid but someone who was feeling something deeply. I was impressed that he hadn't gone to the prom, that this had been on his mind, that he had felt compelled to call me. And it was true. He did have a right. Finally I said, "Okay."

"Was it a boy or a girl?" he asked, speaking quickly before I could change my mind.

"A girl. Eight pounds, thirteen ounces."

"A girl. Jesus. What else?"

I flinched from his voice, his eager interest—and yet it excited me to talk about the baby, to answer questions no one else had asked me. "Very pink," I said. "Red. Lots of dark hair."

"What else?"

I told him that I named her Molly. I told him the name of the hospital where she'd been born, and the name of the obstetrician. I told him the name of the agency that handled the adoption. I quoted to him the profile of the adoptive parents. Then I asked, "Why do you want all this information?"

"I don't know," he said. "I just do."

"Well—" I wanted to get off the phone, back to my book.

"I'm going away to boarding school in the fall, for senior year," he said unexpectedly. "In California."

"Oh." I couldn't think of anything to say. "Cool."

"Yeah." There was a silence. "I wish I could have seen her," he said.

"I'm sorry, Mark." *Just leave me alone,* I thought. Just. Leave. Me. Alone.

"So," he said, and there was another pause.

I told him I had to get going, and we hung up. I ate my crackers and tried to read, but I couldn't. I watched an old movie on TV until it was late and I became exhausted enough to sleep.

I don't remember if I saw Mark again that year. Maybe I passed him in the hall at school or saw him on the street. I don't remember. I didn't wish him any harm, but as far as I was concerned, Mark Erling had ceased to exist.

I wasn't ever really able to slip back into normal life. In senior year I became known as a loner, a slightly peculiar artist—but mostly people ignored me. *Dead Duck* carried on without me. I hardly ever went to a party. Most of my time was spent studying and working on my portfolio for art schools. By the time I left West Dunster, except for Marietta, I didn't have a single good friend. I had ended up dating Neil Hauser for a short time during senior year, and then, even more briefly, a quiet, studious boy named Marty Kelly who was considered weird, but I wouldn't miss either one of them.

I couldn't wait to leave Maine. It wasn't that I no longer loved my parents. I was tied to them in a hundred small ways. But during those months at Edna Quinlan, no matter how much they wrote and visited and called, I had been alone. I couldn't tell them how I felt when I held my daughter in my arms, or about the dark, empty space that opened inside me when I lay in bed that morning in the hospital and made the decision to give her up. I couldn't understand why no one besides Suzanne had ever seen what that had meant, how it was like a little death, like something being ripped away.

After I graduated from Dunster High, I did what I had always been meant to do: I went away to art school in Boston. It was, of course, the city where I had been most unhappy, but it was also the city of museums and cafés and sober, rain-colored buildings. Those four hopeless pregnant months hadn't quite killed my old affection for the place, and I was ready to give it another chance. Both of us, I figured, could start over.

Marietta was going to film school in California. As always, I had only admiration for Marietta, who could leave us all behind and point herself toward a goal that had nothing to do with family, friends, familiarity. But her decision devastated me, it was so far away. I remembered our childhood fantasy of living near each other forever. California seemed like Mars.

"How can you do this to me?" I asked her—only half kidding.

"She was ruthless—driven—in desperate pursuit of success at all costs," Marietta cried melodramatically. "Marietta Donnelly was determined to claw her way to the top, and she didn't care who she kicked aside in the process!" Then she laughed and hugged me. "I'm going to miss you, kid. This is not a joke. I'm going to miss you bad!" She looked me in the eye. "But I'm going."

All that remained to me, I felt, was my painting. It still seemed pointless much of the time, but it was what I did. For most of my eighteen years, it had been a major part of my identity. I wanted to learn how to be a better painter. I wanted to meet other artists and see the world. Without a brush in my hand, I was lost.

• • •

Patrick was firmly set in the sculpture track, and I was a painter; except for an art history class that fall—before I even knew who he was—our paths seldom crossed at school. The sculptors worked in basement studios, in a deafening roar and rattle of machines—saws, grinders, sanders, welding tools. I worked in a top-floor painting studio, where light poured in through the windows and the view was of trees and sky.

Patrick and I met, finally, late one spring afternoon when I was walking home to my little railroad apartment on Queensberry Street, near the Fenway. I was carrying a heavy roll of watercolor paper tied up with twine. My friend Jeanie Volovich and I had placed a bulk order from an art supply catalog, and had had the paper delivered to her place on Boylston Street. At school, I was working in oils, but when I came home I painted watercolors for fun at my kitchen table.

The paintings were chaotic, formless, not very good. They pleased me, though: the chanciness of watercolor challenged me, every painting was an adventure. I would come home from school, set up my watercolors, and paint—quickly, loosely, without thinking much about it—whatever happened to be on the table in front of me: a box of Wheaties, the gas bill, a stack of books, last night's dirty dishes. I thought sometimes about the watercolor still lifes my mother had painted when she was young and hopeful. I had no clear memory of them, but I was sure both my parents would have hated these flawed, messy attempts. And I suppose it's obvious that that was one reason I liked them so much.

On the day I met Patrick, as I was struggling down Boylston with the roll of paper, I had to stop and rest. I set it on a bench and plopped down beside it, sweating. It was a warm March day, unseasonably beautiful for Boston. I leaned my head back and raised my face to the breeze. Then a voice asked, "Could you use some help with that?"

I opened my eyes: Patrick. I recognized him, though I didn't know his name. I wasn't in need of help—just a rest—but when I looked up at him it was as if something fell into place in my brain, or in my heart. Something that had been muddled and confused became simple, orderly. I looked into his tawny-gold eyes and said, "Yes, actually, I could. In a minute."

He sat down beside me. "You do watercolors."

"Sometimes. Mostly I work in oil."

"You're at the school, are you?"

"Yes. First year."

He nodded. "You look a little familiar."

This made me smile; he obviously had never noticed me. I told him we had been on the elevator together once, and he hadn't said a word: just looked like he was having a busy life in some other world. He laughed. "I was probably thinking about lunch. Or about whether I could afford to invest in a new fishtail gouge." He held out a hand. "Patrick Foss."

I took it. Bony fingers, a grip just short of painful. "Wynn Tynan," I said. "You're a sculpture major?" I knew perfectly well that he was.

He nodded. "Right now, I'm working in wood, but my great love is welding."

*My great love is welding:* Only Patrick could make that statement without either irony or self-consciousness. I liked the way he spoke—with a lilt at the end of a sentence. "What's so lovable about welding?" I asked, to keep him talking.

He took the question seriously. We talked welding. We talked watercolor paper. We talked professors and classes. He told me he had an academic scholarship that paid his tuition and rent. I was impressed; scholarships were famously hard to come by at that school. He also worked part-time, welding in a machine shop somewhere in South Boston. We asked each other a million questions. I could have sat there in the sun and talked to him forever, but before we knew it, the sun was fading, and we were still sitting on the bench with my roll of paper between us.

We walked to Queensberry Street, Patrick carrying the paper over his shoulder as if it were a roll of gift wrap. "What floor are you on?" he asked me at my door.

"Fourth."

"Walk-up?"

"Unfortunately."

He bounded up the stairs ahead of me, and when we arrived at my apartment he leaned the paper carefully against the living room wall.

"Thank you."

He was staring at my fireplace. "This is a great apartment you've got."

"The fireplace doesn't work, of course."

"Well, but—look at all the space."

I looked around. The living room was barely big enough for my ratty Salvation Army sofa and a rocking chair and a bookcase overflowing with junk. Beyond it was a glimpse of the tiny, cluttered kitchen.

"I live in one room," he said. "One empty room, mostly. It's got a bed and a table and some twisted old hunks of metal, but that's about it."

I had a vision of poverty, passionate dedication, an attractively wild-eyed fanatic living in a hovel—like something from a film about artists in turn-of-the-century Paris.

"Can you stay for dinner?" I asked.

He accepted with an alacrity that I found flattering but that, I soon realized, was very likely a need for free food. I didn't care. I just wanted him to be there, sitting on the kitchen windowsill while I threw dinner together. Behind him, the sky was turning purple, the lights came on in the apartment building across the way. Patrick's face was bright; his eyes gleamed. He wore a blue denim shirt under his old black sweater, faded jeans with the knees out. I wished I could paint him.

I listened while he compared the merits of European and Japanese chisels. I had never heard anything so interesting. When he asked, I told him about the odd, slapdash watercolors I was doing. I was too unsure of them to drag them out, but he looked at a stack of sketches I had done on one of my weekends home in Maine, and then we got talking about growing up in small towns. Patrick was an orphan who had been raised by his bachelor uncle somewhere in the wilds of New York State. From the time he was a kid, he had worked in his uncle's salvage yard.

"That's where I got my passion for metal," he said. "It was a paradise, that place. Ten acres of the stuff, surrounded by a fence made of corrugated tin that was so beautiful—so old and weathered—that I just wanted to cut hunks out of it and hang them on a wall somewhere. You wouldn't believe how many colors there were in that fence. It's still there—I wish you could see it!"

I wished I could, too. If I had had a car, I would have insisted that we jump right in and drive all night until we got to his uncle's place, wherever in hell it was.

"What about you?" he asked me. "Tell me about where you're from." He leaned forward, his elbows on his knees. I told him about West Dunster, about my grandmother in Greenwich Village, about my father's toys and my mother's photographs and *Dead Duck*. He wanted to know everything, and he wanted to tell me everything. Conversation with Patrick was like a badminton game with a dozen birdies flying through the air. When we sat down to dinner, he smiled at me and said, "On top of everything else, you can cook, too!"—and I was gone: That quickly, I fell in love with him.

What was it? His rough, Irish-and-German almost-handsomeness? His long, skinny body that contrasted so beautifully with his round, boyish cheeks and full mouth? Or was it his voice, deep but oddly musical, with a hint of Irishness about it—a legacy, I later learned, from his mother and his Uncle Austin, both born in County Cork. Or maybe it was the dreamy look in his eyes when he told me about his uncle's place, and how he used to prowl it on early mornings before school, looking for rusty mufflers and wheelbarrows and bits of machinery, piling them up in a corner of the barn until he could turn them into sculpture.

"What I loved, Wynn," he said, "was taking all that ugly junk, all those rusty old pieces of people's lives, and transforming them into something beautiful—something with form to it, and meaning. Making beauty from ugliness. It always seemed to me like magic!"

I loved his enthusiasm, his complete freedom from the need to appear cool or sophisticated. He made me think about things I had never thought about before. That evening, over dinner, he quoted something Tolstoy had written in his diary: *An artist's mission must not be to produce a solution to a problem, but to compel us to love life in all its countless and inexhaustible manifestations.* He recited this, ducking his head a little in embarrassment, and then he looked at me and asked, "Do you agree, Wynn?"

Did I agree? Did I agree with *Tolstoy*? I had of course read *War and Peace* (skipping the battle scenes) and written my flimsy paper on it, but I had never thought about Tolstoy, never asked myself what the artist's mission was. Hesitantly, I said, "Yes, but sometimes maybe you can't do the second thing until you've done the first thing."

Patrick leaned toward me. "That's a very good point," he said. "You're right, of course. Sometimes I get so carried away that I just—" Then he interrupted himself. "But I still think it's really important, what he said. I think we have to keep that in mind all the time, Wynn. Don't you?"

Or maybe it was the way he said my name, in that confiding, intense, deep voice of his—my name as I had never heard it, with the vowel sound prolonged as if it were a syllable in a song.

Whatever it was, I loved Patrick Foss from that very first evening, when he sat opposite me at my kitchen table eating a dinner of Minute Rice and canned tomatoes—the only food I had in the house. His vivid presence filled the room. For me, he filled the city. After that evening, Boston meant Patrick to me. Even now, to this day, the word *Boston* conjures up a complex series of images, and in spite of everything that has happened to me in that city over the years, most of those images are of Patrick. He sits opposite me at my kitchen table. He strides down Huntington Avenue, talking, and over his shoulder is a weathered wooden beam that he salvaged from a Dumpster. He frowns over the sketches of my father and the cats and the Maine landscape, and makes comments that change my art, my life, forever.

• • •

My parents had delivered me to Boston in September, my stuff packed into the back of my father's pickup, but since then I had managed to keep them out of my apartment. This hadn't been easy. They came to Boston regularly and always wanted to stop in at my place—to take me shopping for towels or something, to lug sacks of vegetables up my three flights because they were positive I wasn't eating properly. I made excuses, pleaded busyness, finally had to confess to them that my apartment was in no condition to receive them. I no longer believed in my parents' first commandment: I thrived on chaos, cultivated it, and I could imagine my mother walking in the door, recoiling in horror, then rolling up her sleeves.

I knew I was disappointing them, and they missed me, and I felt vaguely guilty about the situation, so I took the Peter Pan bus line back to Maine every month or so with my sketchbook and a suitcase full of dirty laundry. When I was home, I could fall with a readiness that appalled me into the old easy life of the pampered child, at the center of things and taken care of. The familiar, rigid peacefulness of the house. My mother doing my laundry, sorting the lights from the darks, permanent press from cotton, sewing on a button or fixing a hem. My father's orderly workshop, where I sat by the stove sketching him and the cats and the shelves lined with toys, while he painstakingly attached fat little wheels to a wooden truck.

My parents wanted to know every boring detail of my life at school, things no one else on earth would have the patience to listen to: what my art history teacher had to say about this painter or that, had my landlord fixed the drip in the sink yet, what did I pay for a tube of paint. My father would pick me up at the bus station, and my mother would have a hot meal ready, one of my favorites, and over dinner they would begin their doting interrogation.

For a while this was pleasant enough. It was like being in some tedious movie: not very exciting, but I had the starring role. But by the time I awoke on Sunday morning, I needed urgently to leave. My parents always wanted me to wait for the late afternoon bus back, but I insisted on catching the eleven o'clock. They never woke me up: I know they were hoping I would oversleep and miss it, but I willed myself to wake up in time. Then I ate my mother's huge Sunday breakfast, frantically packed my things, and got driven to the bus station with minutes to spare.

As the bus headed south, it took me a while to throw off the despondency that filled me whenever I was in the company of my parents. If they noticed, I don't think they were aware of the source. They attributed it to the inevitable changes that occur when a child leaves home and is immersed in her own life. To them, the act of giving away my baby had been a tiny blip in the happy course of my life, something a sensible girl like their Wynn would eventually rise above. I doubted that they thought of it very often—perhaps, after all this time, never, and they assumed that for me it was a small, distant, unpleasant memory. And it was true that I managed to put it out of my mind for long stretches. But while I was home in Maine, it returned, and a low-grade resentment simmered behind everything I did.

By the time the bus crossed the Massachusetts border, the cloud would begin to lift, leaving in its place a feeling of relief so dense it was like a real object stored on the rack along with my suitcase. I couldn't wait to get home, and it wasn't lost on me how that word had become transformed. *Home* was no longer that tidy green house with the perfect hedge: Home was the junky apartment where I painted and dreamed of things that were beyond my parents' comprehension.

• • •

When Patrick came into my life, I already had a boyfriend. I met him at a party: Alec Gunther, a graduate student in art history at Harvard. He was six years older than I was, and awesomely steady and reliable. Alec reminded me in some ways of my father. He was less reserved, but he was kind, competent, solicitous of me. He was perhaps a little predictable, a little tame. But he was my first real boyfriend, and I had invited him home that first Thanksgiving because he desperately wanted to meet my parents, and because I was sure they would approve of him. They were impressed with his manners, his prospects, his degree from Yale, his fellowship from Harvard, the wine he brought for Thanksgiving dinner, his knowledge of art, his general air of tidiness and control. They were probably impressed even by his tweed jackets and his tasteful leather weekend bag, monogrammed ACG. Alec Cavendish Gunther. *Husband material*, I could hear my mother thinking. *A good provider.*

The day after my dinner with Patrick, I called Alec and broke our movie date. "I can't see you any more," I said over the phone.

He insisted that we get together for coffee, and I met him at a café on Boylston Street. He was there when I arrived—Alec was always on time—sitting at a table drinking cappuccino. I slid in across from him. "This has to be our last date," I said immediately. "I'm sorry, Alec."

He looked stricken. Maybe I had done him an injustice, maybe he did passionately adore me, but I suspected Alec had enjoyed the idea of having an arty wife, a genteel sort of painter who would be a pleasant adjunct to his career. I was quiet, unthreatening, younger than he, and I seemed stable—Alec didn't like what he called neurotic women. We would hang some of my better paintings in our house, one over the sofa, one over the mantel. When he finished his Ph.D., he would teach, preferably at Harvard. He loved Boston, Cambridge, loved his work. He was writing his dissertation on the influence of the Dutch masters on nineteenth-century French landscape painting. He wanted me to go with him to France, to the village of Barbizon where Delaroche and Millet and Theodore Rousseau had worked. He would write and I would paint.

"I don't understand," he said. "We're a couple, Wynn. We have a future together."

"I don't know what to say. I can't see you any more, Alec. I'm sorry. I'm horribly sorry. But I just can't."

It was true: I was sorry. I was fond of him, and I knew he was good for me. He was mature and responsible, a born teacher, the most erudite person I had ever known. But when he kissed me no sparks flew, and, sitting there across from him, I desired not Alec and his conscientious kisses but Patrick—an unknown quantity, a boy who didn't seem to notice I was female, who was so wrapped up in talking, in shoveling in his dinner, in working, in the virtues of koa wood over

Honduras mahogany, that it didn't seem as if he'd ever have time for a girlfriend.

But looking at Alec, I wanted only to be looking at Patrick.

"Please forgive me, Alec." I kept saying that over and over, with variations. "I know it's sudden, but I don't know what to do about it."

"You've met somebody else?"

I hesitated; then I blurted it out. "I've fallen in love with someone."

"Who?"

"A sculptor."

"A sculptor?" Alec raised one eyebrow, as if in his experience all sculptors were cads or madmen.

"Yes. From school."

"You've been seeing him?"

"No. Not yet. I just met him."

"When?"

"Yesterday."

"Wynn." He smiled and tried to take my hand. "This is absurd."

I pulled away. "I can't help it, Alec. It's the way I feel."

He sighed. We talked a little longer, and finally he held up his hands as if I was robbing him and said, "Okay. Okay. But let me just say this. If this guy doesn't work out, let me know."

I stared at him. I could see that he believed this was what would happen. He sounded more than ever like my father: generous, optimistic, determined to look on the bright side. "He will work out," I said. "Or I will die."

I left him brooding over his second cappuccino. I went to the nearest pay phone and called Patrick and invited him to dinner again.

• • •

I made dinner for us almost every night: rice with tomatoes and bits of stewing beef, or rice and zucchini and chicken wings, or rice with leftover broccoli and soy sauce from the Chinese takeout place on the corner. I used to spend a lot of energy just trying to get a good meal into him. I felt like my mother—like his mother, if he had had one. My stove was a temperamental two-burner, and my cooking was primitive, but Patrick couldn't cook at all. Lord knows what he was living on before I came into his life.

"Is rice nutritious?" Patrick asked me once, wolfing it down.

I had no idea. It was cheap and filling. "Very," I said firmly. "Eat." He ate. Sometimes, after one of my awful little dinners, we would head over to Brigham's for ice cream sundaes—a great treat that we didn't indulge in very often because Patrick was so poor. There was nothing left over in his budget for fripperies like ice cream—or clothes. Any extra money went for art supplies. Being a sculptor, he often said, wasn't cheap.

We ate rice together, we talked, we went for long walks after class, and, two weeks after we met, Patrick and I went to bed together.

I hadn't made love with anyone since that night with Mark. The idea terrified me. It wasn't a rational feeling: I had been on the pill since my Edna Quinlan days, and I knew I wouldn't get pregnant. But though I had dated Neil and Marty during my last year in high school, and then I had been seeing Alec, I hadn't wanted to do more than kiss any of them.

When I met Patrick, everything changed. It seemed an eternity to me, that interval between meeting and getting him into bed. I ached for him. I thought about him constantly, lying in bed at night with my hand between my legs, wishing for him. I have never wanted anything as much as I wanted Patrick Foss.

The night we ended up in bed, he came over for dinner as he had done virtually every night for those two weeks. It was expensive feeding us both: I remember that I was nearly out of money. My parents sent me a check every month—a frugal one, since they believed that poverty in youth builds character—and it was April twenty-ninth, the end of the month. I improvised a dish made of rice and a can of tuna and, I think, some frozen peas, and with it we drank the cheap beer Patrick always brought, and we talked and talked: art, school, exams, professors, welding, watercolor versus oil, metal versus wood, cats versus dogs, city life versus country life, rice and beer versus caviar and champagne . . .

But something had changed between us. For the first time, sex was part of the undercurrent of our conversation, it was with us there as palpably as the gluey rice or the roar of the crowd from the ball park three streets over. We looked into each other's eyes, our gaze holding, our conversation stopping, his hand reaching for mine across the table. I thought I would faint from happiness.

"Wynn," he said, his voice quiet with emotion.

We stood up, we embraced, we kissed, and after a while we went into the bedroom, so hot with the need of each other we could hardly get our clothes off.

Then, when the actual moment came, I froze. I held him away from me and said, "Wait. Please. I'm sorry."

He stared at me, and then he took me by the shoulders and said, "Wynn," very gently. "It's all right. I didn't mean for things to go so fast, you know I would never want to hurt you. Are you a virgin, love?"

I didn't know what to say. For the weeks since I had known him, I had hardly ever thought about my pregnancy, my foolishness, my lost child; I'd been able to think of nothing but Patrick. I had thought Patrick would fill the black void that was always there, vast and gaping beneath everything I did.

Now I knew that if I opened my legs to this man I would fall into it. I sat there shivering, and pulled the sheet up around my neck.

Patrick said, "Wynn, tell me what you want me to do, I'll do it, I'll do anything."

The room was dark. I could barely see his face and hoped he couldn't see mine: the face of a weak and contemptible person. All I wanted was for him to leave so I could be alone with what I was feeling—that immediate, unexpected return of the old anguish. We sat miserably, not touching, and then he said, "Wynn?" and reached out to smooth my hair with such tenderness that I began to cry. I leaned against him and wept into his bare shoulder, loud, hard sobs I had no control over, and he stroked my hair, rubbed my back, wiped my tears with the sheet and lifted my hand to kiss it. "Shh," he kept saying. "It's okay, Wynn. Whatever it is, it's okay, love."

I knew he was bewildered. I could sense his confusion in the tone of his voice and the slight tenseness of his body as he held me. But he never asked me what the trouble was—he was too much of a gentleman to insist on an explanation until I was ready to give it. And I wasn't ready: I knew I couldn't tell him the truth.

How I knew that, and why, I'm not sure, but there was an unforgiving quality in Patrick that sometimes made me uneasy. He was unfailingly loyal to his friends, but he could also be harshly intolerant of art that was overcalculated or insincere, and I knew his attitude didn't apply only to bad art. He never expressed this, but I sensed that he saw himself as a poor boy who had come from nowhere and who was going to make something great of his life no matter how powerful the odds were against him. He had set the highest standards for his own behavior, and he had little respect for anyone who didn't. Disloyalty, dishonesty, and pretense: those were for him the deadly sins.

I thought about telling Patrick I gave away my child as if she were a kitten, or a dress that was too big on me. I imagined him looking at me with alarm and sympathy and asking *why*. And then what?

*It was inconvenient, I wanted to get on with my life, my mother talked me out of keeping her, my own father wouldn't support me, there was no one on my side, I couldn't cope, I was alone. The baby cried when I held her, Patrick, and I panicked. I panicked!*

I heard myself saying this to Patrick, the orphan boy whose parents were gone from his life when he was five, who knew firsthand the meaning of loss and abandonment. I knew how his eyes would change, and the way he said my name, how the look on his face would become detached, appraising.

He stroked my hair, and I lay in his arms thinking of all this. We heard the Fenway Park crowd erupt out of the stadium and onto the streets, fans yelling, cars starting, horns honking, and when there was silence again I said, "I had a bad experience once. Something I don't like to talk about. It makes this difficult for me."

That was all I could say. God knows what he thought—that I had been raped, most likely. I didn't want him to think it, I hated myself for being anything less than honest with him, but the truth, I knew, could take him away from me, and by this time I couldn't risk it.

That was the first night—a disaster. We loved each other, though. There was nothing clearer than that, except perhaps our desire for each other. And so we tried again. He was patient and inventive and persuasive. He won me over because of his sweetness, and because I wanted to be won over, and because I needed him so much.

Making love, finally, with Patrick was like finding myself—my real self. Making love with Patrick was the first ecstasy I had ever known. I had seen glimpses of happiness—in my work, in friendships, in the old days with my parents—even sometimes with Alec. But this terrifying kind of ecstasy—the unexpected rapture that took the place of what I had feared—went beyond mere happiness. Making love with Patrick was my first complete experience: I had never even imagined such a thing, that every part of one's being could be engaged at the same time.

This sounds complicated, but it was really very simple. It was love. I loved him. I loved talking to him, I loved kissing him, I loved being near him, I loved guiding him into me, my hands clutching him—my mouth, my legs, everything open to him, his face above me, his face below me, my fingers in his hair, my voice crying out in a kind of abandon I didn't know I was capable of. It seemed the miracle could happen, the dark void might indeed be filled. Everything, everything was changed.

• • •

I fell in love with Patrick almost exactly two years after my daughter was born, and that piece of my past was the only important thing that I ever kept from him. It was my sleazy little private pain. I hated having secrets, and over and over I tried to find a way to tell him. But when I searched my mind for the words, I was swept with such overwhelming shame and guilt that I couldn't speak.

Strangely, my happiness with Patrick made me imagine my daughter in a way I hadn't before—as if the power of being in love had allowed other, less happy emotions to be released. I thought of her as a real child, one who was getting older, who lived happily with her parents somewhere in the Midwest, who didn't know I existed. I thought of her especially at the end of March, on her birthday—just as my mother did of her two lost sons. Sometimes the world seemed to be made of memories of lost children. Where was she, that dark-haired daughter? What kind of life did she have? What did she look like? Was she blowing out candles, opening gifts? Did she have a pet, did she like being read stories?

The worst thing was that soon after I fell in love with Patrick, a thought began to pick at the edge of my consciousness that at first I could scarcely acknowledge was there. The thought was this: If I had kept that child, what a good father Patrick would have been. We would be a family, the three of us. I had seen Patrick with children—how easy he was with them, how effortlessly he could make them laugh. These were knacks I didn't have. He didn't condescend to them, didn't batter them with questions the way most adults did: *How old are you? What grade are you in?* He just talked to them, simply and with interest, as if his own childhood were still vivid to him, what it was like to be six, eight, eleven. He told them little things about animals, or bugs. Once he told a pack of kids we met in a playground about a pet turtle he'd once had, named Greenback. They wouldn't leave us alone, and when we left the park they called after him, "Bye, Patrick! Bye!" until we were out of sight.

Patrick, Wynn, and little Molly—that mythical happy family—became my favorite fantasy, and, sinking into it, I would feel a painful, shamed relief. At the same time, keeping all this from Patrick was agony for me. But how could I tell him that I had done something it would sicken him to hear? And how could I explain that I was in the grip of a fantasy of such hopeless bliss that by comparison real life, even lying in bed with the lover I adored, could not measure up?

• • •

Once when we were talking about my parents Patrick looked at me shrewdly and said, "What's your problem with them? They sound nice enough, they seem like good parents."

I stared at him. "There is no problem. My parents are great. Why do you ask that?"

"I don't know. You just get that look on your face."

"What look?"

"That *holding-back* look. You know. You've got it now."

I went over to the mirror. To me, my face just looked crabby. I smoothed it out, widened my eyes, put on an inane grin, and turned back to Patrick. "What? This?"

He laughed, but it wasn't Patrick's way to let things go, and later he brought it up again in his oblique, undemanding way. "I don't suppose it's easy being an only child," he said. "Or having one."

"You were an only child."

"Me?" He snorted. "My experience was so out of the loop it doesn't count. A kid raised in a junkyard by an alcoholic Irish immigrant uncle. The fact that I was an only child seems a minor detail."

I was going to Maine less and less often: That spring I had seen my parents only once, when they were both in Boston on one of my mother's visits to Haskell Graphics. I met them at the Ritz-Carlton for tea, and I didn't bring Patrick, though I told them about him.

"You broke up with Alec?" my mother asked, as if I'd said I had decided to have my legs amputated.

"I'm afraid so."

They looked at me with concern. I had braided my hair neatly and dressed with care in a dress my mother had sent me, an aggressively simple green linen shift that I had finally located in the depths of my closet and ironed hastily on the edge of my bed while Patrick, still under the covers, watched with amusement. Looking down at my lap, I could see how inadequate a job I'd done.

"May we ask why?"

"I'm seeing someone else," I said. "A sculptor."

My father looked interested. "What kind of sculpture?"

"Sometimes wood. Mostly metal."

"Metal?"

"Rusty stuff. Old mufflers and things."

"What on earth does he do with it?"

"Probably not your kind of thing, Dad."

He smiled. "Maybe not anybody's kind of thing."

"He's won a million awards," I said, more fiercely than I'd intended to. "He has a full scholarship. He's going to be a great artist, a famous sculptor."

My father still looked dubious. "What's he like?" he asked. "Besides poor and talented?"

I hesitated, looking around the room: pale pink tablecloths, demure tea-drinkers, discreet conversation, waitresses with silver trays. Impossible, in such a place, to describe Patrick adequately. "He's very nice."

My parents looked amused. "Well, I hope so," my mother said. "Bring him up to see us."

I shrugged. "We'll see how things go."

She smiled and smoothed my wrinkly sleeve. "That dress looks sweet on you," she said, and my father asked how my painting was going, and the subject of Patrick was dropped, but the rest of the afternoon was wrapped in an aura of faint doubt and disapproval that, I realized, didn't bother me at all. I had no intention of taking Patrick to Maine.

But he was curious about what he considered my normal childhood, and he wanted to see my hometown, meet my parents. I put it off as long as I could. The prospect of going to Maine with him unnerved me. West Dunster was saturated with my secret past. The place was full of lies. There were people there who knew the truth—not only my parents, but Marietta, old teachers, the Erlings—and plenty more who knew half-truths or who suspected things. I had a panicky feeling that by some subtle osmosis, as soon as Patrick crossed into the town, past the WEST DUNSTER POP. 2,879 sign at the foot of Burbank Mountain, he would see deep into the other Wynn and know me for what I was. And despise me.

But it wasn't only that. It's probably a shameful thing to admit, but I didn't want my parents to know him. With Alec, I hadn't cared—in fact, I enjoyed being in Maine with Alec, seeing him and my parents bond like old pals. But I wanted to keep Patrick for myself. He was mine, *mine*, and I wasn't ready to trot him out for my parents to approve or disapprove.

But in the end there was no getting out of it. In June, Patrick had a few days off from his welding job, and we took the bus to Maine. Once the decision was made, I was resigned: Whatever happened would happen. When I was feeling optimistic, I thought that in Maine I would even find the courage to tell him the truth: I wouldn't be able to hold it back any longer. The truth had become, for me, a paradise, an idyllic place that I wanted more than anything to visit—a sort of Paris, a place I knew was unattainable but beautiful, liberating, full of wonders—a garden of delights, but hedged in by deadly thorns.

Both my parents met us at the station in Dunster. They had approved of Alec on sight, but it was immediately obvious that they weren't so sure about Patrick. I had assumed that his appearance would win my mother over—he was much handsomer than Alec—and that my father would, if nothing else, relate to him as another man who worked with his hands. But I saw their faces when we got off the bus, and suddenly observed him through their eyes: his hair badly needed cutting, he wore a faded CAESAR'S CLAM SHACK T-shirt from a thrift shop. The only shoes he had brought were battered old sandals, and he carried an aged green duffel that had gone through World War II with his father.

My mother kissed my cheek. Then she said, "Patrick?" as if disbelieving it, and was taken aback when Patrick hugged her. My father winced visibly when they shook hands. "I'm so glad to meet you both," Patrick said. "At last! I've been asking Wynn to bring me up here for months now, and she finally ran out of excuses."

My mother looked at me. "Well, we're delighted that you managed to persuade her," she said.

"Yes, it's great," my father said vaguely.

"It is, isn't it?" Patrick said, smiling.

All the way to our house in the car he asked questions about the landmarks we passed, the history of the town, the logging industry and the paper mills, the weather. His happiness at being there was intense, his delight in the rugged landscape and in finally meeting my family. Sitting squeezed beside me in the back seat of my mother's Volkswagen, he kept his arm around me, and once he leaned down to give me a quick, exuberant kiss.

I could sense my mother's horrified realization: *My God, she's sleeping with this hippie slob.* She had asked me once, when I was dating Alec, if I was being careful about birth control, and I assured her—somewhat testily—that she needn't worry about it. That was all that was ever said, but I knew that the thought of my having sex with anyone made her and my father nervous, that the specter of Mark Erling was always with them.

When we got to Brewster Road, after Patrick admired the bright blue front door, the wisteria that flanked it, my mother's cozy kitchen, and the cats who trotted out to greet us, he rooted around in his duffel for the present he had brought: a pen and ink sketch he had done of me dozing under a tree by the river, my hands clasped in my lap, my long skirt spread out around me, my head flung back. He had matted it and put it into a cheap black frame, and when he handed it to my mother he said, "It doesn't do her justice, of course. But I thought you might like it, just because it's Wynn."

My mother looked at it, startled. "But it's wonderful," she said. "You did this, Patrick?"

They were touched. They agreed that it captured their daughter perfectly, and that it was a lovely thing in itself. My father fetched a hammer, and after some discussion they hung it in the living room next to a small drawing I had done years ago of the two of them playing chess at the kitchen table. It depressed me to see the two drawings side by side: next to Patrick's spare simplicity, mine seemed bloated and fussy.

"I can't imagine why you still have that thing hanging up," I said.

"We love that little drawing, Wynn!" my father insisted.

"How old were you when you did this?" Patrick asked me.

"I'm not sure. Fifteen?"

"Fourteen," my mother said. She always knew these things. "The winter you were in ninth grade."

Patrick glanced at me. "It's very good work."

My parents beamed at him—the sure route to their approval was to praise their daughter's art. "Wynn is much too modest," my father said. "That's one thing you'll learn about her."

The drawing, for all its flaws, was full of feeling, full of me, in all my adolescent exuberance. Even I could see that.

"I was a child."

"I think you must have been a remarkable child," Patrick said.

"I doubt it." I hesitated. The drawing I had done suddenly seemed unbearably melancholy; the freedom of it, the ease of the line, were things that had become alien to me. And the affection for the subjects was almost palpable. "But I was a happy child," I said, and was appalled to find my voice breaking. "It was a long time ago."

"Not so long."

"Longer than you'd think."

After dinner, I showed him where he would sleep. Our house had no real guest room, just a tiny attic area under the eaves where there was barely space for a cot. "It's a bit inconvenient, but it's the best we can do in this small house," my father said behind us on the narrow stairs. I had a panicky moment, expecting Patrick to say, "Well, why don't I just sleep with Wynn?" But of course he said no such thing. He flung down his bag obediently, asking my father questions about the age of the house and the changes my parents had made in it.

The sleeping arrangements hadn't been an issue when I brought Alec home; I was quite happy to kiss him good night at the attic stairs and retire to my own room. But it was maddening not to be able to sleep with Patrick for three whole nights. It wasn't so much sex I missed as comfort. As I lay there before sleep in my old bed, I tried to figure out what was wrong. I had dreaded the visit, but it was going more smoothly than I expected. My parents had warmed up to Patrick, though they couldn't spend much time with us. My father was busy; my mother said she had a ton of work piled up in her darkroom. She'd had bronchitis during the winter, and was left with a cough she couldn't shake. She and my father bickered about whether or not she should see a specialist, and one evening when it turned cool my father went across the room and arranged a shawl around her shoulders. It occurred to me that my parents were aging: Was that what was bothering me? That they were inching closer to death, that someday they would be gone—and then what? What would I do with my anger then? And with my old, frayed love for them?

• • •

Marietta was home for the summer; I hadn't seen her since the fall, though we wrote to each other faithfully. She looked glamorous—very thin, artfully made up, her hair cascading down her back. She and Keith and Patrick and I went out for pizza and beer, and the next afternoon Patrick insisted that Marietta and I spend some time together. He didn't mind at all. He would borrow my rickety bike and go for a ride.

"You two are best pals," he said. "I know you're fond of me, darlin', but you've known Marietta a lot longer, and don't tell me you don't need to talk."

Marietta and I spent the afternoon at Osmar Lake rubbing suntan oil on each other and gossiping. She and Keith were just friends now, she said. She was involved with a German boy she had met in her screenwriting class, but he was home in Berlin until the end of August.

I asked her what she thought of Patrick. She said, "I like him a lot. I thought we all had fun last night. Didn't you? At least, Patrick seemed interested in Keith's band."

"Yeah, they got along really well."

My fears about my secret being revealed had been absurd. All Keith really wanted to talk about was the band he was in and their hopes of getting some hotshot producer in New York to record them. Then Marietta and Patrick had a long, amiable argument about the Dodgers and the Red Sox.

"Patrick's pretty intense, though."

"Intense? Yes, I guess he is." I looked over at her. In spite of the suntan oil, she was getting sunburned. Marietta always got sunburned. "Isn't intensity good?"

"It's good for you. He'd wear me out. But you'd probably think Richard was a frivolous twit."

"*Is* he a frivolous twit?"

She turned her pink face toward me and grinned. "Of course! Why do you think I like him?"

"You think Patrick is too serious? He's not really. I mean, no, he is, but he—"

Marietta reached over and pulled my hair. "Hey! Relax! Richard is perfect for me. Patrick's perfect for you. What do you want me to do? Fall in love with him? He's cute, he's terrific, but he's your type, not mine."

I smiled. "I guess I just can't believe that everyone isn't in love with him."

"Perfectly natural, dollink. You're nuts about the guy. He's nuts about you. Enjoy it while it lasts." I just looked at her, and she laughed again. "All right, all right! It's going to last forever. Right?"

"Right," I said. I didn't laugh. "Absolutely right, Marietta."

Marietta raised her eyebrows. "Talk about *intense!*" She looked down at her arm. "I'm burning to death. I'm turning into Joan of Arc, for Christ's sake. Let's get out of here."

"Marietta?"

"What?"

"You won't say anything, will you?"

"About—?"

"About what happened to me. About the baby."

She stared at me. "You haven't told Patrick about that?"

"I couldn't."

"Wynn, you've got to." She reached over to squeeze my hand. "Listen. You've got to get over feeling bad about it. You got drunk and got knocked up. That doesn't make you a whore or anything!"

As always, I was struck by how odd it was that for nearly everyone it was only my pregnancy that concerned them, rather than what came after—as if pregnancy were a self-contained state without consequences, like appendicitis, and giving away a child was nothing.

"It's not that, Marietta."

"Then what in hell is it?"

I sighed and began to gather up my things. "I don't know." I thought of Suzanne Lombard, how we had wept for our lost babies. I remembered her anger, and I wondered what had become of her.

"Wynn?"

"I'm being stupid. I know I have to tell him."

Marietta pressed one finger into her arm, leaving a white mark that quickly turned red again. "Shit, it's not fair. Why do I burn and you tan?"

"Italian granny."

"Damn." She stood up, wincing, and shook out her towel. Then she stood there frowning at me.

"What?"

"I'm worried about you. If you don't tell him, it's going to mess up your whole relationship."

"All right! I'll tell him!"

"When?"

"When I'm ready."

After a moment, she smiled at me. "You really do look devastating with a tan, blast you."

While we were at the beach, Patrick had taken his bike ride, then mown the grass and raked it as finickily as my father would have done, and put the clippings in the compost. He also fixed the brakes on my bicycle.

"Isn't he supposed to be on vacation?" my mother asked.

"Patrick likes to keep busy."

"He's certainly got a lot of energy," she added, as if that were a dubious quality at best.

We were sitting on lawn chairs. Patrick was with my father in his workshop. From across the expanse of grass, we could hear their voices—not just Patrick's but my taciturn father's as well. "What on earth could they be talking about?" she asked.

"Routers, I would guess," I said, smiling. "Or maybe hand saws versus power saws."

My mother laughed, and that made her cough. I went inside and got her a lemonade and a beer for myself. "You've seen somebody about that?" I asked her. She waved a hand, still coughing, and when her cough subsided, she said, "Please don't worry. I know Dad wants me to see this doctor in Portland, but Dr. Rice says I just have to wait it out. He gave me a prescription for some cough medicine, but it makes me so sleepy I only take it before bed."

We sat in silence, drinking our drinks, smelling the fresh-cut grass. It was very beautiful there, and peaceful, the huge square of lawn ringed by flower beds and, up near the house, the carefully tended vegetable garden: my father's rustic pea fence thick with green vines, the rows of tiny pale lettuces, the wooden supports in place for the tomatoes. I was aware, from time to time, that my parents were amazing. They were both well into their sixties, and yet everything they did reflected hard work, discipline, and that implacable serenity I had grown up with and by which I had defined my own life for so many years.

"Wynn?" my mother said suddenly. "Why didn't you want to bring Patrick to see us?"

I wasn't prepared for her question, and I didn't know what to say. I had lost the habit of honesty with my parents. *None of your business,* was my first thought. But of course it was her business. I said, "I don't know. For one thing, I wasn't sure you and Daddy would like him."

"Hmm."

Her face was still pink from her coughing spell. The lines around her eyes and mouth were deep, her close-cropped hair almost entirely gray. I looked at our hands, close together on the arms of our chairs: mine was fleshy and tanned; hers was thin, the delicate skin age-spotted and papery and the blue veins prominent. Her gold wedding band hung loose on her finger.

"I mean, you liked Alec so much."

"Yes." A burst of laughter reached us from the workshop. "What was the other thing?" my mother asked.

I couldn't stop looking at her hand. I remembered how beautiful her hands used to be. How had she become so old? When had this happened?

"What?"

"You said that was one thing, that we might not like him. What else?"

"Oh—nothing, really. Just that. You know. He doesn't have Alec's table manners, things like that."

"Patrick is different," my mother said. "He takes some getting used to. But there's more to him, I think. We both like him very much."

I felt a wave of gratitude. "I'm glad." I reached over and took her hand. "I'm really glad, Mom." At the moment, it was true.

• • •

On our last night, Patrick and I borrowed the Volkswagen and drove to Osmar Lake. We made love near where Mark had gotten me pregnant. I didn't tell Patrick that that particular spot of sand had any significance, I didn't tell him anything: I wanted to, I tried the words over in my mind, but finally I just clung to him, thankful that he was there with me. *Enjoy it while it lasts,* Marietta had said. Her words had chilled me. But it was Marietta who changed boyfriends with the seasons, not me. And I knew she was wrong: It wasn't keeping secrets that would destroy my relationship with Patrick; it was telling the truth.

• • •

One of the things Patrick and I did was to invent our own language. It started as a joke. We were walking down Huntington Avenue, when he suddenly turned to me and said, quite loudly, "Chafanga tee olungo?"

I looked at him. He wore a suppressed smile, and his eyes had that wicked gleam that I had come to associate with his unexpected wacky side—the side that sometimes went beyond Patrick Foss the obsessive, maniacally driven and ambitious sculptor and emerged as Patrick the nut, Patrick the funny little rebellious boy.

I said, "Wayfingo kahbi snoot."

"Woggo," he said, delighted. "Woggo dondolo."

I nodded. "Feekimo."

It became something we treasured, that crazy language—who knows why? At first it was a form of adolescent foolishness, to make people pay attention, try to figure out what tongue we were speaking in that polyglot city. Surrounded by Spanish and Chinese and Polish in our multicultural neighborhood, we were amused by the odd language we called Feekish. And sometimes in bed, Patrick would turn to me and say, "Boofinka, wheemara?" and I would reply, without hesitation, "Humprammi. Whalliko festuna." Eventually, we codified various words and phrases. *Whalliko festuna* meant "I love you"—easier than the English words for two reticent people. *Woggo* was our word for sex. He called me *Wynnooka,* I called him *Pattonino.* It was silly, and yet it was meaningful to us. It was a way of circumscribing our private universe, of being everything to each other, of keeping the real world at bay for a while.

I thought sometimes that I would confess all the awful things about myself to Patrick in Feekish, if I could only figure out the words.

We had some good friends—Jeanie Volovich, her boyfriend Andrew, Patrick's pals Clement Clay and Richie Lippman, and my friend Rachel Lucas, an exchange student from England. But Patrick and I spent most of our time alone together, and that summer we became so inseparable that we began to think it was silly not to share an apartment.

It was the seventies. Living together was in the air; all our friends were doing it. Even fickle Marietta had moved in with Evan—Richard's successor. I half relished, half dreaded the idea of my parents' mild disapproval. Anna Rosa, I knew, would give us her blessing; she had met Patrick at Christmas, and he had passed her test by asking her about her Italian childhood and eating three helpings of gnocchi and sauce at her kitchen table. By the end of the visit, she was calling him doll.

But we hesitated. We talked it over endlessly and decided we weren't ready—some kind of separation was still necessary. Sometimes he stayed at my apartment, sometimes I stayed in his bare one-room on Hemenway Street. When we were apart we missed each other, and we could have saved money by splitting one rent. But

Patrick used to say, only half-joking, "It's not right to be so happy all the time, Wynn," as he kissed me good night at my door. "I'm going home where I can brood about things without looking up and seeing you there and feeling cheered by the sight of you."

As for me, I longed to be with him, but I was stopped by the fear that if we lived together I would be unable to keep my secret, and the real me would stand revealed: the weak and selfish girl who, against her better judgment, had been persuaded to give away a part of herself.

• • •

I struggled with my painting all through art school. The certainties I had been blessed with when I was younger had deserted me, beginning with my bleak collages at Edna Quinlan, but persisting long after that, and continuing to plague me no matter what I did. My painting professor called me a chameleon—not entirely with disapproval, but with something like awe. There was no consistency to my work, no single vision—the only thing my creations had in common, Patrick said, was that distance, the refusal to be present in my work.

"Don't think so much!" he was always telling me.

"But I have to plan it out, Patrick—at least a little."

"You're not understanding me," he would say, and look exasperated. "I don't mean just rush in and throw paint on the canvas, love. I mean crawl into your work, Wynn—live in your painting."

"I don't get what you mean," I said.

I did get what he meant, though: I could remember a time when I did live inside my work. A time when I hardly lived anywhere else, when I was most at home when I was standing at my easel. I was aware that I was doing something else now, but I couldn't, for the life of me, see how to change.

"Maybe I should transfer to B.U. and major in English," I said to

Patrick one day. I had already, in fact, sent for a catalog and an application.

"Maybe you should stop worrying about it," he said. "It will only make everything worse." Then he put his arms around me. "Wynn, don't blow this out of proportion. You're a good painter; you're very talented. You've produced some amazing things."

"Then how can I paint such crap, Patrick?"

"Shh," he said, holding me close. "Don't say such things. You just need to find your voice, darlin'. You need to find out who you are."

"I know who I am."

"I don't think so."

I pulled away from him angrily. "Don't patronize me, Patrick! How come you know who *you* are? You don't have this problem."

He looked at me earnestly. "Wynn. Listen to me. I'm a much simpler soul than you are. I'm easy. I'm a guy who carves things out of wood and welds bits of metal together—that's all I've ever been." He took my hand. "Think about it, love. It's all I do. Aside from my bloody work and you, I don't have much of a life."

In a way, it was true. Patrick wasn't antisocial, but he didn't talk on the phone for hours as I did, he didn't read much, he'd never waste a whole evening devouring terrible old movies on TV. He rarely drank to excess, he didn't smoke pot or cigarettes, he refused to drop acid. He hardly ever took a day off, or even an afternoon. Occasionally on a beautiful summer day I could persuade him to go on a picnic or take a walk. He worked every chance he got, and his friends were the same way; when he and Richie got together for a few beers, they always talked about art—what they were doing, what other people were doing, what they had seen in a museum or a gallery, why one thing was good and another bad.

"And that's all I'm ever going to need." He grinned at me. "Pathetic, isn't it?"

Even while he was still in school, Patrick was beginning to sell his sculptures. A middle-aged couple from Brookline—both doctors—encountered his work at a student show, and they bought one of his smaller pieces immediately. They introduced Patrick to other collectors they knew and, gradually, he began to sell things—not for a lot of money, but steadily—and he stopped being painfully short of funds. He bought a couple of new sweaters, including a beautiful golden-brown one at Brooks Brothers, exactly the color of his eyes. He took me to Red Sox games—he had a crazy affection for that doomed team. He bought some of the burled maple he had been craving, and a set of Japanese chisels, and he began to talk about, someday, when he could afford it, having one of his welded metal works cast in bronze.

When we had been seeing each other for two years, he made a killing: a large metal piece was bought by the Brookline doctors, and Patrick treated us to a trip to Mexico on spring break. We flew to Mexico City, then took a bus north to the town of Querétaro. Jeanie and Andrew were spending a year there; Andrew was taking Spanish at the Instituto Allende in nearby San Miguel and Jeanie had wangled a grant to research the architecture of the area and make paintings of what she saw. They had rented a house in Querétaro, and we had agreed to baby-sit their plants and their cats for ten days while they went off to the coast to explore the Mayan ruins.

When we arrived, it was late evening, and the town was asleep. We took a taxi to the little house in the hills, where we found the key, as promised, under the mat. In the dark, we could barely make out the keyhole, and we were completely unaware of the charm of the place. It seemed only cold, silent, alien. We were exhausted from our long trip, and we stumbled inside, fed the cats—Pablito and Rosalia—and collapsed onto the huge carved bed, behind a huge carved door, and fell instantly asleep.

In the morning, we woke to paradise. The tiny house consisted of a kitchen, the bedroom, and a large back room that opened into a courtyard. The courtyard was full of flowers: geraniums, bird of paradise, miniature roses, cacti of all kinds, vast drooping festoons of bougainvillea. An orange tree was in blossom, wafting its sweet scent into our windows. The cats slept in patches of sunshine.

Patrick and I made breakfast from the cold cereal, milk, oranges, and tea Andrew and Jeanie had left for us, and then we went out to the courtyard and sat in the sun with Pablito and Rosalia. Four hours later we were still sitting there, dazed with the beauty, the smells, the street noises, the Spanish music from at least three nearby radios, and the excitement of being together in a foreign country. Finally we roused ourselves and went out into the street to investigate.

The house was up the hill from the vast Friday *mercado*. We bought fruit and vegetables, bright tin toys and straw dolls, carved wooden animals, a brilliant shawl, cheap shoddy espadrilles, fresh-made tortillas, a roasted chicken. And Patrick bought me a necklace of turquoise beads strung on a silver wire. When he fastened it around my neck, he kissed me gently on the cheek and said, "Whalliko festuna, Wynnooka."

I looked into his face. "No." I shook my head. "Say it, Patrick. Say it."

He had never really said it, except in Feekish. He had said *I'm crazy about you,* and *You're the greatest,* and *How did I ever get along without you.* But he had never said the words, and suddenly, standing there in the middle of the crowded market, my arms filled with bundles, the scent of roast *pollo* rising up between us, his fingers fumbling with the clasp of the necklace—suddenly I wanted to hear it, in English.

"Say it. Please. Now."

He smiled and bent his head down to me. He put his forehead against my forehead. His eyelashes brushed my eyelashes. "I love you, Wynn," he said. "*Te amo*. Whalliko festuna." And then again, "I love you."

We stood there as the crowd surged around us: Mexican grandmothers with bright plastic shopping bags. Beautiful, well-behaved children clutching their mothers' skirts. Sellers bargaining with buyers. Tourists with cameras. And the two of us smiling into each other's eyes, saying over and over, "I love you. Whalliko festuna. *Te amo.*"

We didn't do many of the things tourists do. We didn't sightsee or take pictures or even make sketches. We bought postcards that never got sent. We took long walks, but we didn't go to see the Palacio Municipal or the Convento de la Santa Cruz. We never rode the bus to San Miguel de Allende or to check out the craftspeople at San Juan del Río. We didn't go dancing at the just-opened disco; we didn't hear a concert or see a ballet at the Académia de las Bellas Artes. We did happen to pass the Jardin Obregón one Sunday evening when a band concert was in progress, and we sat among the decorous family groups and listened. We occasionally drank margaritas at El Rincón, a bar where a sad-eyed flamenco guitarist played.

But mostly we stayed in Jeanie and Andrew's apartment. We made love in the big carved bed, on the kitchen floor, in the bathtub—once on the terrace, late at night, in the dark. And for long, blissful hours, we did nothing at all—just sat in the courtyard with the cats on our laps, talking about our future together, our hopes, our prospects. It was the first time we discussed marriage, how we would live, the children we would have.

Despite my promises to myself and Marietta, I had never been able to tell Patrick about my past. The more involved we became with each other, the more I doubted that he would understand my story, and as time went by the simple fact that I'd concealed it for so long became bizarre and indefensible. Once, a boy we knew from school had made up a stupid lie, absurdly inflating some trivial accomplishment, and Patrick, telling me about it, said, "That guy's a pathological liar!"

I raised my eyebrows. "Isn't that a bit of an exaggeration, Patrick? It sounds like he was just trying to impress people."

Patrick said, "Call it what you like—but I feel I can never really trust him again."

How could I tell him I'd been lying to him for years? I was forced to continue to lie: an ever-expanding circle of deception that I didn't know how to break through, and that, in time, even my painting became part of.

I had become aware that my artistic failures were troubling to Patrick; I sensed his bewildered impatience while he waited for me to figure things out, for some direction to emerge from the confusion of works I was producing. "Don't dream such small dreams," he said once. "Don't ask so little of your art, Wynn!" This talk made me weary: Everything seemed so much more complicated than Patrick made it sound, his ideas as irrelevant to my concerns as if we were different species.

During one of these conversations, he said, "An artist has to be honest above all—don't you think? Even if the process is agony?"

He wasn't referring to me; he was brooding about the roots of his own obsession with collecting damaged, cast-off objects and trying to create beauty from them. But my heart fluttered unpleasantly at his words.

"I don't know what you mean by that," I said. I know I spoke more sharply than I'd meant to. "That sort of blanket statement always puzzles me. What is honesty, exactly, for an artist?"

Patrick thought for a few seconds, then grinned at me. "You're trying to say I'm being pretentious."

We were sitting at my kitchen table, drinking beer. "Something like that," I said, and I had to smile back at him. As always, his own candor, his openness disarmed me. They also made me uneasy. That evening's rice dish was bubbling away on the stove, and I got up to check it.

He went on, "I guess all I mean is that in my own case, there are certain feelings that I have to trust. When I was doing all the wood carving, it never felt right to me, not really. Not the way working with metal did. The old pieces of junk have a life of their own, they tell me some kind of truth." There was a pause. "I'm not explaining it very well. It's just that the work has to feel honest—you have to pull it out of your soul, Wynn—and you can't be making it for any other reason."

Needlessly, I kept stirring the rice, breathing in the hot steam that rose from the pan. I was remembering the dark, belligerent collages I'd done at the Edna Quinlan Home. On one of my trips home, I had burned the whole stack of them in the fireplace, a few at a time, and astonished myself when I was done by bursting into tears. It occurred to me that those collages were perhaps the last honest art I'd produced.

"Do you see what I'm saying?" Patrick asked.

"Yes," I said. "But I'm not sure I agree." I sat down again, abruptly. My face was sweaty from the steam, and I wiped it on my sleeve and took a long drink of beer. Patrick looked at me in surprise. I continued, feeling reckless, "Maybe honesty isn't always so positive. We all have things in our pasts that we don't want to face, that we just want to forget—don't we? Doesn't everyone? And maybe—sometimes—if we give it time—something can come out of that, Patrick. I mean, something grander than we're aware of. The way a shadow sometimes has more power than the actual object."

He was frowning. "You're talking about a kind of pathological art," he said.

"No! That's not what I mean, I don't mean hidden crimes or perversions or anything sick, just—" I looked at him helplessly. "Just things."

He seemed truly baffled. "What *things*, Wynn? I don't understand."

I took another sip of beer. The knot in my stomach combined with the smell of the boiling rice made me think I might throw up. The simple fact was that I needed to tell him the truth, all the truth, the vital truth of my life without which it was impossible for him to know me at all. I was convinced in that moment that not to tell him was wrong, self-destructive, mad. It was the closest I ever came to letting it all spill out, to saying, *Patrick, Patrick, there's something I haven't been able to be honest about, something important, and I'm going to tell you now, I have to tell you, because if facing the truth is agony, hiding it is worse.*

I studied his face. His expression was perplexed, quizzical—but also, I perceived, oddly wary, as if he were nervous about how I might answer. *Like a child about to hear bad news,* I thought. Looking into his eyes, I saw the vastness of the gulf between us, and how his own innocence walled him off and made him unable to comprehend something like a friend's silly, insecure lie, or my confession of abandonment and deceit.

I stood up, went back to the stove, said it was too hot to argue. We changed the subject, and I served dinner, feeling more alone than I had in a long time.

But sometimes I could almost make myself forget that other unsavory, guilty, secretive Wynn, and in Mexico she virtually disappeared. Yes, we would be married someday. We would have children. Patrick wanted a daughter. Maybe two. What about me? *Whatever comes along,* I said around a lump in my throat. *A son, maybe. A son who looks like you.*

Back in Boston with our little tin trucks and our serapes and my lovely turquoise necklace, we decided that we had to live together.

My parents' reaction was mixed: They could see how happy Patrick and I were, and I know they were relieved that things were working out for me. They even sent us a check so we could buy some decent furniture. But my mother wrote to me in a letter, "Don't let Patrick bury you. Your work is just as important as his." My father said we were too young for such a commitment, we should wait a couple of years, and in the next breath asked why we had to live together, what was wrong with just getting married?

But when I called Anna Rosa, she was delighted. "Kids are smart today. Don't rush into marriage. Get to know each other first."

"I thought Catholics weren't supposed to approve of stuff like this," I said.

"What's right for one person isn't right for another," my grandmother said. "That's what the church can't seem to get through its thick skull. You kids are going to be okay."

"If you didn't approve, I don't think I could do it," I told her.

"You're my honeybunch, Wynn," she said. "And don't you forget it."

I put Patrick on the phone, and she said, "Good luck, doll. God bless you."

Patrick said his Irish Catholic Uncle Austin might be a problem, and so we made an overnight trip to Livingstonville to break it to him.

We drove there in a rented truck—Patrick was hoping to find some choice rusty junk to bring back. I had met Uncle Austin once, when we stopped in to see him en route, somewhat circuitously, to New York City for a weekend. I was intrigued by the fact that this solitary man, inexperienced with children and a natural loner, had successfully raised the little orphaned boy who turned out to be Patrick. I wanted to know him better.

But he was a daunting figure to me. That first time we visited, on a bright winter afternoon, the three of us were awkward and a bit shy.

We sat on seedy upholstered chairs in the living room and talked, fitfully. Uncle Austin had trouble meeting my eyes; my presence seemed to embarrass him. He offered us beer, then tea, then some of the baked beans he was cooking, all of which we declined. He seemed hurt by this, and I felt intrusive and apologetic the whole time we were there, which was about an hour. I was also distracted by the stark beauty of the landscape through his windows: the golden stubble of the fields poking above the white snow cover, the blacks and grays of the distant hills, the shabby houses with thin breaths of smoke coming from their chimneys, and, above it all, the fiercely blue sky. It reminded me of Maine, but it was quieter, less dramatic, and as Patrick and his uncle made dutiful chatter about the junkyard and Patrick's scholarship and some cousins back in County Cork, I kept imagining how I would paint it.

On the second visit, things loosened up. It was as if Uncle Austin had given himself a talking to and had resolved to accept the fact that Patrick was grown up now, he was a man with a girlfriend, and the girlfriend was a presence to be reckoned with. Gradually, I realized he had also had a few drinks. But it didn't matter. He was charming. He shook my hand warmly and said he was glad to see me, and the three of us took a tour of the junk yard, Uncle Austin pointing out certain prized sights—like the skeleton of a Model T that had been rusting there since World War II—as if we were at Disneyland. Eventually, Patrick and I went out and brought back two pizzas and a six-pack. Uncle Austin drank whiskey along with his Budweiser, keeping a brimming shot glass on the table circled by the fingers of his left hand. He drank beer and smoked cigarettes with his right.

"We came to tell you we're going to move in together, Uncle," Patrick said. "I hope you won't mind. And we came to take away some metal. I saw a couple of interesting pieces out there I thought I might be able to give a home to."

Uncle Austin smiled. He was a small, wiry man with a pot belly and Patrick's light brown eyes. When he smiled, there was a gap between his front teeth. His hair was as thick as Patrick's, but wavy instead of straight. He looked like a picture of a leprechaun in a book I'd had as a child.

"Are you accusing me of not being broad-minded, laddie?" he asked. "Are you calling me an old fogy? Why should I mind it if you've found the right girl? And it seems to me you have. As for the junk," he added with a wink at me, "take whatever you like. You always have, why stop now?"

"Then you won't mind if Wynn and I sleep in the same room while we're here?" Patrick asked.

"I'd think it was pretty strange if you didn't."

Patrick stared at him. "You're sure?"

"Sure I'm sure!" His uncle's eyes twinkled. "What's the matter with you, Paddy my boy? Where'd you get these old-fashioned notions?"

We finished the pizza and the beer, and Patrick went up to bed early, tired out. I stayed up chatting with Uncle Austin. He got talking about the old days, and I found my chance to ask him how he had come to adopt Patrick. *Had he had doubts?* I wondered. *Had anyone tried to talk him out of it?* "Wasn't it strange to have Patrick left to you?" I asked. "Suddenly to have a five-year-old boy in the house?"

Uncle Austin pondered that, and then he said, "It seemed strange that my only sister was gone, just like that. Smashed up that green Nash Rambler they drove—they lost control going around a curve, and crashed into a wall of rock. No seat belts in those days. They had to cut the damned car open like a tin to get them out. My sister Katie and her husband, Ted."

My eyes filled. "God, I'm sorry," I said, as if it had been yesterday.

Uncle Austin took a sip of whiskey. "They were good people," he said. "Ted Foss was a blacksmith, you know—a huge fellow, bigger than Patrick, and strong as a bear. It must be in the blood, Patrick and his fascination with all that metal stuff. The rusted part of it I guess he gets from me." He chuckled. Then he shook his head and was silent a moment. "And Katie—well, she was a pretty young thing, and full of fun. I was that fond of them both, it was like a light going out. But having young Patrick come here to live only seemed strange for a time. There was no choice, really. The poor little fellow didn't have anybody else. The only other relatives were in Ireland, and a shiftless lot of good-for-nothings they were, too. I got used to the situation quickly enough."

The old, nagging guilt made its prompt appearance, as I knew it would. "That was—it was wonderful of you, to do that."

"Nothing of the kind! I was glad to do it. Besides, you know how Patrick is." He smiled. Uncle Austin had a wonderful smile, frank and a little goofy because of the gap in his teeth. "He's a likable lad."

"That he is," I agreed. I had to wipe my eyes.

Uncle Austin's fingers left his shot glass and reached across the table to pat my hand. "I'm glad to see you're tenderhearted," he said. "And you're a good mate for that boy, I can tell. I've never had a mate myself, nothing that took, if you know what I'm saying. But I've got a feel for these things." He picked up his glass again and sipped. "I'm a Catholic, you understand. Not much of one, but I'll never shake it, I know that by now. And I'm well aware that all this, this living in sin, is not what the pope would consider a good idea. But—" He paused. "Well, you two are in it for life, aren't you?" I said that I was pretty certain we were. "All right, then," Uncle Austin said. "I can't see a problem. Good luck to the both of you. And now I'm going to do something that's not like me at all. Completely uncharacteristic. Maybe a first."

He got up and went to a cupboard over the sink where he found a second shot glass. He brought it over to the table and filled it, then pushed it across to me. "I'm a cheap old bastard," he said, "but I'm going to give you a taste of my Jameson's. Twenty-some dollars a bottle and damned hard to find in these parts. Go ahead. It won't hurt you. Put it down where the flies won't get it."

I drank it down, and only with difficulty kept myself from coughing at the taste of the fiery, smoky stuff. But I immediately felt more cheerful; the guilt diminished, fizzled to nothing.

Uncle Austin looked at me expectantly. "What's the verdict?"

"It's lovely," I managed to say, and he smiled approvingly and poured me another one.

Uncle Austin and I stayed up half the night drinking whiskey and talking about Patrick's youth. I learned about the time he rescued a dog from the well, the art prizes he won at his school, the comic books he made in which his dead parents appeared as superheroes, the deficiencies of his old girlfriend Deborah, the way he persuaded the owner of the body shop in town to give him welding lessons because he couldn't get them at the high school, the crazy art he had begun to make from rusted auto parts and old tools. I listened, enthralled, to this, far into the night. And I'm afraid that in the process I acquired a taste for Irish whiskey.

When I finally stumbled up the stairs, I lay there beside Patrick, my head spinning, the dark room full of tiny, quivering points of light. My last muddled, drunken thought was that the terrible decision I had made five years before was part of what had led me here: to this house, to Uncle Austin whistling softly as he puttered in the kitchen, to my love snoring softly beside me in his old metal bed. And so it couldn't have been all bad—could it?

I woke the next morning with a hangover from hell.

"You *what*?" Patrick roared with laughter when we awoke at seven. He called down the stairs, "Uncle! You debaucher of young women! Why did you let her do that?"

"What was I going to do, I ask you?" his uncle called back. "Refuse a lady when she begs for a drink?"

"Please!" I moaned. "My head."

Still grinning, Patrick left me to suffer and headed out to the salvage yard. He and his uncle hoisted into the truck the rusted metal pieces Patrick had picked out: a large piece of corrugated tin, a couple of oil drums, and a tractor seat that dated from the thirties, plus what looked like some blades from an ancient windmill. When they were done, Patrick came upstairs. "A gold mine," he said. "I just loaded a gold mine into the back of the truck."

I sat up in bed, my head pounding, and mumbled something incoherent.

"Wynnooka," Patrick said. "For you." He handed me a mug of black coffee and perched beside me while I sipped. Then he put his hand on my bare leg. "Woggo, Wynnooka?" he asked.

"Are you crazy? I can hardly focus my eyes together, and you want to have sex!"

"Ssh," he said, grinning. "Not so loud." He leaned over and kissed me. "It's just that you're so cute when you're hungover."

The two of them ate a hearty breakfast—I think Uncle Austin actually made flapjacks with maple syrup—while I tried not to look. I drank more black coffee and took aspirin and groaned. But by the time we left I felt better. We backed the truck out of the driveway, honked the horn at Uncle Austin waving to us from the porch, and then Patrick reached over and took me by the shoulders. "Admit it," he said, shaking me, trying to hide his smile. "Life is damned good, Wynn. Admit it!"

I laughed and admitted it, and we sat for a long moment with our arms around each other before we drove our truckful of rust back to Boston, singing old songs that we translated into Feekish.

• • •

In September, we gave up our two tiny spaces and found a larger, grandly grungy apartment on the Fenway that had a back terrace where we could sit and play the Boston Spanish-language station on our radio and pretend we were still in Mexico. It was good being together in that apartment, but Patrick sometimes did become morose: He brooded, as he had warned me. Our very happiness, he said, made him uncomfortable and scared.

"I'm not used to this kind of happiness," he said once. It was the orphan talking, the cast-off child. "What would I ever do if it was taken away?"

I felt cold suddenly: The black void opened before me. What would I do? Where would I be without him?

"It won't be taken away," I said. "How could it? We have each other forever, Patrick."

"How do we know that?" he asked, when he was in one of these moods. "How can we know such a thing?"

I stroked the back of his neck. "Because we love each other," I whispered. "And because it's our mission to love each other in all our countless and inexhaustible manifestations." I kissed him. "Isn't that the way it goes?"

He smiled. "Something like that."

These crises never lasted. We were both busy, working hard, and Patrick, as always, was obsessed with his sculpture. He rented a studio in a warehouse down by the boatyards, and he routinely got up at dawn so he could spend a couple of hours there before his first class. Marietta was right about his intensity. He was a cheerfully unapologetic workaholic. Sometimes he drove me crazy, coming in at three or four in the morning after working all day. There were times I wouldn't see him for thirty-six hours at a time. Or he would be silent for long periods, sitting tensely at the kitchen table or on the terrace, frowning as if hell had opened before him. Then he would jump up and say, "Holy Jesus, I think I've figured it out, Wynn," and be off again. But he was the star of the school.

• • •

That November, Anna Rosa fell on a patch of ice and broke her hip, and died in the hospital of pneumonia. I hadn't been able to see her before the end—everything happened so quickly—and when Patrick and I took the train to New York for her funeral none of it seemed real to me. Even her little neighborhood church was like a picturesque movie set, with its stained glass and statues of obscure Italian saints—someplace my grandmother might have taken me when she was alive, whispering loudly about how pretty it all was and lighting a candle for the soul of my grandfather.

The funeral was surprisingly well attended. My grandmother had a lot of friends in the neighborhood, and there was a contingent of Upper East Side ladies she had sewed for. My Uncle Henry, widowed and rather reclusive—we hardly ever saw him—was there from Florida. He and my father embraced, tears streaming down their faces. In the middle of the Requiem Mass, Anna Rosa's old beau Roy broke into loud sobs. This was somehow shocking: Roy was a large, overweight, gray-haired man who hardly ever spoke; next to my tiny grandmother he had been like a huge, kindly tree, or a small mountain. He was sitting beside me in the pew. I put an arm around him and tried to comfort him, but seeing him collapse was like seeing a monument crash to the ground: It made me realize that my grandmother was gone, and in a moment I was crying as hard as he was, and the two of us just sat there and wept.

After the funeral, Patrick and I, along with Roy and my parents and my Uncle Henry and a few neighbors, went up to my grandmother's apartment. We crowded into her living room and ate Italian cookies from a bakery and opened a bottle of her sweet yellow wine. All I could think was that I would never be in that apartment again, never smell those smells and eat that food and curl up against my grandmother's plump back while she talked me to sleep. I looked down into the backyard of the Bleecker Street restaurant we had never been to: The garden was white with snow, the tables gone, the strings of lights put away until spring.

A few weeks later my father sent me a box of Anna Rosa's costume jewelry—sparkly beads, all her pierced earrings, some lovely old Bakelite bracelets—and an envelope of photographs. That was all there was.

Then my parents left West Dunster. My father sold his business, and they moved to Florida for my mother's health. They had been talking vaguely about moving south, but when they actually did it, it was a shock. In the past few years, my mother had developed a bewildering array of minor medical problems—the persistent cough, shortness of breath, headaches. They all stemmed from a chronic bronchial condition that worsened during the frigid Maine winters, when she was almost always sick. I knew she had given up the business of greeting card photography; she told me she was tired of it. She was now seventy, and it was time to retire. I had no idea her health was bad enough for them to take such a drastic step.

They said they didn't mind leaving Maine—they had nothing to keep them there—but I knew it was actually quite difficult for them to go. It wasn't my parents' way to dwell on such things, however. My uncle had a condo in Fort Myers; my parents knew people in Miami. They had visited the Keys, and when they heard about a little pink stucco house for sale on Key Largo, with a view of the water, they flew down and, impulsively, bought it. They acquired an old wooden boat, took up saltwater fishing, grew orchids and avocados in the backyard. My mother's health seemed to improve for a time.

They came to Boston to see us during the summer of Watergate, and we watched the hearings in their air-conditioned hotel room.

Patrick and I went to Florida that Christmas—a peculiar tropical Christmas without my grandmother. They took us fishing, and we all went whale-watching—my mother in jeans she had embroidered herself with flowers and ladybugs. I painted my parents and Patrick sitting on the veranda playing a furious game of poker. My mother made a time exposure photograph of the four of us standing in front of their boat, the *Anna*—Patrick in a beaded headband, my long crazy hair blowing in the wind, my parents standing between us, grinning, with their hands on our shoulders. I still have those photographs; we all seem to glow with happiness and well-being. My mother looks absurdly healthy.

But her symptoms came back. For a while, her doctors were convinced she had developed emphysema, but eventually—belatedly—the problem was diagnosed as lung cancer.

No one expected it to be terminal. My parents planned a summer trip to Italy, my mother renewed her driver's license for the next five years. At Christmas, one lung was removed, and she seemed better, though she was very weak. Then she got sick again, worse than before. The cancer had moved rapidly: The other lung was found to be affected, and it had spread to her liver. She was given six months; she didn't live five.

It was horrible to watch her suffer. She could hardly breathe, even with oxygen, and the sound of her rasping, shallow struggles for air filled the house. Whenever Patrick and I visited, we lay awake listening to her wheezing in her room down the hall. She was unable to eat, her eyes were huge, her hair fell out from the useless chemotherapy. When I was with her, I couldn't bear to look at her, and I couldn't look at anything else.

She spent her final, terrible week in the hospital, deeply medicated for the pain, hooked up to tubes and a respirator, unable to control the tears that ran down her gaunt cheeks. She moaned, sometimes, in a long, quiet, relentless monotone that I don't think she was even aware of. This undignified anguish seemed the wrong end for anyone, but especially, somehow, for my mother, who was always so in control, so composed and elegant, who always coped and made everything all right.

Nothing was going to make this all right. I knew that. All I could do was be with her. My father and I took turns at her bedside. Sitting next to her, holding her hand, rubbing lotion gently into the dry skin of her arms and face, I remembered the only other time I'd been in a hospital, when I had lain in bed at the hospital in Boston and my mother had sat beside me, and how she broke down when she told me the baby was a girl who looked like me. I remembered her stern profile, her distress when I said I wanted to keep her. I had never stopped regretting the loss of my child, but as I sat there listening to my mother fight for breath I reminded myself that she had done what she thought best. I longed for her to get better, to be herself again, so we could talk about it, forgive each other, get it clear between us. But she was beyond that; she was lost in her own pain.

Her last day was torture for us all. Her doctor had put her on a morphine drip, and she drifted in and out of consciousness. When she was awake, she was restless, tossing and turning, trying to get out of bed. Once I was certain she wanted to tell me something. Her face contorted with the effort, and she clutched my hand. All her strength, it seemed, was in that wasted claw. One of her nurses was there. She kept saying, "It's okay, Mrs. Tynan. Don't fight it. Just let go."

"No!" I cried. I gripped my mother's hand in both of mine. "Don't, Mom. Please don't."

The nurse—Lorraine was her name—put her hand on my arm. "You've got to let her go in peace, Wynn. I know it's hard for you, but don't make her keep fighting. Let her go."

"I can't."

"Wynn," Lorraine said gently. "You've got to."

I had another flash of memory, the social worker in the hospital saying, when they took the baby from me: *You've got to let her go.* How alike they were, birth and death: fear, pain, and helplessness. And everything changed forever.

Lorraine's shift was over and she left. My father went out to get coffee. I stayed by my mother, listening to the desperate rasp that was her breathing. Each long, slow breath seemed as if it would be her last, but then, from some great depth, she would summon up another one, and my tensed body would relax. How could I let her go? I didn't care what Lorraine said. I touched the beautiful bones of my mother's face, her winged eyebrows, still dark. They had given up on the chemo, and her hair had begun to grow back, stark white and perfectly straight. I remembered how she used to struggle with my hair, how combing out the tangles she cried as much as I did. Once she had thrown down the brush and said, "Oh God, it kills me to hurt you, Wynn." We took a break, and she laughed and showed me myself in the mirror—one side of my head tamed by her brush, the other half still wild. "My two daughters," she said, kissing me. "Both of them beautiful."

*How can anyone do this?* I thought. *How can anyone bear it?* Her breathing stopped, then started again. "Mommy," I said. "Please don't die." She opened her eyes and looked at me, and tears gathered and spilled down her cheeks. I wiped her face with the sheet, I smoothed her hair, I rubbed her hand. I wanted her to know I was there. Then, suddenly, as I sat and watched her face, the room became strangely quiet. At first, I didn't know what had happened, and then I knew her breathing had stopped. Her face didn't change; she continued to look at me, but her blue eyes were blank. "Mom," I whispered, and then I put my arms around her and held her to me, I buried my face in her hair. She weighed nothing.

Her death was a release for my father, but it put him into a state of despair and something close to panic. In less than two years, he had lost his mother and his wife. It was a terrible thing to see my parents' marriage end so painfully. They had been married for thirty-seven years; their affection went deep, and so did their dependence on each other. Dad was lost after her death; he became a different person—bitter, depressed, and, eventually, unwell himself. When I visited him or talked to him on the phone, he was peevish, complaining about his neighbors, his brother, Henry, who never called him, the weather, the odd aches and pains he had developed. I hoped he would get over it, and some version of his old, placid, practical personality would reassert itself, but that didn't happen. Within a few months he became—suddenly, appallingly—old, and difficult, and sick.

For me, it was a double loss. My mother's death devastated me. Who arranged the world so that she could suffer like this and have her life cut so short? I missed her every minute, and I missed her angrily, outraged at the cruelty of her death, and at the lack of a resolution between us, all the things unsaid. For months, when I thought about her, I wept.

Trying to deal with my own grief, I became impatient with my father's. It made me feel terrible to talk to him—his long dejected sighs, his running complaints about how tired he was, how much there was to do without my mother there to help him, how I didn't visit often enough.

I tried to be understanding, but I was so agitated all the time that I couldn't work, couldn't study, and I had to take the first Incomplete of my life. Patrick and I were always spending our scarce funds to fly to Florida and sit at my father's kitchen table with him in numbing boredom, while he complained about everything from his lawn to his investments. We were forced to neglect Uncle Austin; we had no time to visit him, spending every possible holiday and bit of time off with my father in Key West. I called Dad twice a week. I wrote him letters, sent him slides of my work and Patrick's, told him funny stories about student life. Nothing broke through the gloom; he was interested only in his own suffering. Patrick was wonderful with him, trying to engage him in conversations about chisels or chip knives, listening patiently to his long phone diatribes while I paced the floor and gnashed my teeth and made strangling motions with my hands. For a while, my father's suffering eclipsed my mother's death and left me little time to think about it, I was so busy trying to come up with ways to comfort him.

Gradually, of course, I got used to my mother being gone, and to my father being someone else. I had Patrick; my father had no one. I knew that, and in time I did learn how to deal with him, how to distract him from the emptiness at the center of his life—at least not to let his moods affect my own so drastically. I began to work again, and when Patrick and I went to visit him, it was good for a few days: The three of us could play poker, or go fishing, in some kind of harmony, before Dad began to feel sorry for himself.

But he and I were never as close as we had been, and though he took joy in my existence, my painting, my life with Patrick, a part of my father was always unreachable—always, it seemed, listening for a voice that wasn't there, seeking a comfort that was no longer available to him.

His sorrow was especially poignant because I was sure that was what would happen to me if I ever lost Patrick. During that time, Patrick and I became very close; we made love more often than ever, simply because we were alive, we were young and healthy and strong, we were together.

I had lost everything: my child, my mother and father, my grandmother—even my painting had become chancy. What I had now was Patrick: *Patrick,* who was enough, who was everything.

I thought often, perhaps too often, of what Patrick had said when he was in one of his black moods: *I've gotten used to happiness. What would I do if it was taken away?*

# *Question Three*

# Why Did You Run Away?

After graduation, Patrick and I moved to New York, to a loft on SoHo's extreme eastern fringe—a vast, bare, primitive place on Lafayette Street, with no proper kitchen, rough wooden floors, a toilet and a shower. The heat was unreliable in the winter, intense in the summer. Our huge filthy windows looked out across the broad street to a bank and a grungy bar. Derelicts sometimes slept in our doorway. The neighborhood was ugly and desolate, dangerous after dark, not entirely safe in the daytime. We loved it.

Our rent was $150 a month, and we could just scrape it together. Patrick worked part-time as a welder at a machine shop in Queens. Every Monday and Tuesday morning at 6:30 he would rouse himself out of bed, grumbling, so he could be in Long Island City by eight, and he would arrive home after seven in the evening, grumpy on Monday, buoyant on Tuesday, always starving and filthy. Four days a week, I waitressed the lunch shift at Fanelli's, which in those days was a workingman's bar.

We were hard up but not destitute. For emergencies, I had a little money left me by my mother, and from the beginning in New York Patrick had some small, erratic success with his sculpture. Soon after we moved to the city, he sold a piece for a thousand dollars to our landlord, an uptown lawyer who wanted it for the reception area of his office. Then he had two things in a group show at a gallery on West Broadway; his name was mentioned in a review, and one piece sold. After that, he showed his sculptures regularly, always in modest group shows, and he received a couple of small grants. By then, he was working entirely in metal, and his pieces had become large and unwieldy, and not cheap to produce. They also weren't easy to store. Our loft was full of his work, but he had to keep some of it at Uncle Austin's, loading it in pieces into a rented truck and storing it in the decrepit barn behind the house. He ran an electric line out there and made himself a country studio and sometimes, when we felt the need to get out of the city, we drove upstate and stayed for three or four days. Patrick would go out to the barn and work far into the night on one of his pieces, hammering and welding, while Uncle Austin and I drank whiskey in front of the TV and prayed that he wouldn't set the place on fire.

I've never known anyone who worked as diligently as Patrick did, with such single-minded intensity. He worked on his pieces, but he also spent time making phone calls, taking the subway uptown to the galleries on Fifty-seventh Street, making the rounds of places in the neighborhood, talking to people, trying to get his work shown, trying to find buyers, commissions, grants. He complained about all of it, how it took time away from his work and often ended in futility, but he kept at it, and it began to pay off.

Occasionally he had enough money ahead to create an assemblage of found objects and have it cast in bronze, an absurdly expensive undertaking. "Making art is a luxury," he often said. The money he spent producing it, and the dollar value he was able to put on his work astonished me—especially those bronzes—not because they weren't worth it, but because he was so confident. Ultimately, that belief in himself contributed to his success. He never held himself cheap, and so neither did anyone else. Of course, it helped that his work was wonderful: huge and rough, but lyrical and haunting, and expressive, always, of that unmistakable joy in living that filled everything he did.

And I woke up every morning with the miracle of Patrick beside me, feeling awe and gratitude for the life we led, and with the old, rarely spoken fear that we both felt—he the orphan, me the bereft mother—that it would somehow be taken from us.

• • •

I was painting, too, of course: Patrick's industry shamed me into working hard. But during those New York years I was beginning to realize that my heart wasn't in it. I began to look forward to going to Fanelli's, whole afternoons when I spent hours on my feet carrying trays and dealing with customers: It was a pleasure compared to struggling with a painting that I knew was doomed. I think now, looking back, that, aside from the problems I had creating honest art or finding a voice in the midst of my inner confusions, I let myself be influenced too much by Patrick's work. I was trying for the same abstract boldness, the same largeness and energy that he achieved in his sculpture. And yet I continued to paint small canvases because that was what always felt right to me. The combination was hopeless.

What I liked best was working outdoors: Painting the city, I grew to love it. Like a lot of newcomers to Manhattan, I used to take endless walks, exploring the streets north of SoHo in the Village with my portable French easel on my back. My street paintings were the best things I did, maybe because I didn't have time to think, I was constantly having to deal with the changing light and the crowds and the weather, the occasional hostility of a shop owner or doorman, the curiosity of tourists. I was oddly at ease there, and even Patrick had to admit that my work had some of the old warmth and freedom. What he didn't say—though we both knew it perfectly well—was that the paintings were also not terribly interesting—just conventional representations of quaint Village scenes. Still, they were the best I could do. When the weather kept me inside I forced myself to work on something or other, but nearly everything I produced was worthless.

On my travels, I often walked by my grandmother's apartment building. The dry cleaner had been replaced by a candle shop, and Anna Rosa's third-floor windows were no longer curtained in the elaborate swagged draperies she had made. Once I stood by her doorbell—O'TOOLE/MEROLA it said now—wishing I could ring it and bring her back, remembering how, when I heard her voice on the intercom, I would yell, "It's us, Anna Rosa!" and she would say, "Who is *us*? Burglars? Men from Mars?" Then she would buzz us in, and we would climb the stairs to her exuberant hugs and tins of Italian cookies and the unique smell of her apartment: sugar and herbs and tomato sauce overlaid with dry-cleaning fluid. I made sketches of the old building and always meant to paint it, but I never did: That place was so clear in my head, so beautiful the way I recalled it, that to put it on canvas would have been to destroy it. Someday, I told myself, when I'm working well again, I'll come back and make a wonderful painting of it. But not now.

The city's beauty and richness and variety—even its sordid dangers—seemed the ideal background for Patrick and me and our love for each other, the delight we took in each other's company, the refuge we found together in our sunny loft, our mattress on the floor. We worked in the daytime and often went out with friends at night. We got to know Santo Peri, who would eventually become an important gallery owner, and his lover, the painter Ralph Pritchett, and Frank and Gwen Maxwell, who lived over on the Bowery and were just beginning to experiment with their photographic collages. We hung out at the Broome Street Bar with them and some of the other pioneering artists in the neighborhood. Those were good times: We were a close little community, we helped each other, we were excited by each other's successes.

And then, one day, as I had feared, everything ended.

My father had bought us a television, and Patrick and I were idly watching the news on the April evening when the story about Molly McCormick's murder was first broadcast.

I can remember it with the clarity with which people say they remember a mugging, or a car crash. Even now, in my mind, I see it as a slow-motion film, with odd irrelevant details: the mug of coffee I was holding, the way dusk was just beginning to fall outside the windows, Patrick slouched in an old wing chair we had salvaged from a Dumpster, the announcer's staccato delivery of the facts of the case—the monstrous, shocking facts. A nine-year-old child tortured, violated, then strangled to death by a father who had been systematically abusing her since she was a baby. Death, it seemed, was merciful. A picture of the father, a drab man in handcuffs. A picture of the mother, an overweight woman with a black eye. A picture of the child, Molly McCormick of Kansas City—a cute, skinny little thing with masses of dark hair and a crooked smile.

My first thought was: *That could be my daughter.* It didn't come out right away that she was adopted, but even then, in that initial story, I think I knew. I stared at the screen, turned to stone, trying not to know, trying to deny it. The photograph wasn't a very sharp one. There was more of an impression than an actual child. But the resemblance between us was unmistakable—that and the name. I waited for Patrick to say, "That child looks so much like you!" But he only gave an exclamation of disgust. "Jesus, what is *wrong* with people?" he said, and was depressed about the story all evening. I don't think he noticed my reaction, my silent horror, or if he did he assumed it was merely my response to a particularly dreadful news story. I remember lying awake that night beside him, wondering if it could be true, if this had been the fate of the red baby I had held so briefly in the hospital nine years before, then deciding that it was impossible, my imagination was out of control, life couldn't be so cruel.

The next day, when I read about it in the *Daily News*, it all came clear. An adopted child named Molly, exactly the age my daughter would be, a Midwestern couple, and a clearer photograph, a recent school portrait. It was uncannily like my third-grade photograph. The dark unruly hair, the triangular face, the light eyes. She was thinner than I had ever been, and her eyes were older than any nine-year-old's should be. Her face showed the marks of strain and suffering, and her smile was forced, false, eager to please.

It was a Monday. Patrick had gone to work. I sat at the table in our loft reading the article over and over, studying the pictures: the unhappy child, the drab father, the battered mother. I knew it was my daughter, and I remember thinking: *I did this.* The second thing I thought was: *I need to tell Patrick.* And the third was: *I can't.*

In all our happy years together, I had never managed to summon the courage to tell him I had given away my child. As time went by, as people I knew became parents and I got to know their children, what I had done, the way I had gone against my own conscience, seemed even more shameful. I saw women artists who were raising children and continuing to paint. I knew single mothers managing to have good lives with their kids despite everything. An acquaintance of mine had not one but two children when she was in her teens; she managed an uptown gallery, worked on her sculptures when she could, and was devoted to her two adorable boys.

That gap between Patrick and me, that failure of confidence, was a constant anxiety, and I never gave up trying to find an opening, a way to reassure myself that he could know this about me and still love me. One night we were in the back room at Fanelli's having one of those tipsy bar discussions about love: *What does love really mean, what are its limits?* I asked him, "What if I did something wrong, Patrick? Something terrible?"

He just smiled at me. "But you wouldn't. I know you, Wynn. I know exactly what you're capable of."

"But let's just say I did. Would you still love me?"

His smile disappeared, and he got that same wary look in his eyes that I remembered. "The idea is ridiculous."

"But *what if,* Patrick? It's just a theoretical question."

He said nothing. His whole face closed up. His golden eyes narrowed with impatience. He must have known that all I needed was an assurance that he would love me, no matter what; it was only a drunken conversation, it meant nothing, we'd both forget it in the morning.

And yet he wouldn't say it, because it wasn't true.

Now everything was immeasurably more horrible. I couldn't tell him. I couldn't tell anyone. And, I thought, why should I confide in anyone? What right did I have to seek comfort? I couldn't even cry. If I had cried, I would have hated myself even more—crying was so cheap—but I couldn't have cried if I'd wanted to. I was a stone.

For a long time I couldn't do anything. I hadn't slept much the previous night, and I remember that I woke that Monday to a gray, rainy day. Across the vast room was the painting I had been working on, a drab semi-abstract still life of a pile of books on the windowsill. The sight of it sickened me. *I gave away a child so I could paint,* I thought. *A child died because I wanted to be a painter.* I thought of my mother, and my thoughts weren't forgiving: I wished she were still alive, so she could see what she had done. I imagined calling her on the phone, screaming at her about this child on the news, confronting her with the nightmare of it, letting out some of the rancor that had lived in me for nine years.

I was in agony—literally: my stomach hurt, my head pounded, my chest was tight. I thought seriously about killing myself, and I despised myself because I couldn't do it. *There is my wretched painting on the easel, and somewhere my child is lying dead.*

I was in bed when Patrick came home. I told him my head was splitting, I thought I was coming down with something. He was very quiet, very kind. I lay still, breathing evenly, while he fixed himself some food, read a newspaper, and then finally got into bed beside me. He fell asleep immediately, as he nearly always did, and once he was safely asleep I went over to the window and sat staring out at the bleakness of Lafayette Street in the dark.

It was still raining. I remember the sepia look of the street that night, the way it gleamed gold where the light fell on it. I watched a man walking slowly, staggering from time to time, to the corner of Houston, where, as he turned toward Mulberry Street, he fell. I saw him fall, watched him lie there in the rain, did nothing—just watched. I hated the world, and I hated myself with an intensity I didn't know I was capable of. I hated my own existence. I hated the parents who had inflicted it on me. I even hated Patrick for his innocence, his implacable goodness in the face of the evil in the world. I sat there cold and dry-eyed, hunched in a chair, full of loathing and shame and horror, until, toward dawn, I fell asleep.

Patrick awoke soon after and was sympathetic to what he assumed was the flu coming on. But he had slept later than usual and was in a rush to get to work. I could barely speak, and though I wanted nothing more than to lie in his arms and let him comfort me, I had to force myself just to kiss him good-bye, feeling that he debased himself by touching me, and that I in some strange way made myself even more loathsome by allowing it. When he left I went back to the window and sat there all day looking out at the street.

I can see now, so many years later, that I was in shock, the way certain kinds of crime victims become numbed and zombielike afterward. It's a clinical condition. It can be identified and treated. There are books about it, articles. If this had happened today, I could take a taxi to a crisis center of some kind, tell my story, and be helped. At that time I knew none of this, I knew nothing, and I wouldn't have helped myself if I could. I wanted to die. Failing that, I wanted to be like a dead person.

For days, I went on like that, letting Patrick blame my silence and remoteness on the stubborn headache, a vague flulike malaise. I tried to act normal. I cooked dinner for us and attempted to eat. I brushed my teeth and put on clean clothes. Sex wasn't an issue; I didn't feel well enough. Patrick was working on a sculpture in his corner of the loft—slabs of wood combined with random metal objects, one of the pieces he was going to have cast; it was at a crucial point, and he was completely absorbed. I tried only to stay out of his way. I spent my time walking, sitting in cafés, strapping my easel to my back so Patrick would think I was going out to paint.

The murder, with its hellish details, was an important story, dominating the news for days. At that time, reports of child abuse were uncommon. When the news magazines came out that week, I bought them all, and saw more photographs, took in more details of Molly McCormick's life and death. Everything I read confirmed what I already knew. There was a color photograph of her when she was about three, wearing red pajamas, sitting on the floor beside the Christmas tree. I knew that somewhere, in a box of old junk, was a photograph of myself at that age, in red pajamas at Christmastime, and when Patrick was out one afternoon I searched until I found it, and compared the two. We could have been twins. The pale blue eyes, the masses of hair, the general shape of our faces. I stared at those photographs, went over them with a magnifying glass. There was no escaping it. Our noses were different, our jawlines; her face was thinner; and she had her sad, desperate smile. But everything else was eerily similar.

One night when I came home, Patrick had turned on the news. Molly McCormick's funeral was being shown. Unable not to watch, I sat down beside him. There was a weeping aunt, a priest, a little playmate looking bewildered. The social worker who had handled the adoption was interviewed. Patrick said, "You have to wonder what this kid's real parents would be feeling if they were watching this." His mouth was twisted with anger. On the television screen, the casket was being lowered into the earth in some Kansas City cemetery. "It's bad enough to give up your kid—I honestly don't understand how anyone could do that. But then to just turn your back, refuse to take responsibility, let whatever happens happen—that's a mystery to me."

"I think sometimes—" My voice came out in a whisper, and I cleared my throat. "Sometimes it must seem like the best decision. To give a child up and then to bow out."

"People can convince themselves of anything," he said. "When I hear about something like this, I—" He broke off. "I don't know. I don't even want to talk about it." He went to the refrigerator to get a beer.

I cut out, carefully, all the pictures of Molly McCormick. I put them into an envelope and hid them between the pages of my sketchbook, taking them out obsessively to look at them. I couldn't keep away from those pictures for more than an hour or two. Sitting in cafés, I pulled them out and stared into Molly McCormick's blue eyes, thinking of my careless, privileged life—my own untroubled childhood, the drunken evening with Mark Erling, my years of happiness with Patrick while that child was being beaten and tortured, my lame, failed, boring paintings.

Patrick kept asking me if I was okay.

"Yes, I'm okay." I forced myself to smile. "Just female stuff, plus a small artistic crisis."

"You want to talk about it?"

"Not yet. Right now I need to think."

Absorbed in his work, he accepted that.

When I made my weekly call to my father in Florida, we chatted about his perennial border, what was thriving, what needed replacing. We exchanged comments on the weather. He brought me up to date on his arthritis pains and the medication he was taking for his sinuses. He didn't mention the Molly McCormick story. I half wanted to confront him with it, to inform him we were no better than murderers, he and my mother and I. I wanted to ask him some of the questions that were seething in my brain. *Was it because she had lost two sons? Was that why she wanted me to lose a child? Or was she punishing me somehow for surviving when my two brothers had not? Or was she simply evil, cold, hateful?*

I imagined my father's cowardly mumbles, his automatic defense of my mother, the phone slammed down in denial. And, of course, I said nothing. In the end, I was relieved that my father hadn't realized the truth. My shame was my own. No one knew what I had done, that I had in effect killed my own child. I had thought of her as my lost daughter. Now she was more than lost: She was dead.

I called in sick to work. I roamed the streets, and whenever I saw children playing, children walking hand in hand with their parents, I could hardly keep from sitting down and crying—if I could have cried. I walked until I was exhausted, returning compulsively to my grandmother's building on Cornelia Street. I wanted her back: She was the only one I wanted to confess to. I stood in front of her building and was filled with a longing that was almost unbearable, wishing I were six years old and could curl up beside her on the scratchy brown horsehair sofa while she told me about her boss, Mr. Sax, at the tailor shop and the basil she used to grow in Italy and how she fell in love with my grandfather in Maine because he was tall and handsome—like a Yankee Rudolph Valentino.

Eventually, I had to go home, where I would sit by the window looking out, folding and unfolding the pictures of Molly McCormick and trying to avoid Patrick. I didn't know what to do.

And then, suddenly, I knew what to do.

More than a week had gone by since I'd first seen the Molly McCormick story on television. It was the next Tuesday morning. I had been awake since dawn. I stayed in bed while Patrick hauled himself out, showered, ate breakfast. Before he left, he came over and kissed me gently on the cheek. I didn't stir. Then I heard him go out the door, lock it, and open the outer metal door to the stairwell. It slammed behind him. I sat up in bed and called, "Patrick!" He didn't hear me, of course. I didn't mean for him to hear me. I was saying good-bye.

I had received a letter from my old friend Rachel Lucas. After graduation, she had gone home to London to teach art at a school for disturbed children. Rachel had written:

*I'm sorry to hear your painting isn't going well, though you seem to be weathering it cheerfully enough. You'll get it figured out—if it's any help, I have faith in you. And I know you're firmly entrenched in New York with Patrick. But if you weren't, I'd tell you to come over and apply for this job that just came vacant here. The last teacher quit after six months—we do go through teachers quickly, chew them up and spit them out. But I've been here more than three years now—incredible!—and I think you would like the place, too. I know you'd love living in London. For me, it's been a great inspiration. It might do the same for you. Maybe you just need a change. I know this is hopeless, and believe me I'm not trying to talk you into something you don't want to do, but—who knows? I thought I'd mention it.*

It came to me suddenly that I had to give up painting, and I had to give up Patrick, and I had to leave New York. I couldn't allow myself to have the things that made me happy. I found paper and wrote a note. I didn't think about what to say, just scribbled it: *I'm leaving you because I have to. Please don't ask me why.* I left money with it; the rent was coming up, and the Con Edison bill. Then, quickly, I packed: some clothes, the photographs of Molly McCormick, my sketchbooks, a few personal things. I debated whether or not to keep the few photographs of Patrick that I had, sketches I had made of him. In the end, I put them into the Dumpster behind our building, but I kept everything he had ever given me: the turquoise beads, a tiny stuffed cat, a leather belt, a sweater I loved. I knew I had to keep those things, whether I deserved them or not.

I took my portable easel out to the street and left it outside a studio on Spring Street that held life-drawing classes: some struggling artist would find it and give it a good home. I packed my leftover clothes, shoes, books into bags and lugged them to the Goodwill store. Then I went to the bank for travelers' checks and took a taxi to La Guardia, to the British Airways terminal. I bought a ticket for the next available flight; it left in four hours. It was only then that I placed a phone call to Rachel in London. She had just come in. I asked her if the teaching job was still available, and could she get me an interview. I didn't care if she could or not. I would go anyway. The connection was very bad, but she said she'd be thrilled to see me, I could stay with her as long as necessary, and she told me how to get to her place from Heathrow.

Then I called my father and explained that Patrick and I had broken up, I was upset, I was pretty sure Rachel could get me this job in London, things had happened very quickly—that was all I said. He was sad about my being so far away, but didn't ask many questions, and he didn't sound particularly surprised. I suppose it seemed natural to him that things wouldn't last, that people he was fond of would disappear from his life.

I sat in a plastic chair with a stack of magazines that I read through systematically. I couldn't let myself think, couldn't let myself imagine Patrick arriving home to find me gone. I read fashion magazines, recipes, articles about the stock market, movie reviews. Then my flight was called, and eight and a half hours later I was knocking on the door of Rachel's flat.

And all the time I could hear Patrick's voice in my head: *I'm getting used to happiness. What would I do if it was taken away?*

• • •

The pay at St. Clement's wasn't great, and I lived austerely in London. I found a bed-sitter in a run-down row house near Regent's Park. It wasn't far from the London Zoo, and I used to be awakened in the morning by the roaring of the lions. I liked London, but I never loved it as I had New York. And that was fitting. That was exactly the way I wanted things to be.

The only kind of satisfaction I allowed myself was connected with my work, and that took a while. St. Clement's was an amazing school, staffed by people who truly cared about the children—children who had never been loved, who had been removed from abusive homes and placed there. The school was privately funded, with a large endowment and an impressive list of prominent backers. It was well known as a place that, in the face of enormous odds, could produce remarkable results, and it was a blessing, a haven for the children fortunate enough to find their way there—

desperate, angry, ancient children who had never had childhoods.

I hadn't known what I was getting into: I had simply fled the hell that New York had become. I thought St. Clement's would be a refuge, but at first it was more like a pit where all my demons lay in wait. The children seemed like my enemies. They pulled at me, they pushed me away, they intruded on my life, they laughed at me and broke down in front of me and threatened me. I spent most of the time feeling completely inadequate, bewildered, half sick with a whole new set of anxieties. For the first month or so, I went home every night exhausted, too tired to think, too beaten down even to analyze how I felt about being there. I didn't know if the place was making everything worse, if it depressed me or was healing me, if my decision had been a stroke of genius or the worst mistake of my life.

Rachel told me she had wanted to quit almost constantly during her first couple of months. Once she had gone in hysterics to Mr. Munro, the headmaster, and resigned, but had let herself be talked back into her job. Within six months, she said, she was hooked. She couldn't imagine quitting now. "Leave those kids?" she asked, and laughed. "At this point, I need them as much as they need me, Wynn. Maybe more."

Gradually, I began to see what she meant. I became used to the place, the way you get used to the frigid water in a lake that, when you first jumped into it, you were sure was going to kill you. *The kids just get to you* was what we all said—kids who would tear your heart out if they didn't frighten you to death. A large minority of them were violent, some were suicidal, all were depressed, and with many of them, we failed. I witnessed anguish and fear at St. Clement's that I will never forget. I saw a boy slash his wrist straight across, twice, three times, with a piece of glass from the window he broke, the blood spurting all over us as we tried to get to him. He held us off with the glass until he passed out from loss of blood. The ambulance arrived before he bled to death, but as soon as he was released from the hospital he tried it again, and that time he didn't survive.

That was probably the worst thing. That and the time a girl named Violet, one of my prize students, left the grounds, hitched a ride north on a frigid January day, and drowned herself in a half-frozen lake somewhere outside Manchester, her hometown. And there were other, less spectacular disasters—self-mutilations, petty cruelties, breakdowns and hysteria, occasional attacks on the teachers.

And all that time, the memory of the fate of Molly McCormick ran through my mind like a dark river in which I feared I might drown.

I had kept with me the pictures of her, and I still took them out from time to time to look at them. When I did, the shame and guilt returned—worse, perhaps, because I worked with children like Molly every day. Their lives were disturbingly real to me. I had merciless recurring nightmares about rescuing abused children, about fleeing with them through gunfire, carrying screaming babies across battlefields, struggling to stay afloat in deep, greasy water with two or three small children clinging to me. I would wake up from these dreams in terror—sweaty, breathing hard, with the echoes of my own panicked voice lingering in the air of the stuffy little room.

At St. Clement's, what kept me going was that some of these children thrived, even blossomed, in the art classes that Rachel and I taught. They fought against math and grammar and languages. Some of them even refused to play sports. But St. Clement's, wisely, stressed art instruction; at least a year of studio art was required of all students. Through art, they were freed—if only for those few hours every week—to say or do or explore anything. For many of them, it was the first time in their lives that they weren't afraid to be themselves.

It seemed wrong, at first, that the students not only enjoyed my classes, but began to like me,as well. I didn't want anyone to like me.

I wanted to punish myself, I wanted my life to be unfulfilling in every way. I don't know what I had expected, what kind of teacher I had planned to be—some stern and strictly functional automaton who would give a prim lecture, a brief critique, then disappear out the door. At St. Clement's, of course, that was not an option. To punish myself would mean I must punish the children, who more than anything needed the contact of humans who cared about them. I knew I was going to be changed by that school, the place was going to invade my heart whether I wanted it to or not. In each of those needy children I saw my daughter, and I felt that the only way I could even begin to redeem myself was to give them whatever they wanted from me—to give them myself.

This was dramatically illustrated in a little boy named Timmy. Half a dozen circular scars from cigarette burns dotted the backs of his hands; there were rope burns on his wrists and jagged white gashes across one cheek, just below his eye; he limped; his hearing was impaired. He was the saddest child I ever met. Six, but small for his age, and thin, as most of our children were, he never spoke. We were told that he screamed in his sleep. He was terrified of everyone. He would actually shake with fear when I tried to get him to draw with a crayon.

Then, after a few weeks, he seemed to get used to me, and after a few more weeks he wouldn't leave my side. Gradually, all he wanted was to sit on my lap. Nothing else satisfied him, and he would cry if I had to put him down to do something else. He was like a baby, or an insistent puppy, who couldn't understand the inconvenience of what he demanded. It became increasingly difficult for me to do any teaching in the classes Timmy was in. Eventually, I requested a conference with Mr. Munro, the headmaster, and Mary Kirk, the school's head social worker. It was decided that for a while I would do nothing for an hour each afternoon but sit with Timmy on my lap.

"He trusts you, you see," Mary said. "I feel it's important that we capitalize on that."

"We can try it for as long as you can stand it, Wynn," said Mr. Munro.

"I can stand it," I said. "As long as he needs it."

And so after lunch every day, while the children were in their rooms for the official rest periods, I would sit in a big comfortable chair in Mr. Munro's office, and lift Timmy onto my lap. And we would sit. And sit. That was all. He demanded nothing more. He didn't want to be told a story, he didn't fall asleep, he didn't move. He wanted only to snuggle there peacefully, perfectly still, his head tucked beneath my chin, one of his hands holding one of mine, his skinny legs dangling down like sticks.

For me, that hour or so with Timmy every day was a kind of therapy. I won't say it did me as much good as it did Timmy; to say that my own horrors in any way equaled his would be nonsense. But that time was incredibly important to me. I was never bored or impatient. Even in the summer, sweating from the contact with Timmy's warm little body, I never wished him elsewhere. We would sit there, breathing in unison, and the time would go by in a dream. I was always astonished when Mary poked her head in to tell me it was three o'clock, and I had to teach my watercolor class.

At first Timmy cried when he was taken away, but it wasn't long before he could accept it. He knew he could come back the next day, and the next. Those quiet afternoons were perhaps the only good thing he had ever had to look forward to—surely the only affection he had ever received. After a few months, he was talking, and beginning to play with the other children. At the end of a year, he was well enough to be placed with relatives in Cornwall. The day he left I broke down and wept—the first tears I had shed in a very long time.

St. Clement's saved me. Rachel, Mary Kirk, Henry Munro.

Timmy. Poor, doomed, suicidal Violet who could paint rings around me. A physically and sexually abused girl who went from white-faced catatonia to an Oxford scholarship. A pair of twins—Derek and Richard—who had been raised in a cage and, until Mary began working with them, knew almost no words but obscenities. The green and fragrant garden behind the brick buildings, the predictable routine, the amazing art the children made—all this gave me more than I can say. Working with the kids at St. Clement's was far from a constant joy, it was so often frustrating, difficult, insanely demanding, and futile. And sometimes a child was just plain hateful, or terrifying. We didn't succeed with every one; our failures were frequent and heartbreaking. But we saw many of them become happier and more trusting under our care, and go on to lead something approaching normal lives.

• • •

I had never planned how long I would be away, but I ended up teaching at St. Clement's School for four years.

I wrote to my father every week, phoned him when I could afford it, and twice a year I flew to Florida for a visit. He had begun to regain his good spirits, and he didn't talk so much about my mother any more. He flirted with a well-off, three-times-widowed woman named Sophie Hope, whom he met at the marina, and eventually they began dating. She was a fisherman like Dad—an overweight, talkative, pretty woman with a loud laugh, a little older than he and very different from my mother. She called my father Jim. She told me, in gory detail, about her two face-lifts, showing me the white scar under her jawline, and once she took me aside and whispered to me that my father was really amazing for his age, if I knew what she meant. She wore red lipstick and blue eye shadow, and favored printed dresses with plunging necklines that showed off her freckled cleavage. She reminded me a bit of Anna Rosa.

Dad seemed genuinely happy with Sophie, though his health

wasn't good. He still complained about his arthritis, his chest pains. I could see him getting older, more frail every time I visited, and he would fall asleep in his chair after dinner. This was especially disturbing to me, who was used to seeing my father rise at dawn, work all day, and then play poker or chess far into the evening.

And, of course, watching my father age, I saw myself getting older, too.

On those trips back home, I never got in touch with Patrick, and I waited, half in hope, half dreading it, for my father to say Patrick had phoned or written him, looking for me. It never happened. Nor did my old friend Gwen mention him in her infrequent letters. Or Jeanie, with whom Patrick and I had stayed friendly after she and Andrew married and moved to San Francisco.

I wrote to Marietta, who was working as an assistant producer at a very minor studio in Hollywood, giving her my new address and explaining that Patrick and I had broken up; I told her I couldn't talk about it yet. She wrote back: *Please don't push me away, Wynn. When you're ready, tell me all about it—please.* I never did, of course; I implied something vague about his work coming between us, and she said she was sorry, but she wasn't surprised. The idea that Patrick would let his work separate us seemed a particularly vicious untruth but I couldn't be honest about it even to Marietta. We wrote to each other regularly, and I sometimes expected a letter from her saying Patrick had written to ask if she knew where I was. But there was no evidence that Patrick had ever tried to track me down, and I was grateful to him for respecting what I had asked in the note I left: *Please don't ask me why.* He was, of course, better off without me. I knew that, and I assumed he did, too.

Still, I wondered constantly what he thought, how he had taken it, where he was, did he ever think of me. I bought a small, carved wooden box at a junk shop near the zoo, and into it I put the Mexican turquoise beads, the tiny stuffed cat Patrick had bought me at a Village street fair, a few clippings about him I got from art magazines. He was in a major group show, he got a Guggenheim. One of his sculptures was purchased by a Japanese banking firm for their New York office; with this notice there was a small photograph of him, a side view, standing beside a huge metal assemblage. It could have been any tall, unsmiling, dark-haired man, and yet of course when I looked at it—the set of his head, the angle of his shoulders—I saw the man I would always love, the man I had abandoned, and I touched my fingers to his face, his mouth, his body, forcing myself to remember, to want him back, and to understand deep in my soul that I would never have him.

I kept the box on the table beside my bed; it was the last thing I saw at night, and the first thing I saw in the morning. I wish I could say I was able to laugh at the pathetic absurdity of it—of clinging to these shards of our past while Patrick, it was obvious, was getting on perfectly well with his life. But I didn't laugh. I didn't cry, either. I just sat there with the beads wound through my fingers, the little cat pressed to my cheek, the bits of paper spread out around me.

• • •

Painting in New York had been difficult, even humiliating. In London I had renounced painting, as I had renounced Patrick. I didn't miss putting paint on canvas the way I missed, daily, hourly, the presence of Patrick in my life. But it was harder than I had expected. I was always working with paints, involved daily with the production of art. Many of my older students were incredibly gifted—almost as if the suffering they had endured qualified them in some subtle way to see more sharply into the world, as if art had been given to them as a compensation. I knew from my own experience as a student that the best and most democratic way to teach was to paint along with them, and to let them critique my work as I did theirs. In a way, I was sorry to miss out on their honesty, even their brutality. They could be cruelly tactless with each other. I thought sometimes that if I allowed myself to paint at St. Clement's, my paintings could no longer be dishonest: I would have no choice but to paint what was in my heart.

At the end of the day, when my student helpers and I tidied the studio and cleaned the brushes, I would breathe in the smells of turpentine and oil and have such nostalgia for the life of a painter that I would nearly break down. And that was the way it should be, I reminded myself. *My child died so I could paint.* Denying myself was the point.

• • •

Rachel was married a year after I arrived in England. Will was in his late thirties, ten years older than Rachel; they resembled each other, both short, energetic, and sandy haired with chubby, angelic faces. Will had a struggling rare-book business in Bloomsbury, but he was a painter, too, and he and Rachel used to invite me to go with them on painting excursions. We would ride the bus out of the city on our days off, to places as close as Kew or as far away as the Suffolk downs, and they would paint while I sat under a tree with a book.

Rachel, of course, asked me why I wasn't painting.

"I need a break," I said. "It was going so badly in New York. I think I just need to quit for a while and recharge."

"Maybe you were too influenced by Patrick's work," she said.

"I often thought that was true," I admitted.

"I miss seeing your paintings."

I laughed. "I don't."

"Is that why you left him so suddenly, Wynn? Because of your painting?"

I had lied to Marietta in a letter, but I couldn't lie to Rachel face-to-face. Several times I was, in fact, sorely tempted to tell her the story. When I first arrived, and she asked what had happened, I said only that we had broken up, that it was painful and I couldn't talk about it. I decided as time went on that it was unfair to her to be so secretive, and so that night I told her the bare bones of the truth: that I'd done something shameful when I was young that had terrible repercussions, and decided that I couldn't simply go on with my happy life. I needed to make a change in it. And that was why I left New York: to atone.

She looked at me doubtfully. "Did you say *atone*?"

"Yes. I mean—I've always been so selfish, Rachel. I wanted to do something for someone else for a change."

"And what did Patrick say to that?"

"I didn't tell him. I just left."

Her eyes widened. "And he didn't know why?"

I shook my head. "I couldn't tell him. He would have hated me. I could stand anything but that."

"Patrick?" Her voice was incredulous. "What do you take him for? Unless I'm remembering him wrong, Patrick couldn't hate you for some foolish thing you did a million years ago."

*Patrick*. In a rush, his image came back to me: his face, his broad back, his golden-brown eyes, his smile. I remembered the first time he told me he loved me, when we were in Mexico and he fastened the turquoise beads around my neck and I made him say the words. *I love you, Wynn*. Te amo.

"Patrick couldn't hate you," Rachel said again.

"Then he would have been wrong."

Rachel stared at me. "Wynn, what on earth was this dreadful thing you did?"

I only shook my head. I couldn't tell her. I couldn't. Maybe I should have overcome it, but my mother's reticence lived in me. We dropped the subject. It was obvious that Rachel disapproved of my mad flight, my silence, my assumptions, but I was convinced that if she had the whole story she would agree I'd done the right thing. And if she didn't, I didn't really care. I had done what I had to do, and I didn't want to—*couldn't*—discuss it. I didn't want to be talked out of my feelings of self-disgust, my sense of horror at the horror I had perpetrated.

In my three years in London I had two brief romances. The first was with an absurdly self-important young solicitor named Colin, who was tall, toothy, bearded, and always hungry. He and I took up cookery together, concocting elaborate meals in his kitchen, a sauce-spattered cookbook open on the counter in front of us and Colin, in a filthy white apron, chopping and slicing, chatting all the time, like a lean, male, British Julia Child with a big ego.

By the time I quit seeing Colin I was a pretty good cook, and when I began dating Brian—a shy, balding little man who painted picky dry-brush watercolors of quaint architectural treasures and sold them to tourists—I often made dinner for him on Saturday nights. He couldn't cook at all. He would bring wine and sit in the kitchen talking to me while I cooked. The food was immeasurably better, but the ritual reminded me so vividly of those awful rice-centered messes I used to concoct for Patrick on Queensberry Street that I sometimes became too depressed to eat.

I drifted away from each of them, puzzling them, I'm sure, first by my passivity, then by my indifference. It wasn't that I didn't give them a chance. Both those men had their virtues, and in spite of myself I did have fun in their company. But the twin truths of my life were the knowledge of my daughter's fate, and the wrenching pain of my separation from Patrick; those two private wounds made everything else seem trivial. Sometimes I'd go out with Will and Rachel and get roaring drunk in some pub, flirting halfheartedly with the men I met and becoming moderately proficient at darts. But usually, when I wasn't working, I preferred to be alone in my room, listening to the lions roar.

• • •

On one of my visits to Florida, my father and I had dinner with Sophie at her rather posh condo—an ultramodern space crammed incongruously with the torrent of kitsch Sophie had apparently been collecting since her girlhood: Hummel figurines, silk flowers, fancy sofa pillows, stuffed animals, music boxes, china cats, her first husband's World War II medals, a wooden rack displaying souvenir spoons, a glass case containing dolls in different national costumes. The living room windows had a view of the golf course where her third husband had dropped dead one day trying to get his ball out of a sand trap, an event she talked about with her handkerchief to her eyes.

It was odd at first to see my father in the midst of the jumble, sharing the couch with a pair of teddy bears in little sweaters, but it was clear that he felt comfortable at her house, and I could see how its cozy warmth could be like an embrace for a lonely widower. Under her influence, he had changed in small but significant ways: He was wearing his hair longer, and had acquired a wardrobe of bright bow ties. He played country music on his new CD player, with a special fondness for Emmylou Harris and Lyle Lovett. And once I heard him muttering to himself, "Now where the fuck did I put my glasses?" I sometimes thought that without Sophie my father would have wasted away to a dry stick of a man, and died of dullness.

After dinner—one of Sophie's typical casseroles, heavy on the sour cream—we got talking about my childhood. Sophie, for all her husbands, had no children, and she could get very sentimental about me. "Your father has told me so often about what a dear little girl you were, Wynn," she said. She leaned forward and laid her plump hand, with its bright pink nails, on my arm. "And every time I think about that sad thing that happened to you, my heart just goes out to you, honey. What a terrible experience for a young girl to have to go through."

I stared at her, then at my father. Dad was looking down at his plate, and I was sure he would clear his throat and change the subject: *Yes, and then there was the time Wynn won that art contest, she couldn't have been more than four . . .*

But he surprised me. He said, "I think about that often, Wynn. And I'll never get over wishing we'd handled it differently. We let you down when you wanted to keep that baby, and it took you away from us. I know it did."

I just looked at him, unable to speak. I wondered if he had talked the whole thing over with Sophie and she had made him see how wrong it was, or if my mother's death had freed him to say what he had really felt all along.

He glanced up at me fleetingly, then back down at the remains of his dinner. "I wish things had been different," he said.

I still couldn't say a word. I could only think of that poor dead child. Sophie sat looking at us, her eyes brimming, and then she stood up, patted my shoulder, kissed my father's bald spot, and headed for the kitchen. "I think it's time for a piece of key lime pie," she said. "That'll cheer us all up."

I realized then that the knot in my chest and the burning sensation behind my eyes were the components of a trembling fury that threatened to spill over. I stood up. "I don't want any pie," I managed to say. "I'm going for a walk." I felt their gaze on me as I stumbled out of the room, and I could picture Sophie's bewilderment when the door slammed shut behind me.

Outside, the air was fresh and cool. It was early evening, still light, and there were a few last golfers on the course. I went down Sophie's front walk, taking deep breaths, trying to calm myself; I was shaking, my heart was racing. Skirting the green, I set off through the parking lot to where I knew there was a path that led to a lagoon. I hardly knew where I was walking, I just knew I had to get out of there, away from my father's pathetic admission and Sophie's muddled kindness, before I said something terrible, something unforgivable—something that no amount of anger could justify saying to two old people who loved me and meant well.

The fact was that as I made my way across the lot and down the path, I knew that it wasn't my father's cringing, belated apology that had made me furious. It was my mother. I knew—I'd known for a long time—that my father, for all his lovable qualities, was a weak and timid man. The time was still vivid to me when I'd called him from the Edna Quinlan Home and asked for his help, and he had refused to oppose my mother's wishes. He'd actually said that, not seeing the shame in it. As if my mother were a dictator and my father part of her secret police, an automaton without a conscience who was there only to carry out the will of the leader. How sick, I thought, to let anyone have such power over you, but how much sicker was the need to wield that power. I would never know, now, what made my mother tick: She was safe in the land of the dead. She couldn't tell me anything, even if she wanted to. She was gone, but the hurt she had inflicted had cut deep—deeper than anyone could have imagined. It had left a scar that wouldn't fade, no matter what I did.

I stood by the water while the sun slowly sank behind the clubhouse. The peaceful scene maddened me: the lily pads with their spiky blooms, a silently gliding family of ducks, a rustic bench flanked by pots of geraniums. Everything nice, everything pretty, and yet nothing, I thought, none of the world's fatal niceness could make up for my decade of sorrow and rage and emptiness. I thought for the first time in years of that ride back to Maine from Boston after I gave away my daughter, when my mother pointed out to me that it was spring, the world was a beautiful place, and I should be happy. I remembered the green buds on the trees that day, and my mother's complacent smile. *Life goes on,* she had said.

I sat down on the bench, put my head in my hands, and wept.

• • •

I tried not to open the wooden box very often—my absurd little Patrick museum. The cat, the clippings, the hazy photograph—they were like a dangerous drug, or a medicine I was getting too dependent on. I tried to ration myself, knowing that when I opened the box, in the midst of the torment, there was also a kind of solace to which I had no right.

But my thoughts were not so controllable. I couldn't get Patrick out of my mind. At idle moments I would slip into fantasies of being with him, poking through the rusty junk at Uncle Austin's place, sitting across the table from him at the Broome Street Bar. Most of all, of being with him in our bed. I would feel his young, strong body hard against mine. I would breathe in the delicious, slightly animal, clayey scent of his skin. I would see his face above me—eyes closed, lips parted—as slowly, voluptuously he thrust into me until we were both crazy with the pleasure of it. And his smile when we lay beside each other afterward, his hand on my breast, our legs entwined, our sweat mingled, and a feeling of simple well-being that was more intense than any feeling I had ever known. The feeling that I was where I was meant to be, that this man was my rightful home, my destination, the best part of me.

Sometimes I indulged myself in imagining seeking him out to confess everything to him—just letting the whole story tumble out, beginning with Mark Erling and me by the lake, and ending with the yellowed news clippings I kept with me. I imagined the relief I would find just by saying those words to him, no matter what his reaction was. Even if I lost him. Because I'd lost him anyway. But in my most secret, shameful fantasy, he didn't condemn me. He absolved me. Somehow, he made it all right. I hid my face against his shoulder, he stroked my hair, and peace, peace returned to us both.

In my saner moments, I knew he would not forgive me. I remembered what he had said about people who gave away their children, and when I caught myself having those foolish fantasies, I wrenched my mind away, guiltily. But I never succeeded in banishing Patrick from my consciousness. And, increasingly, I read about him. While I was in England, he became quietly famous. During those years, as he turned thirty, he progressed from emerging artist to one of the new stalwarts of the New York art scene. The boom years of the eighties were just beginning. Patrick was making money, selling his work to collectors and museums and corporations in New York and in Europe. My little clipping collection grew. Our old friend Santo Peri, now a successful art dealer, was photographed with Patrick at someone's opening. Patrick taught for a semester at the Rhode Island School of Design, the city of Boston commissioned a piece, he got another big grant. I wondered how all this was affecting him, what he was like, whom he was with. On especially bad days I tortured myself picturing him with other women—better women than I. He was better off without me, and I knew Patrick, my beautiful lover, wouldn't be alone for long. And that, too, was no more than I deserved.

One day in March I saw a notice in a London art paper about an exhibit at a small gallery near Portobello Road. Four young sculptors, two Americans, two Brits, were showing drawings of their works. "Working Drawings by Rising Artists," it was called. Patrick Foss was one of the artists.

I took the tube over there on a rainy Saturday afternoon when, it seemed, the rest of London had, quite sensibly, decided to stay home watching TV. The streets were sloppy and cold, the tourists at the street market looked wet and unhappy, and the gallery itself was a tiny, unpromising place squeezed between a bicycle shop and a dentist's office.

Inside, though, it was the usual pristine white space, with the usual dressy, bored young man behind a desk. "Good afternoon," he said. "Quite a day, isn't it?"

I agreed that the weather was frightful. Not surprisingly, no one else was in there. I put my umbrella in the stand. I could see Patrick's drawings on the wall beside the desk. I didn't need to see his name in tasteful little black letters. I recognized several of them instantly. They had been stuck up on the wall of our loft with pushpins. One of them—clear to me even at a distance—was the beautiful pen-and-ink drawing of the sculpture he'd been working on when I left him.

"Oh God," I said involuntarily, and the elegant young man said, "You're still shivering. Here—would you like me take that wet coat?"

"No, I'm all right."

"You're sure?"

"Yes. Thank you," I added belatedly. I went to the wall and stared at the drawings. There were eight of them. They were overwhelming. I looked at the drawings, and I saw Patrick as clearly as if they had been self-portraits.

"He's a beautiful draftsman, isn't he?"

"Yes," I managed to say. "He is."

I knew Patrick could draw, and most of the drawings were familiar to me, but they seemed unexpectedly lovely in their austere frames against the white wall. The sculptures themselves were massive and disturbing, but the drawings were almost delicate, the line expressive and very simple, the complexities of Patrick's vision whittled down to pure form. As always when I saw his work, I was stunned by his talent. It was something I had never gotten used to or taken for granted, even when I lived with him.

As if he read my mind, the man at the desk said, "Foss—he's going to be one of the greats."

I felt a surge of affection for this man, and I turned to him with a smile. "Yes. He certainly is. His work is wonderful. I knew him," I said. I couldn't stop myself. "I knew him in New York."

"Is that so?"

"We were in school together. We were—we were friends."

"Really?" He folded his hands under his chin, smiling, expectant. "So you know his work pretty well, then, do you? Well, tell me—"

I interrupted. "Was he here? In London? I mean, did he come over for the opening? Or did he hang the drawings himself? I mean—I wondered—is he still here, do you think? Does he ever come in?"

The gallery man's smile became a little strained. "He couldn't make it to the opening, alas. Couldn't get away—some other commitment, I believe. No, he hasn't been here. We've dealt with him entirely by post."

"I see." I turned back to the drawings. "They are lovely, aren't they? Really lovely. Do you have—?"

"Take one of our postcards." He picked one up and held it out: four small reproductions, one for each artist. Patrick's was one of the drawings that was new to me, a study for a work in progress.

"They're so small."

"It's just a little promotional thing," he said stiffly.

"You don't have a book, some kind of—?"

"No, I'm afraid not. This is just a very small exhibit. We hope someday to have something more substantial. Why don't you get on our mailing list?"

"Yes—yes, thank you. I'll do that." He handed me a book. My hand was shaking; if they could read my name and address, it would be a miracle. I turned back to the drawings, drinking them in. Patrick. *Patrick.* How many times had I seen him bent over the drawing board, frowning ferociously, one hand gripping the pen, the other tugging at his hair. I remembered suddenly the drawing of me he'd given to my parents the first time I took him to Maine. Where was it now? It must be somewhere at my father's. I would call him when I got home, ask what happened to it. I wasn't sure I deserved to actually possess it, but suddenly I needed to know where it was, and that it was safe.

"Check out Martin Steinberg over there before you go. Now there's an interesting artist. Another Yank, from California. He's been working in plate glass and tar. Very intriguing stuff."

"Yes," I said. With reluctance, I abandoned the wall of Patrick's drawings. I retrieved my umbrella from the stand. "Yes, I will, another time," I said vaguely. I smiled again. I know my eyes were full of tears. He must have thought I was a madwoman. "Yes, thank you. Thank you very much," I said, and went out into the rain.

• • •

On my next visit to Key Largo, my father's health was dramatically worse. He hadn't really been well since my mother died, but his complaints had been vague and minor—fatigue, arthritis, twinges of pain, once a dizzy spell. All this seemed to improve once he started seeing Sophie. "This woman won't let me get away with feeling sorry for myself," he said, beaming at her.

"Damn right," she would say. "Don't bother me with your ridiculous aches and pains." In her eyes was the anxiety of a woman who had buried three husbands. "You're healthy as a horse, Jim."

But this time, when Dad picked me up at the airport in Miami, he told me he had to have open-heart surgery. He had blacked out when climbing a flight of stairs, and his cardiologist said he needed a triple bypass.

I went with him to talk to the surgeon. Dad wanted to schedule the operation during my Christmas vacation, so I could be there. This was September, just before the fall term was due to begin. The surgeon was dubious about waiting three months. Both of us urged him to have it done sooner. Sophie would be there, and I was pretty sure I could get time off.

But Dad was stubborn. He got Dr. Martinez to admit that the statistics were against his dropping dead if he didn't have a triple bypass tomorrow, and the operation was scheduled for mid-December.

My father put on a plaid bow tie and took me and Sophie out to dinner that night, and while we waited for our appetizers he broke the news to her. She burst into tears, and my father said, "Oh, Sophie, for pity's sake"—sounding just like my mother. Then he seemed to catch himself, and he did something that seemed to me amazing. He got out of his chair and went down on one knee—right there in the Colony Lobster House on a crowded Saturday night—and said, "I'm going to come through it all right, honey. The statistics are on my side. And—listen to me, Sophie, stop crying—when I recover I want you to marry me."

She raised her head. "Do you mean it, Jim?"

"I mean it." He took her hand and kissed it. "Will you?"

"Will I?" She began to laugh. "Of course I will! Oh Jim!"

They stayed there with their hands clasped, looking into each other's eyes and laughing. They'd forgotten anyone else was there—the waiter hovering with our shrimp cocktail, the interested people at the next table—and me, sitting there with wet eyes, grinning from ear to ear.

The next day we all went shopping for a ring—a hilarious, extravagant outing. My father was more excited than I could ever remember seeing him. He insisted on buying a huge diamond, flanked with rows of tiny emeralds—"my best one yet," Sophie pronounced it—and then we went out and drank champagne and ate caviar. Three days later I flew back to England. In early November Sophie called me to say my father had died in his sleep.

I flew to Florida for the funeral, to settle my father's estate and to weep with Sophie, who kept twisting her diamond on her finger, raising it to her lips, covering it with the fingers of her right hand as if it were a wound that hurt. She took me to dinner at the Colony, requesting the same table where my father had proposed, and we sat looking out at the marina and watching the sunset sky, talking about him.

"I know I could never have been to him what your mother was," she said. "Jim told me frankly that she was the love of his life, and I came in a distant second."

"He said that?" I was appalled. My father seemed to have gone straight from kindly, dignified reticence to an alarmingly rude candor.

"I forced it out of him," she said, and leaned toward me in her confiding way. "I said to him: Jim, tell me honestly. How do I measure up to Molly? She was a fascinating woman, and don't try to tell me different. She was thin and beautiful and educated and accomplished. I'm fat and older than you and I've never done a thing with my life but go shopping and take care of my husbands. And he said, I'll be honest with you, Sophie. I worshipped Molly. I don't worship you. But she didn't always make me feel good, and you do. There was always something a little unattainable about my wife, he said. Well, that's one thing you can never say about me, I said. And he laughed." She was smiling. "I know he didn't love me as much as I loved him, Wynn, but that was okay. I need to know these things. I need to know where I stand. The truth can be painful, but it's like that Gelusil I take—I have to have it or I feel sick. He was fond of me. We had a lot of good times. And I'm not just talking about bed, although—" She broke off, fumbled for a clean tissue. "Ah God, Wynn, I'm going to miss that man."

She began to cry again. I sat there in silence while she wept, glad that two lovable people had found happiness together. It seemed unbearably poignant that he had died in the midst of it. I was tempted to say something to Sophie about my mother, that she wasn't the paragon she seemed, and that Sophie with her uncritical love had perhaps, in the end, made him even happier. But I knew this wasn't something I should do. I looked at Sophie in her black silk suit, her shoulders shaking, a crumpled tissue held to her lips, her eye makeup running, and I put my arm around her shoulders. "I'm sorry," I said. "Oh, Sophie, I'm so sorry he's gone." And I realized that somewhere mixed with grief for my father I was sorry for myself, too—for the fact that the possibility of that kind of happiness seemed remote, seemed impossible, and still seemed wrong. My father had begun a new life in his seventies. My life had ended when I was twenty-six.

I returned again to Florida at Christmastime to clean out my father's house. The house was small, but everything in it was reminiscent of my childhood—those idyllic years of my growing up in Maine. Slightly shabby possessions I had taken for granted or barely noticed when I visited were now unbearably dear to me. But how could I return to my tiny room in London with my old high-backed bed in tow, and my mother's boxes of prints and negatives, my father's toy collection, the bookcase he made for me when I was twelve, my old dollhouse? And Patrick's drawing of me—I found that, too, carefully wrapped in newspaper with some of my old paintings, stored in a box labeled "Wynn—Artwork." I gave it a quick look and wrapped it up again. On top of everything else, that was too hard; the little drawing was not something I could cope with.

I was going through my mother's filing cabinets, where she kept the endless business correspondence from her career—my father hadn't thrown out anything—when I came across an envelope with my name on it in her handwriting.

It was a while before I could open it. I sat looking down at the letters of my name, feeling slightly foolish, like a character in a play. The fateful letter. The dead hand. The revelation that will change everything, move the plot forward, explain all. Then I laughed at myself and opened the envelope. It was probably nothing. A few baby pictures she'd put away. Old spelling tests. A mundane letter begun and never finished.

The envelope was not sealed. Inside was one sheet of paper, densely covered in my mother's handwriting that was as meticulous as typescript. I read it slowly:

Wynn dear,

I'm writing a letter I may never send. Maybe I'll destroy it as soon as it's written. Or maybe I won't, and you'll find it somewhere years from now, when I'm dead. Or maybe someday I'll be able to sit down with you and say what I'm about to write. I hope I can do that. But I know myself, and I'm afraid I never will, and so I have to write this.

I need to tell you I'm sorry, and to ask you to forgive me. I wish I could have let you find a way to keep the baby. I know how much you wanted that, and I disappointed you. Yes, there were things we could have done. But I discouraged you because I knew that was right. I have to say I was afraid of that baby. I am aware of your capacity for devotion, and for passion, and for uncompromising love. I know those things about you, Wynn. I was afraid that motherhood would take you over, you would give up your soul to that baby, and you would forget you're an artist before anything. Motherhood! You were only sixteen, my daughter. A child yourself. Life is complex enough without adding teenage motherhood to it.

The baby haunts me every day, the little girl with your face. But that doesn't change my mind about what we did. I just hope that someday you'll forgive me, maybe when you have a daughter of your own. And I hope that your life will be happy. You grew up too fast, you grew away from Daddy and me. Don't think I don't know that, and don't think I don't regret it. I only wish—

It broke off there.

• • •

This letter shattered me. I kept going back to that day in the hospital when we had simply stared at that baby, she and I. Saying nothing. Now I had seen her madness in print, I knew exactly what she had been thinking. *I was afraid that motherhood would take you over and you would forget you're an artist before anything.*

*And look at me now, Mother,* I thought. I was not an artist. I would never be an artist. My mother's insane ambition ruined my life, and my daughter's. She made me give her up; by giving her up, I caused her to die; her death made it impossible for me to paint. There was a poisonous satisfaction in plotting out this circle of waste and futility. I hoped my mother, sitting in her particular, complicated purgatory, was aware of what she had wrought. I hoped the knowledge ate away at her worse than any flames of hell.

One sentence stayed in my mind: *I just hope that someday you'll forgive me, maybe when you have a daughter of your own.* The heartlessness of it. I had a daughter of my own, I thought. I had a daughter! And thanks to you my daughter is dead.

I ripped the letter into tiny pieces and burned them in the kitchen sink.

• • •

I lingered in Key Largo for nearly two weeks, packing and cleaning and putting my father's house on the market, sitting alone in restaurants eating fish called snook and grunt and mutton snapper. I wasn't sleeping well, and when I did sleep I had strange, unsettling dreams about the Edna Quinlan Home, about my mother on her deathbed, one horrible nightmare about a dead and bloody child. But it was hard for me to leave. I wanted to get over the bitterness I felt, the pure devastating anger, and I couldn't find a way. I wanted to see Sophie, but she was visiting friends up north for Christmas. I needed someone, and as I walked along the beach and lay open-eyed in my father's guest room, I felt more alone than I'd ever felt in my life. I wanted my father, who was dead. I wanted Patrick, who was lost to me forever. I wanted Marietta, Rachel and Will, Jeanie—they were all far away, they had their own lives. I had no one. I was close to no one. There was only me, Wynn, and I wasn't nearly enough.

I knew that it was time for me to leave England. I would hand in my resignation when I got back and then store everything until the end of the school year, when I would return to the States. It wasn't just the need to find a home for my childhood icons. It was that I had lost so much—everything I loved—and I felt that I needed at least to be on my home ground.

I would move to Boston, I decided. I adored New York, but I couldn't live where Patrick lived. And with my parents dead Florida meant nothing to me, nor did Maine, where I no longer knew anyone. I remembered how Boston used to be our city, mine and Patrick's, how every inch of its pavement was full of our love for each other. And I remembered, too, how I had lived there those four long winter months when I was pregnant. Boston would be difficult, a painful place to settle down in. But it was familiar, too, the baggy gray city on the river where I had always felt at home. In truth, I had nowhere to go. And it wasn't my business to shrink from a little pain: Hadn't I made pain my mission?

Leaving London wasn't easy—my job, my friends, the lively streets, the diverse accents. I had inherited from my father enough money to live on—modestly, but with a degree of comfort—and I knew I could return to England for visits when I liked. But it would never be the same. During those last months of that warm and fragrant spring, I worked hard at my job, trying to give my students as much as I could. But I spent my spare time going for long walks around London. I took endless photographs, wishing I were still a painter, so I could have gone out there with my easel and kept the England that I loved alive in my heart in the best way I knew how. *You're an artist before anything,* my mother had written. And I had to admit that there was still truth in her statement. It was just that I was an artist who didn't paint.

Saying good-bye was painful, but when I finally got to Boston that summer, I was happier to be home than I had expected. I rented a sunny apartment in Cambridge near the Fogg Art Museum, and had the contents of my father's house shipped there. I kept my mother's photographs and other things stored in boxes—they filled me with anger and disgust, but I couldn't bring myself to get rid of them. The memory of the day she died, the way the tears ran down her face and her breathing went silent and stopped, came back to me in flashbacks at unexpected moments and made me cold with sorrow. There were even times when—desperately, childishly—I still missed her. But I couldn't bear to see her photographs on my wall.

I arranged a row of Dad's old toys on a shelf, and I slept in my childhood bed, with the old quilt folded at the bottom. I thought of how many times I must have walked right by this building with Patrick on the way to the Fogg, little knowing that some day I would sleep there alone, thinking of him. I didn't realize until then how apprehensive I had been about coming home. Lying in bed, listening to the traffic noises in the street, I was visited by the old familiar grief, but with something new added to it: the consciousness that my life was slipping away and that all I had to show for it was memory, loss, anger, and these shabby treasures from my youth. I had to remind myself that that was only right: I had what I deserved.

• • •

Without a job to keep me occupied, the days were very long. I felt strangely disoriented. I took walks. I bought books at the Harvard Co-op, brought them home to my apartment, read them, went back for more. I watched movies on TV. I applied for a position teaching art at a private school in Brookline; they rejected me because I had never taught "normal" children. I applied for a receptionist job in a Boston gallery, but they said I needed to know how to type, and when I inquired about a bookselling job at the Co-op they said I was overqualified. Those were the only jobs I came across for which I seemed even remotely suited.

One hot, aimless day in July I woke up possessed by an impulse I couldn't resist. I didn't examine it, I just did it: I went to the spare-room closet, unpacked my brushes and paints and set them out on a table. I began sorting the tubes of paint. Some were dried up, hopeless; others were fat and ready to use. I examined my brushes, looked for something to pour turpentine into, searched in vain for my old stapler. I made a list of what I needed and then walked over to Heller's and bought paint, canvas, stretchers, a stapler, an easel, and lugged it all home in the heat. I couldn't wait for them to deliver. I had to paint. I had to paint *now.*

I spent the afternoon preparing canvases—stretched half a dozen and sized them. The next morning, I set up the new easel in front of my dresser, and painted a hairbrush, a pair of earrings, a folded scarf. I painted the light as it slanted through the window, a portion of the window with its striped curtain, and the vague reflection of myself, painting, in the mirror. I did what I had done all those years ago when I began art school: I painted what was there, but now I worked in oil, not watercolor.

It was a large painting. It took me most of two days. I stayed with it, eating only when I began to feel faint, sleeping badly and waking up early on the second day, painting in my nightgown, with my morning coffee cooling nearby. My apartment was hot, but I forgot to turn on the air conditioner. I didn't think about the heat, or about being hungry. I didn't think about anything. I just painted.

When it was done, I couldn't look at it. I cleaned my brushes, and then I went outside for a walk. It was early evening, the humid end of a hot summer day when the air was like the inside of a plastic bag. I walked down to the river and over the bridge and back again, going fast, my brain empty except for registering the glassy look of the water, the chopped brown grass where languid students hung out in shorts and T-shirts, the old brick buildings rising up between the trees. When I got home again, I was sweaty and sick, my heart pounding. What I felt was a kind of terror, as if I had committed a crime and knew I must turn myself in.

I stripped off my clothes and stood under the shower. The cool water poured down on my head and shoulders and my closed eyes. I raised my head to drink it. I stood there a long time, letting the water calm me down. Then I put a towel around my hair, wrapped myself in a bathrobe, and went down the hall in my bare feet to look at the painting.

It was crap. In one quick glance, I took it all in—the insipid colors, the timid brushwork, the awkward, pointless composition, all of it overlaid with a sort of eager desperation. It was the work of a student trying to impress. It was the work of an amateur. It was a huge, ugly, meaningless painting of nothing. The thought that I had kept down during my long, hot walk, that would have edged into my mind if I had let it, came to the surface: *My daughter died so I could paint.* I looked at the painting and saw myself, my presumption, my sins, my punishment.

• • •

Near the end of that year, an odd thing happened. A letter came from Santo Peri, forwarded from England. It was two months old. Santo said in his letter that he was curious about my work and would love to see what I was doing now. Could we get together the next time he was in London?

He wrote on his gallery's letterhead stationery: the Peri-Prezio Gallery on Fifty-seventh Street. I agonized over whether or not to answer, but finally what decided me was simple loneliness. I longed for some human contact, even with an old friend I hardly knew any more and hadn't seen in—how many? Four years? Someone from my old life. I didn't tell him I had no work to show him. I only said I had left London, I was back in Boston, I would like very much to see him if he was ever in town.

He had to be in Boston on business, and we arranged to have lunch. It was a cold spring day. Santo came to my apartment, and we stood in my front hall talking while I found my coat and scarf. Santo was fatter, sleeker, definitely more prosperous. His present lover was a stockbroker and art collector—the Prezio half of the gallery. Santo wore a spectacular camel-hair coat, and when he hugged me I smelled expensive cologne. I had made lunch reservations, but he wanted to see my paintings first.

"Where is your studio?" he asked. "Or do you paint here at home?"

I said, "I'm afraid I lured you here under false pretenses, Santo. I don't paint anywhere."

He frowned. "I don't understand."

"I don't paint any more." I knotted my scarf around my neck, trying to keep my voice casual. "I've stopped painting."

He spread his hands with a small, puzzled smile. "So—what are you working on, then?" His dark eyes twinkled, as if he expected me to take him into a studio full of art pottery or marble sculptures.

"I'm not working on anything."

"Nothing?"

"Nothing."

"I see." He waited for me to say more, and when I didn't he looked at me for a moment in silence. Then he said, "Well, I'm sorry to hear it. I'm *shocked* to hear it. But of course it wasn't just your work I wanted to see. I'm delighted to see you looking so well and so—" He gestured vaguely. His face—dark, handsome, a bit jowly—gave me no clue to what he was thinking. He forced a smile. "Shall we go to lunch?"

We walked the three blocks to Vittorio's. I heard myself nattering on about Cambridge, the weather, the buildings we passed. I pointed out a little bakery where I bought bread, showed him a shop where I had found the scarf I was wearing. Santo was silent, and his disappointment, disapproval, plain stupefaction at what I'd said hovered around us like a sour smell.

When we were seated at the restaurant, I stopped babbling. We looked at the menu, ordered wine and food, then sat staring at each other. "Wynn," Santo said. "Wynn, what is it? What's going on?"

I didn't know how to reply. He was looking at me with the kindness and affection that I remembered from years ago. The waiter brought our wine, and a basket of bread. I took a piece of bread and sat there holding it. I knew I had to say something. "Santo," I got out finally. "Why did you want to see my work? My paintings?"

"Why?" Santo unfolded his napkin and tucked it into his collar, smiling. He took a sip of wine. "Why do you think, Wynn? Because you're a talented artist. Because I always loved your work. Because of all the painters I knew in New York in those days, you were the one I thought would make it."

"Santo, I was painting so badly!"

"Yes, you were," he agreed, his smile still in place. "But you were painting badly in an interesting way. Your work was never boring. It was like a good wine, maybe a fine burgundy like this one we're drinking, that's still a bit too young, it needs mellowing, it's not there yet. But it has all the ingredients, and you can drink a glass and enjoy it, not for what it is but for its promise." His smile became a grin. "Forgive the pretentious claptrap, Wynn. You know what I mean. I'm saying I believed in you as a painter. I thought that by now you'd be a superstar."

The buzz of excitement I felt took me by surprise. Could it be true that those chaotic, directionless paintings I was making in New York had had some value—had been interesting failures? It had been a long time since anyone had praised my painting, or even said anything at all about it. How long since I'd talked about my work? *My work.* I thought of the wretched canvas I had produced during those two hot July days—that alien, pathetic mess—and took a quick sip of wine. "What you say means a lot to me, Santo," I told him. I had always respected his opinion, his eye, even years before when we were all struggling and Santo was just starting out. "If I did have any work, I would love to show it to you, I'd love to hear what you thought of it."

"My gallery is doing very well," Santo said, "and one thing I like to do is give exhibition space to emerging artists—young people with talent who haven't been discovered yet. I admit I was looking forward to discovering you."

"I—yes," I said. "I know about your gallery." I hesitated, not knowing how to go on. I kept seeing that painting, imagining Santo's face if I'd shown it to him, his stumbling attempts at tact. There was an awkward pause.

Santo gave me an ironic smile. "And?"

"Well—"

His voice became very gentle. "Wynn, I meant what I said. I would be willing to give your work a serious look, if it were the way I remember it. And not just because we go way back. You have it in you to be a very, very good painter." His smile deepened. "I'm a businessman, not a philanthropist."

"It's not that."

"Then—are you saying that—assuming you did have anything to show me—you wouldn't want my gallery to consider representing you?"

"No, that's not what I mean."

"Then what *do* you mean?"

I took a deep breath and looked down at the tablecloth. "I don't know how to say this, Santo. I didn't come back to the States to return to my old life or to get involved in the New York art world. I'm not ready to do that." I raised my head. "It's a personal thing. I can't really talk about it."

Santo had very large, deep-set, liquid brown eyes, thickly lashed. He studied me for a moment with his steady gaze, as silently and thoughtfully as he would examine a painting, and I could see the questions forming in his mind. I knew he was curious about why I had disappeared, why Patrick and I had broken up. *What in hell is wrong with you, Wynn? Why aren't you painting? Why did you just walk out on that guy?* I looked right back at him, and my eyes were as unflinching as his. *Forget it, Santo. It's nobody's business but mine.*

"I haven't seen you, then," he said. "That's what you're saying. Am I right? If anybody asks, I haven't seen you, and I don't have a clue as to where you are or what you're doing."

There was another pause, while we stared at each other. Then I reached across the table and squeezed his hand. "Yes," I whispered.

"Is that all, Wynn?"

"Yes." I spoke around a lump in my throat. "Thank you, Santo."

For how could I tell him of my fears? That Patrick would find me, would confront me in anger, would reproach me for what I had done—anger and reproaches that I knew I deserved, but that I knew I wouldn't be strong enough to endure. And that would turn to horrified disgust if I could bring myself to explain why I did it. Santo looked at me, shaking his head, and then he picked up my hand and kissed it. "Ah, Wynn," he said.

A few days later I got a note from him. It said: *I didn't know if I should tell you when I saw you, but I think maybe you would want to know this.* He enclosed a photograph, cut from *The New York Times*, of himself and another man. They were both in black tie. Standing with them was a stunning blond woman in a slinky black dress. She was holding the arm of a third man, also in a tuxedo, and that man was Patrick. The caption underneath the photograph read: *At the American Cancer Society Art Benefit, Douglas Prezio and Santo Peri of the Peri-Prezio Gallery, Sonia Shapiro of the DGA Gallery, and her husband, sculptor Patrick Foss.*

• • •

I had bought myself a little red Toyota, and one morning a few weeks later I got into it and made the long drive west on Route 90 to the part of New York State where Patrick's Uncle Austin lived.

I had wrestled with this idea since it came to me, trying not to give in to it, but I was a wreck, and I needed to do something. The photograph of Patrick and his wife had awakened a part of me that I had been beating down for years. I felt—what was the word for it? I felt *cheated*. It was a feeling I hadn't really allowed myself. Of course I was cheated! My life was about cheating myself out of life. I was paying for a crime. This was what remorse was, and atonement.

I knew all this. It was a bargain I had made with myself. But looking at Patrick with his beautiful Sonia—this new Patrick who had a wife and went to benefits and sold his sculptures for big money, who stood there before the camera impeccably dressed and smiling—I felt I was seeing a stranger, someone completely unlike the man I had known, and the idea rose up in me that I had to find out who he was, and what path he had taken to reach that point. I had to reconnect in a way that was more meaningful than the hoarding of clippings in box.

I wept over that photograph as I had wept over nothing else. All the furies of jealousy rose up in me and made me crazy. Jealousy and humiliation and rejection, as if it were he who had abandoned me. And in a way he had, I told myself unreasonably. Why did he never try to find me, never make one inquiry about what had become of me or where I'd gone? Weeping, I crumpled the picture in my fist until it was the size of a marble, and then I flushed it down the toilet, and after a sleepless night I dozed toward dawn and awoke with the confused idea that I had to do something, anything, and the only thing I could think of was Uncle Austin, who had been kind to me and fed me whiskey and said he knew Patrick and I were in it for life.

It was a long ride, and not a pleasant one. I drove too fast, ticking off the dull green Thruway miles, frantic to be sitting at Uncle Austin's kitchen table again, talking to someone who could explain to me who Patrick was.

I left the highway after it crossed the Hudson, and began to drive south. I found Route 146 easily and followed it into Livingstonville, where I stopped for gas and used the bathroom. In the murky mirror I tamed my hair into a braid and put some blusher on my pale cheeks. Then I got back into the car and turned up the state road that led to Uncle Austin's junkyard.

When his house came in sight at the top of a small hill, I was suddenly afraid. I stopped the car at the foot of the driveway. What if he was dead? What if he refused to speak to me? What if Patrick was there? All these things were only too possible, and I decided I had been insane to come.

Up the drive, I could see nothing but a pickup truck—fairly new, but nothing that a rising New York artist might drive. No Porsche, no Jaguar. I tried to imagine Patrick folding his long legs into a Porsche, but ever since Santo sent me the photograph, I hadn't been able to imagine Patrick at all.

I headed up the driveway slowly, ready to reverse out of there if Uncle Austin emerged with a shotgun: This thought was only half humorous. I remembered the rusty fence Patrick was so fond of, the tumbledown barn, the small house with its big porch and behind it the low, wooded hills that always reminded me of Maine. The house appeared freshly painted, but otherwise the place was exactly the same.

I parked next to the truck and paused before I walked up to the porch. I had brought a bottle of Jameson's. What I really wanted to do was open it right there and take a long drink of the stuff. As I hesitated, the front door opened, and Uncle Austin came out. He stood on the porch looking down at me. "Jesus Christ," he said.

"Uncle Austin," I said. I went up the walk, holding the bottle like a peace offering. "How are you?" There was no response.

He didn't move. Uncle Austin hadn't changed much either. He wore his usual faded jeans and flannel shirt and old leather bedroom slippers. Even the slippers looked like the ones he had worn around the house back when Patrick and I used to visit. He looked no older, his hair hadn't thinned, his eyes were encased in the same wrinkles. It was as if time had stopped. *If only it had,* I thought.

His voice came again, gruffly. "What the hell do you want?"

I reached the porch and held out my hand. There was a pause, and then he took it limply, gave it a shake, and dropped it quick. This wasn't going to be easy, but I hadn't expected it to be. "I just wanted to talk." I handed him the bottle. "This is for you."

He made a sound I couldn't decipher, but he took the bottle and went into the house. I followed because he didn't tell me not to, and we passed through the stiff little living room into the kitchen. Uncle Austin bent and put another log into the woodstove, moved things around with a poker, stood up again red-faced. The kitchen was very warm.

"Do you mind if I sit down? Can we have a drink together?"

"I don't drink much no more."

"Then would you pour me one?"

He went to the cupboard, exactly where I remembered, and took down one shot glass, then after a pause another one, and set them down hard on the table. He took out his jackknife and cut the seal from the bottle, looking at me when he was done. "I can't believe you came here," he said. He unscrewed the top and poured us each a shot.

"Neither can I." I picked up my glass and drank half. The whiskey burned going down, and I broke into a sweat.

"What's it been? Three, four years?"

"Almost four. Last time I was here was in May of 'seventy-eight."

He sipped at his whiskey, then looked at his glass as if he would have liked to throw down the whole thing. "Before you walked out."

"Yes," I said evenly. "Just a month before I walked out."

He sipped again, not speaking. I took off my jacket. It must have been eighty-five degrees in there. I didn't remember him keeping it so hot. I wondered if he had been ill. I was so used to old people dying, I felt a rush of gratitude that Uncle Austin was still alive.

"How have you been?" I asked. "You look well."

"I'm fine. Don't you worry about me."

We were silent again. I drank down the rest of my whiskey, and he pushed the bottle toward me. I poured. The clock over the sink said 4:15. I was remembering the last time I was there, the May weekend of my twenty-sixth birthday, when Patrick and Uncle Austin had cooked spaghetti and meatballs for dinner while I planted some perennials out in front—hollyhocks, shasta daisies, a couple of peony bushes, and some ivy that was meant to twine picturesquely around the porch. I hadn't noticed anything but bare dirt when I came in. Presumably it had all dried up and died years ago.

"You going to ask me how he is?"

It was a moment before I took in his words. "Patrick?"

"Who the hell do you think? Are we going to talk about him, or are we going to sit here making idle chitchat all day?"

Of course. This was why I had come. "No—yes," I said, and I had to struggle to keep my voice from breaking. "Please. Tell me how he is."

"He's better."

I stared at him. "What does that mean?"

He stared back at me. "Do you remember, I used to have a picture of the two of you in a little frame over the cupboard there?"

I hadn't remembered, but now I did. A picture of Patrick and me on the porch, smiling, his arms around me in a bear hug. I looked where he pointed. "It's not there any more."

"I broke the glass and took out that picture and burned it in my stove," he said.

I couldn't look at him. I stared at the label on the whiskey bottle. Bow Street Distillery, it said. Dublin, Ireland. Since 1780. After a moment, Uncle Austin leaned forward across the table. "Let me tell you something. You listen to me now. You walked out on that boy, and all you did was leave him some kind of note. He loved you, he wanted to *marry* you—" Uncle Austin's voice rose, and he pounded his fist on the table. "And you just left him, as if he was your roommate, as if he was a pile of shit, a *nobody*. Do you hear what I'm saying? You left him, and you wouldn't even tell him why. And do you want to know what he did when he got home from work and found your note—your fucking little *note*, whatever it said?" His face was tight with anger, his eyes narrowed; it was a look I had never seen before, and I had never heard him use such language. "When he figured out that you really weren't coming back? Do you want to know what was the first thing he did?"

I remembered that Tuesday in June, and how the weather was perversely glorious and sunny. As I had done a hundred times, I imagined Patrick reading my note when he came home from work. Beyond that, I could picture nothing. It was a blank. Patrick without me: the alien Patrick, the man I never knew. I leaned my head on my hand. "Tell me, Uncle Austin," I said. "What did he do?"

Uncle Austin finished his whiskey and poured himself another. "He got in that truck he used to rent and came up here," he said. "It's a wonder he made it without cracking up. Going off the road and killing himself. And when he got here, he was a wreck. He just stayed overnight. He told me what happened, and then he came outside with me and helped me haul some stuff. He hardly said another word. I know he didn't sleep that night. I heard him up till all hours. He was like a zombie, like a crazy man. I could hardly talk to him. And then the next morning—do you want to know what he did?"

I couldn't say a word. I just nodded.

"He went back to New York and began to hit the bottle," Uncle Austin said. "He didn't tell me much about this, but I knew what he was doing. I'd call him at night sometimes, and he'd be half out of his head with drink." He reached across the table and gripped my arm. "I'm not talking about a couple of friendly drinks with his pals. I'm talking serious boozing. He drank himself into a stupor. Listen to me, girl," he said, digging in his fingers. "He went on a binge. And he didn't come out of it for a long time. I'm talking a *long* time. He didn't come out of it until not that long ago."

He let go of me and leaned back in his chair, drank down the shot, poured another, and sat there in silence, looking at it morosely. I rubbed my arm, trying to believe what he had just told me. It was another thing I couldn't imagine: Patrick as a drinker. For the first time in all those years, I understood with perfect clarity that I had done something not only to myself but to him.

"He kept working," I said.

It came out sounding defensive and whiny, and I expected Uncle Austin to lash out at me again, but when he answered it was in a different voice—less belligerent, maybe a little drunk at that point. "Sure. After a while, he did. He worked on his sculptures, and he drank. He could escape into those big hunks of metal, and he could escape into the booze. I suppose it's a mercy he had some kind of outlet."

I thought about the first photograph of Patrick I'd cut from an English art magazine: unsmiling, in profile, standing beside one of his massive works. If I went home and looked at it again, would I see that he was a suffering man?

"I'm sorry," I said, but the words evaporated in the hot air of the kitchen, they were so small, so meaningless. I looked out the window at the fresh green of the sloping hills, the white sky. A bead of sweat ran down my back. Neither of us said anything. I wondered if there was any more to say, and I looked over at Uncle Austin, thinking maybe the heat and the whiskey had put him to sleep, but he raised his head just then and said, "Do you remember the first time you ever came to this house? How you asked me about adopting Patrick, what it was like just out of the blue to have a kid around. Remember that?"

"Yes. I said you were amazing, the way you just took him in, took care of him. Became a father to him."

"Well, I'll tell you what's bloody amazing. It's how Patrick turned out a sane man after what happened to him—his parents being wiped out, overnight. Just gone. And nobody but his rough old uncle to care for him. He was a mess, that kid, when I got him. He was five years old. He wouldn't talk, he wouldn't let anybody hug him or even touch him, he didn't want to eat—and he did these daredevil things."

"What things?"

"He had this little bicycle, with the training wheels, and he would ride that thing into the road, right across Route Sixteen in the traffic. Or he'd light matches—he had an unholy fascination with fire. And he used to run away. I'd go out in the truck and find him half a mile down the highway. I had to watch him every minute." Uncle Austin picked up his glass and sipped. Then he tossed down the rest of it, wiping his mouth on his hand. "Jesus, the kid terrified me, and that's the truth."

"How did it end?"

He thought for a minute. "It was like he made up his mind. He got interested in the rusty junk in my yard. He started helping me work with it. And pretty soon he was acting like a normal little kid. He started first grade, he brought friends home, he got hooked on baseball. But I'm serious, Wynn, for a long time I thought the boy was done for." He smiled a little. "I thought he'd end up in the bughouse, for sure."

I took heart. He had called me by name. He was becoming more like his old self. I started to say something, but then, suddenly, Uncle Austin leaned forward out of his seat and slammed his fist on the table in front of me. "And then you go and do it to him all over again!" He sat back down. "By Jesus, I didn't think he'd survive it a second time."

I put my head in my hands. Was this the news I had come for? That I had not only destroyed my daughter, I had nearly destroyed the man I loved? All the horrors of the last four years washed over me again as if they were brand new. At the same time, there was a curious justice about being there and, finally, talking about it—even in being condemned. Maybe this was what I had needed all these years—someone besides myself to tell me I had done wrong.

I looked up at him. I had to ask. "Will you ever forgive me?" He just stared at me. The smile was gone, and the leprechaun twinkle in his light brown eyes—Patrick's eyes. He sat there impassively, his fingers curled around his empty glass. "I didn't mean to hurt him, Uncle Austin," I said. "I didn't mean to hurt you."

"Forget me. It's him." He kept his unblinking stare on me, and I realized he was very drunk. "Forgive you," he said, his voice thick with whiskey. He let out a bark that I suppose was meant for a laugh. "Not bloody likely, missy," he said. "Not bloody fucking likely."

• • •

I found a school for disturbed children north of Boston that would have been a half-hour commute from my apartment. The headmistress was very nice, but they didn't have an opening, and if they did, they preferred teachers with master's degrees. I checked M.A. programs in art therapy in the Boston area; there were several good ones, but it was too late to apply for the coming fall, and none of them offered summer courses that sounded right. Finally, I began volunteering twice a week at a program in Somerville, doing after-school art projects with the younger children and teaching oil painting to seventh- and eighth-graders.

I fell immediately back into the rhythms of teaching. And my students were so easy! After St. Clement's, dealing with a bunch of American public-school kids was like a perpetual picnic. I wrote to Rachel about it, and she replied, "You mean you don't have to watch your back? Nobody's tried to knife you this week? You're in paradise!"

Gradually, while my students worked, I got into the habit of sketching them—quick, impressionistic little drawings that were all I had time for in between making the rounds, critiquing their work, helping them out, keeping a lid on the goofing off. But from time to time they would settle down and get involved in what they were doing, and then I would perch somewhere and draw.

At first the sketches went badly—they were almost as inept and depressing as the painting I had attempted. Gradually, though, I got to like what I was doing, and the kids began to take an interest, too, complimenting me on a good likeness, complaining when they said I made someone's nose crooked or ears too big.

The whole experience—the teaching and my drawing—was a shaft of sunlight in the dark and tangled garden that was my life, a paradise indeed, and I began to look forward to those Tuesday and Wednesday afternoons as I hadn't looked forward to anything in a long time. I was reminded of the first months after I returned from the Edna Quinlan Home, when I had had such a hunger for people's faces and couldn't stop drawing and painting them. I wasn't sure, this time, why the sketches of those absorbed, healthy young faces gave me so much satisfaction. Partly they filled my need to make art, and partly they came out of my delight in my students and in their work. But I think that drawing was also something I turned to in sheer desperation after Santo and the photograph, after Uncle Austin and his anger; it was one way to survive all that, and to diminish the image of Patrick and Sonia, the woman who had led him away from alcoholism and despair, the woman who had made him forget me.

I taught my classes through the end of the school year, and when June came I taught in a Cambridge summer program—oil painting for teenagers plus a class for adults. In the fall I went back to Somerville, but by then I also had two private students: an incredibly talented fifteen-year-old named Justin, and a young mother named Margery who worked diligently and made progress but mainly just needed to get out of the house and away from her two toddlers once a week.

I was walking home from a class one November day when, crossing Harvard Yard, I heard someone call my name. At first I thought I had been mistaken. I hardly knew anyone in Cambridge. But the voice called again. I turned, and there was Alec Gunther, my old beau from college.

Rather awkwardly, we shook hands. Then we walked across the Yard together, and ended up having coffee in a place in Harvard Square. It was a dusky late afternoon; Christmas carols played over a loudspeaker.

"The last time I saw you was in a coffee shop," he said as we sat down.

"A long time ago."

He thought for a moment. "Nearly eleven years."

In eleven years, Alec had become a distinguished man. Even in school, he had had a certain elegance, but now in his mid-thirties he was even more polished. He was just my height, with neatly trimmed blond hair, a long nose, a sensitive mouth. He was wearing glasses—little metal-rimmed ones—and a fine silk tie, a suit so soft I wanted to touch it. I felt rough and dowdy in my jeans and boots, a ratty red sweater, my hair jammed under a wool hat.

He told me what he'd been doing. He was an associate professor of art history at Harvard, and he had written a book that had been widely praised, about Millet and the Barbizon School.

"My first artistic passion," I said with a smile.

"I remember," he said. "I thought of you while I was writing it." He was abruptly silent, stirring his coffee. A chorus sang: *O'er the fields we go, laughing all the way, ha ha ha* . . . "Actually, Wynn, I've thought a lot about the past this last year or so, probably because the present hasn't been terribly satisfactory."

He was looking into his coffee as if into a book, and I studied his bent head. I could tell he was searching for exactly the right words to finish what he wanted to say. Alec had never, to my knowledge, done or said anything impulsive, and it was a comfort to know that some things never changed. I felt a wave of affection for him. "I'm sorry to hear that, Alec," I said. "What's been happening? What's the trouble?"

He raised his head. "You're not with the sculptor any more?"

I said that I wasn't with the sculptor any more, that he was married to someone else. I told Alec about my job in England, my mother's death, my father's, and my decision to return to the States.

"I'm sorry to hear your parents are dead. I liked them both."

"I miss them. Especially my father. After my mother died, he turned into a crotchety old bird for a while—you wouldn't have known him—but he was mellowing out like crazy when he died."

"And what about you? What made you decide to come back to Boston?"

"Nothing but homesickness." I had no idea how to explain to Alec all that that word implied.

"Do you regret it?"

"No—I love being here. But I feel rather aimless."

"Still painting?"

"Not much. I'm doing a little teaching, and I'm enjoying that more than doing my own work at the moment." He let that pass, for which I was grateful. "I have no family left, and I don't know a soul in town any more." I grimaced. "It's odd to be in this city and not to be in school. It makes me feel elderly."

"Well—now you know me." His eyes were eager behind his glasses. "Maybe that will help." He looked at me for a moment—I saw him drop his gaze to my breasts—and then he said, "I was married to a colleague of mine for several years."

He stopped again. We sipped our coffee. *Oh, what fun it is to ride in a one-horse open sleigh. . . .* It was warm in there, and I took off my hat; my hair sprang out like a caged hedgehog. Alec didn't speak, but he seemed to want to talk, and so I prompted, "And what happened?"

The story poured out in a torrent, as if he had never had anyone to tell it to before. The marriage had broken down over issues of professional jealousy. When his book came out, he was promoted and tenured at Harvard, and he became an international authority on his subject, with more travel and speaking engagements than he could cram into his schedule. Meanwhile, his wife's contract wasn't renewed, and she found herself without a job. She was bitter. They fought all the time. She became cruel, he said—without specifying what he meant. I imagined how easy it would be to be cruel to Alec, who was always so reserved and courteous, and I also imagined that behind his simple story—he was more successful than she, they quarreled, they divorced—there must be layers of torment.

We sat there awhile, comfortably, talking, and then he walked me home. In the weeks that followed, we began dating. It all seemed very logical. Alec was a nice man; he could be quite interesting behind his reserved manner. We spent Christmas at his place, in bed, drinking champagne; neither of us had anywhere else in particular to go. As the winter progressed, we were constantly together. Alec lived well. After the divorce he had bought a lovely old brick house on Brattle Street and filled it with antiques and Oriental carpets. He was the way he had been eleven years before, but more so: He knew about rugs, he knew about classical music and jazz, he knew about wines, he knew all the best restaurants, he could cook. He showed me parts of Boston and Cambridge I had never seen before. He took me to parties where I met his colleagues, some of them awesomely famous. He made love to me slowly, seriously, considerately. He praised my little sketches. I gave him one for his birthday, of the footbridge and the river, and he hung it in his study.

But when Alec asked me to marry him, I resisted. I knew I didn't love him—I loved Patrick, I would always love Patrick, whether he was married or not, whether I ever saw him again or not. No one else could come close to what he had meant to me. I knew that. And I wasn't sure Alec loved me: It seemed sometimes that I was just another treasured possession, like his house or the antique armoire he brought back from his last trip to France. But he said he loved me, several times, and finally it seemed petty and cruel not to believe him.

He proposed once formally, over dinner at a Russian restaurant, complete with champagne and a ring. I said I couldn't marry him, I didn't love him enough. But a week later he asked again, with more champagne, the same ring, a witty sonnet he had written. He was charming; he made me laugh. Impulsively, a little drunk on champagne, I said yes.

Why did I marry him? The simple answer was that he wanted it so much. The more complex one is that I had lost everything, everyone. My daughter was dead, Patrick was married to someone else, my parents were gone, I had no real job, my friends were scattered, my beloved Boston was a lonelier place than I had expected it to be. It seemed like a good idea to make someone else happy, and in doing so I would find comfort, peace, purpose. *We'll have a good life,* Alec had said, and I believed that that was true.

"You have no idea how much this means to me," he said as he slipped a ring on my finger—a dainty but far from small diamond he had found in an antiques shop in Paris, where he had just been to a conference. His voice was very serious; his eyes shone. My heart turned over. I wished I could love him that much, but it was no longer true that I didn't love him at all—how could I not? Who could measure such a thing? Who could balance it out? And was love ever equally given and received?

As I considered the life we would have together the thought came to me—a thought I had banished for years—that it was time for me to have a child, that I needed more than almost anything to have a child. I imagined having children with Alec: a little boy in glasses, an artistic, graceful little girl. I put my arms around Alec and kissed him.

We were married the following autumn. On our honeymoon we went to Paris, a city Alec knew as well as he knew Boston; he spoke decent French and had friends there—pleasant, English-speaking art historians and museum people. We took a side trip to the town of Barbizon, where I did some obligatory sketching—his old dream of the perfect life. He would turn to me at odd moments—in the shop on the Champs Élysées where he bought me perfume, in the Café Loup while we waited for our table—and say, in his modest way,

"Hasn't this turned out well, Wynn?" And he would take my hand and kiss it.

We were sitting in the Jardin de Luxembourg when we first discussed having children. The French children fascinated me. They seemed, all of them, to be fine boned, beautifully dressed, well behaved. I could see Alec and me with a child sitting on the bench between us, that imaginary little daughter. We would buy her a balloon from the stand at the entrance. She would wear the smocked dresses my grandmother had made for me, still stored away in tissue paper in my closet. Alec would teach her little bits of French.

When I brought up the subject, Alec said, "Let's wait a while. I'm too involved in my work right now. I know I couldn't be the kind of father I would want to be."

This was a reasonable thing to say. I knew what kind of father Alec would be when the time came: creative, attentive, passionately involved. I linked my arm through his. "When do you think would be a good time?"

Before he could answer, something strange happened. It was a soft September afternoon, sunny and dry. Alec and I were sitting by the pond, where a small boy in a striped T-shirt and pale blue shorts was sailing a boat. He was perhaps three. His mother and an older sister stood by, talking quietly in rapid French. Suddenly the boy turned and looked right at me. *"Maman!"* he called. *"Maman!"* He started toward our bench. My heart leapt: Instinctively, I smiled and reached out my hands. Then the child looked confused, spotted his mother and ran toward her. We were both frizzy haired, both in pale dresses. *"Maman!"* He clasped her around the middle, and she lifted him into the air and kissed him.

I sat back against the bench, my heart thumping, wanting to laugh at myself but too upset to laugh. I didn't need to know French to understand *maman*. For that quick, mad moment a child had reached out to me, called me mother, and it had left me horribly shaken.

Alec just chuckled; he didn't notice my reaction. Absentmindedly, he watched the two children with their mother for a moment, and then he said, "Let's see how it goes. Of course, you know we'll be doing a lot of traveling. Think how difficult that would be with small children. We would either drag them along or you'd have to stay home with them. Either way, it would be intolerable." He took my hand. "And I have to admit, I like the idea of being alone with you."

I watched the little boy with his mother. He smiled shyly at me over her shoulder. His sister spun on one foot, her white skirt filling with air. I could still hear that shrill little voice: *Maman! Maman!* "Alec," I said. "What does that mean? You'll always be traveling. That won't change."

"All I'm saying is let's wait a while, Wynn. I just don't feel ready." He looked into my face. "You weren't thinking of getting pregnant on our honeymoon, were you?"

I managed a laugh. "No, but—I thought, maybe, soon. I would like us to have a child."

He gestured toward the little French boy and his pinafored sister. "It's easy when you see cute kids like that to think what fun it could be," he said, smiling. "But we have to think of the reality."

Back in Boston, I became caught up in my husband's interesting life—his classes, the research he was doing on a new book, the academic issues surrounding his job. Who would be promoted, who would get tenure, who had a book coming out and how was it received: Those were the things that drove our lives. It was a relief for me to focus in on Alec's world. There was so little in my own.

As time went by and I still wasn't painting, I could see that Alec was disappointed. He had the art historian's reverence for people who actually produced the stuff. *You've got to paint,* he insisted. *You're a painter. Forget getting another degree, forget looking for a job, don't get bogged down with teaching—you should be painting.* I thought of my mother, but I let him persuade me to fix up a studio in the tall, third-floor attic, bringing some of my parents' things out of storage to furnish it with, funky old objects that wouldn't have fit into Alec's house. I loved that studio, with its bare wooden floors and sloping ceiling, my precocious painting of Snarly on the wall along with a few things my students had produced. Justin and Margery came up there for their lessons, and when Justin went off to Yale and Margery's husband was transferred to Baltimore, Samantha and Alice took their places—a teenager and a woman in her forties, both with more talent than money, that I taught for practically nothing. I had a mini-fridge and a hot plate in one corner. Near a window that looked out over the dignified rooftops of Cambridge was my old bed heaped with pillows. If I'd wanted to, I could have moved in.

From time to time, I even tried to paint there. I would get out my oils, find a suitable canvas, make marks on it. I even finished one, a view of the rooftops that I had sketched a dozen times. The drawings were promising. The painting was like a bad translation from a foreign language.

I still had my little box of Patrick mementos stored away in a drawer. I had considered getting rid of them, but I couldn't, any more than I could get rid of the envelope that held the Molly McCormick clippings. From time to time I added new information to the Patrick file—a major exhibit, another grant, a commission—conscious always that the man I read about was someone who, most likely, despised me. For years, the visit to Uncle Austin haunted me—his hostility and, by extension, Patrick's. I didn't care: I had to know where Patrick was, what he did. I had to know he was still there—that he was, in some sense, all right. And like someone biting down on a toothache, I looked in art magazines and in the newspapers for items about Sonia Shapiro, but though I occasionally found something about the DGA Gallery I never saw her name. She was probably busy having babies, I thought, and the toothache intensified.

Alec was perpetually busy with his students, his research, his conferences. I traveled with him sometimes, especially when he went to Europe, but I didn't mind staying home alone hanging around in my studio, reading, writing letters to Marietta and Rachel, absurdly overpreparing for my classes. I had moments of restlessness when I longed to do something more useful or more active, and the abdication of that simple need to get away from myself by putting parts of myself on canvas was a wound that couldn't heal.

But Alec was right: We had a good life. He was a model husband, always coming up with ways to please me. It was a tradition that he serve me Sunday breakfast in bed—the bed was huge, the omelettes perfect, the mimosas made with fine champagne. He loved buying me presents; any occasion, no matter how trivial, was an excuse to give me jewelry. (One Groundhog Day, I found a pair of black pearl earrings on my pillow.) We threw elaborate dinner parties, cooking together amicably in the kitchen. Alec considered vintage jazz the perfect music to cook by, so he would put on Harry James or Louis Armstrong or Jack Teagarden and sing along as we chopped and sautéed. People seemed to like coming to our house. It was so beautiful there, and the wine was always good.

"You people are *exactly* like an ad for something on TV," a French professor named Lydia said once after her third or fourth martini. "I don't know what, but whatever it is, I would *definitely* buy it."

"How do you manage to get along so well?" another Cambridge friend asked. She was recently divorced. "I've never heard you disagree about anything. I've never even heard you raise your voices to each other."

We were at a dinner party. Alec smiled across the table. "Have we ever disagreed, Wynn?"

I pretended to think. "There was that time you thought the brie wasn't runny enough," I said, and everyone laughed.

It was a joke, and it wasn't true.

More and more, we disagreed about the issue of having children. Years went by. Alec wasn't ready. He was too busy. We traveled too much. The responsibility was staggering, the expense was insane, the world we lived in was no place to bring children into.

Once he said, "My students are my children. Overgrown babies, all of them. Believe me, I don't need any of my own!" Then he held up both his hands in that way he had. "Okay, okay," he said. "I know you don't feel that way. I'm well aware that teachers all over the place are producing children right and left. But sometimes I'm overwhelmed. You've got to give me some time, Wynn."

I gave him a year, five years, ten. He never said a definite no. There were times when I thought about children constantly, eyed them on the street, burned with envy while some young mother pushed a stroller as casually as if it contained groceries instead of a small person she had given birth to. I can even remember certain ones. The little Parisian boy in his blue-striped T-shirt. A sweet-smelling baby I held once, briefly, in line at the supermarket while her mother struggled with a screaming toddler. A tiny brother and sister, hand in hand, making their slow, solemn way around the skating rink at Harvard, who suddenly, simultaneously, looked up and smiled at Alec and me. I almost understood those pathetic women I sometimes read about who stole other people's children, plucked them out of carriages or met them as they came out of school and spirited them away.

Periodically, we would talk about names (Eleanor, Jon, Iris, David). We decided the back bedroom would be perfect for a kid's room, with its wall of built-in cupboards for toys. Alec took a lively interest in the children of our friends, picked out wonderful gifts for them, sent his sister and her children in Michigan an elaborate Christmas box every year.

These were good signs, I told myself. I kept hoping; I didn't let myself consider that he might never be ready for a child of his own.

Occasionally, I considered telling Alec about my daughter, wondering if it might influence him—if he could see how profound my need of a child was, how far back it went. I was stopped not only by the old feelings of guilt and shame, but by our lack of real intimacy: Our best talks were about food and furniture and art, not about how we felt, especially when the feeling was painful.

And of course, I was never entirely convinced I deserved another chance. I had had a child, I had given her up out of selfishness and weakness. I still thought often about Molly McCormick: her sweet, eager face, her terrible life and death. I could imagine Alec asking: *Why should you produce another one? What makes you think you'd be a better mother this time?*

I talked about some of this once with Marietta, when I flew out to California to visit her—something I did every year or so since my return to the States. Marietta had become a moderately successful screenwriter, valued for her ability to doctor an ailing script, but she had made most of her money from her second divorce. After a brief, foolish first marriage to an actor with a bad cocaine problem, she married a well-known producer who left her after seven years for an English actress and felt guilty about it. One of the things Marietta acquired was a weekend place in the Santa Monica Mountains overlooking Malibu. "He got the bimbo," Marietta said, when she recovered her sense of humor. "But I got the house."

It was a wonderful house—not large, but low and sprawling, fitted neatly into the landscape, and circled by a veranda. Below it, to the west was a blue glimpse of ocean, to the east a dramatic and spectacular canyon, and, all around, the dry brown hills like a chain of placid elephants.

Marietta invited me to spend a week with her there the autumn after my fortieth birthday. She was finishing up a job, so I brought my sketchpad and a couple of books to read. The nights were chilly, the days hot and dry, and while Marietta worked in her study I read and dozed and sketched the view from various vantage points. I loved the colorless landscape, all browns and khakis—the eucalyptus and succulents, and skeletal trees I didn't know the names of. Hummingbird feeders hung from the veranda roof, and from time to time a bird would dart in, feed quickly, and flit away with a tiny chirping noise.

Marietta and I took occasional breaks to swim in the pool, and one afternoon we had a sweaty hike up one of the fire trails that bordered the canyon. In the evenings we would meet for a drink on the veranda, then put on sweaters and drive down the mountain for dinner, sometimes with friends of hers in the film world, but mostly alone, so we could talk.

Over the years, Marietta and I had discussed in depth her turbulent romantic life; there didn't seem much to say about my placid marriage. But on my last evening, when we were sitting as usual with our glasses of cold wine, I told her about the dissatisfactions of my life with Alec, and my desire for a child.

"So go off the pill," she said.

I looked over at her. She was lying back on a teak lounge chair, holding a cigarette, wearing what looked like a black silk sunsuit, her long, pale legs crossed. Her red hair was streaked with white—a stunning effect that I knew wasn't entirely Mother Nature's doing. She smiled at me. "Well? Why not? He's being unreasonable, you want a kid, you're completely within your rights. What's he going to do?

Divorce you? Kill you? Drug you and haul you off to an abortion clinic?"

I laughed. "Don't think I haven't thought about it."

"Well?"

I shrugged. "We don't have sex all that often any more," I said.

"Then, in that case, Wynn, why do you want to have a baby with him? I mean—what kind of marriage are we talking about here?"

"It's not perfect, I suppose. But it's what we've got."

"Oh, *please*." She took a drag on her cigarette and exhaled with a sigh. "It's the kid, isn't it? The one you gave up. That's why you want one so badly."

I hesitated again before I answered. "Yes. It's partly that. I would like to have another one before I'm too old."

"Then you *should*, for heaven's sake!" Marietta sat up straighter. "Why in hell don't you just leave him and find somebody else and have a baby?"

"I've thought about that, too."

"And?"

"It's not that easy. We've been married a long time, Marietta. Alec adores me. And we depend on each other."

"Oh God, Wynn. It sounds so tepid! You never should have married him."

I wasn't sure that was true, but even to Marietta, I couldn't tell the story of why I had married Alec, or how the marriage had saved me from my solitary despair, or that the deal I had made with myself was: *Make someone else happy, and the past will loosen its hold on you.*

*And has that happened?* I imagined her asking. And what would be my answer?

She startled me by saying, "You know damn well you should have married that crazy Patrick."

"He married someone else, Marietta. I told you that."

"But Wynn—why did you dump him in the first place? That never made a bit of sense to me. You two were perfect together."

I hesitated. It was all so long ago: Why tell her now? I thought of my sad little box of clippings—all I had left of Patrick. And that was the way it should be: I didn't want to bring it all back. In my fashion, I had learned to live with it. The death of my child, those black days in New York, my panicky flight to London, the years of aimless emptiness: Dragging the story out now, on this sunlit terrace, seemed crazy.

"We weren't as perfect as we seemed. It wasn't working, Marietta."

"Why couldn't you *make* it work? Why wasn't that important to you? Jesus, Wynn, you worshipped that guy! Did you even try, or did you just give up, turn your back, and run away?"

*"Shut up, Marietta! Just shut up!"*

We stared at each other. "That's better," she said, and then, gently, "Wynn—what's with you, sweetie? What's the matter? What's been the matter all these years? And don't tell me nothing."

I lay back on my lounge chair and closed my eyes. The sun beat down on my eyelids. "Nothing," I said.

She snorted. "OK. Tell me this. Why didn't you bring your paints? Where's that nifty little portable easel you used to have?"

"You know I don't paint much, Marietta."

"Much? What does that mean, exactly?"

I opened my eyes. "*Hardly ever* is what it means. Is that a crime?"

"Might be. I was brought up to believe that if you don't use the talents the Lord gave you, it's a sin."

"The Lord seems to have taken the talent back."

"Oh, give me a break."

I shrugged.

Marietta got up from her chair and came over to kneel beside me.

She took my face between her two hands. "Wynn. What the hell are you doing to yourself? Who is this person who doesn't paint any more, who's married to a man she doesn't love and doesn't have sex with and who won't give her any children? Who the hell are you? God damn it, you're not the Wynn I grew up with. She wanted a *life,* for Christ's sake! Now where the hell has she gone?"

"I don't know, Marietta," I said helplessly. "Don't badger me. Don't hate me. I don't know, I don't *know.*"

Marietta sat back down, looking out at the view with a frown. "I remember when you came back from Boston. When we were in high school. You were kind of pudgy, kind of distant. And you were so sad, Wynn. I'd never seen anything like it before, in my frivolous little life. You were like a tragic heroine in a novel. Tess of the d'Urbervilles or something. You were so different. It made a big impression on me. And I thought to myself: *My God! Things matter!* I can't explain it very well, but it was the first time I'd ever realized that actions have repercussions—you know? Life was serious. And I thought, she will never get over this, her whole future will be colored by this thing." She picked up her wineglass, sipped, looked at me. "Was that true? Does it all go back to that? I mean everything—not just wanting a kid but marrying Alec, dumping Patrick, not being able to paint—the whole package?"

"Probably." I couldn't say any more. I looked out at the mountains that, obscured by the tears in my eyes, seemed even more like clumsy, well-meaning animals. Marietta reached out a hand, and I took it.

"I'm sorry," she said. "God, it's not fair how things hang on, how things we did when we were babies, when we didn't know any better, when we were like puppies or kittens, we didn't have the brains of a hummingbird—how stuff from those days can keep haunting us." She released my hand, sat back in her chair, sipped her wine, and sighed. "I love you so much, Wynn. You're my oldest friend. I want you to be happy, for Christ's sake. Someday. I just want you to be happy with your life."

I wiped my eyes on a napkin, pressed my cold glass to my hot face, took several deep breaths. "I'm not that unhappy, Marietta." My voice was shaky, and I waited until it steadied. "Believe me. I've been unhappy, I know what it feels like, and this doesn't even come close." I knew what a lie this was, but I hoped she didn't. I loved Marietta, too, but I needed for the conversation to be over.

She smiled. "You are an amazing person. Did I ever tell you that before? I don't understand everything about your life, Wynn. For a busybody like me, you're annoyingly private, and I know there are huge pockets of stuff you haven't told me and never will. But I know this—you're the strongest person I've ever met."

We finished our wine and drove down the mountain to Marietta's favorite restaurant, where we had dinner with a film editor friend of hers, the twenty-two-year-old starlet who'd just been signed for Marietta's new movie, and a man named Gregory who owned a winery in the Napa Valley and who was destined to become Marietta's third and last husband.

When she drove me to the airport, Marietta hugged me and said, "Think about what we talked about, sweetie. Okay? Promise? This is the only life you get."

• • •

As I felt my chance at motherhood slipping away with the years, Alec and I discussed it less often, because when we did there was more open animosity. Our arguments were never resolved, and they left a legacy of bitterness that we buried under our social life and trips abroad and little kindnesses to each other.

Those small, thoughtful acts that comprised our lives, it occurred to me one day, could be more hostile than any fight.

Through the summer program I taught in, I became friendly with a woman named Hannah Rickert. She painted in watercolors, and her husband, Jay, was a potter. Hannah was a tall, shy woman with bright brown eyes and long gray hair who dressed in vivid, dramatic clothes she made herself: capes, blouses with billowy sleeves, flowing skirts that swirled around her ankles. Jay was blunt and quiet, usually in denim overalls; he reminded me of my father. They were older than I, their two sons were grown and gone, and soon after I met them they moved to the Cape, where they lived a retired life in one of those weather-beaten hamlets on the way to Provincetown.

Alec didn't much like the Rickerts. I forget exactly how he put it—some polite euphemism—but it was clear that he found them boring and unintelligent, and, though they were certainly neither, it was true that their world was very circumscribed. They never traveled; they seldom even drove up to the city. They were nearly self-sufficient in their old shingled house with its ragged garden mulched with seaweed—a house full of pictures of their handsome sons, their sons' wives, their grandchildren. What I liked most about Hannah, aside from her quiet humor and her blazing talent, was her love for every living thing. Hannah could get excited about saving a bee that had wandered into her living room; I saw her do this once, and when she had managed to catch it in a glass jar and release it out the front door, her face beamed with satisfaction.

The Rickerts had three goats whimsically named Vera, Chuck, and Dave, and on summer evenings Hannah and Jay would sit on lawn chairs in the goats' enclosure, reading and talking. "They like to be near us," Hannah explained. The Rickerts also had a flock of chickens, and ducks on their pond, and they had lost count long ago of how many cats inhabited the barn. When they could, they had them spayed, but if kittens arrived, they were welcomed, named, fed.

They took care of me with the same gentle affection. At times my life with Alec seemed so sterile and pointless that I had to escape it, and I would drive south down Route 6 to visit the Rickerts for a few days. Hannah and I would walk out on the dunes with our sketchpads, or down to the shore to make drawings of the boats, the gulls, the tourists. In the evenings the three of us would eat immense seafood dinners off the plates Jay had made, and then we would sit a while with the goats—Hannah in a long dress and big straw hat, an assortment of cats on our laps, the goats coming up to have their backs scratched with sticks. Sometimes I helped can tomatoes or pack up a shipment of Jay's pottery. I always returned from the Rickerts' feeling refreshed, loved, consoled, with jars of Hannah's jam and tomatoes, and one of Jay's pitchers or bowls which Alec wouldn't like, and which I would have to keep upstairs in my studio.

At various times I considered telling the Rickerts the story of my life. I knew perfectly well that they were serving as surrogate parents to me, and I longed to talk to them honestly and obtain some kind of absolution, or a closure that was impossible for me now with my real parents. Many times I came close to confessing to Hannah, but silence was a habit, a way of life, the road I went down every day, and in the end I didn't want to dredge it all up, I didn't want to have to find the words to explain it, and I didn't want to burden them with it. And it still seemed to me that I didn't deserve anyone's sympathy. Marietta's reproaches, Uncle Austin's anger all those years ago—those were part of the sentence I had imposed upon myself. Hannah's gentle, motherly understanding didn't fit into the picture.

But I couldn't have survived without the Rickerts, and my visits to Marietta, and my letters from Rachel. I heard myself saying that to someone one day—Marietta, probably—and was struck by how odd it sounded. As if my life were full of affliction instead of pleasure. As if it weren't a good life after all, but something else entirely.

• • •

As years went by, Alec's interest in art expanded beyond nineteenth-century French landscape painting. He became fascinated with an obscure Spanish painter named Victor Ignoto de Madera, who had been a friend of Millet and Rousseau in France and was much influenced by them. After a stay in Paris, de Madera retired permanently to Mexico, where he painted very French-looking landscapes until his death in 1877. Alec did some research on de Madera, wrote an article about him, and began planning a book. For our fourteenth wedding anniversary, we took a trip to Mexico during Harvard's winter break.

Alec was on the trail of some of de Madera's letters and sketchbooks from his years in France, and we spent a week in Mexico City so he could visit the museums and go through their archives. He met with scholars at the Museo Nacional de Arte and at a lovely little place called the Museo de San Carlos, while I wandered the galleries looking at bloody portraits of saints and the stone heads of Aztec gods. Then I would sit in cafés and courtyards, reading and sketching.

Returning to Mexico was a wrenching experience for me, and I found myself thinking about the town of Querétaro, six hours away on the train, where Patrick and I had once been so happy together. Alec and I were staying at a grand hotel called the María Isabel. We went to dinner every night with Mexican scholars and art historians, part of Alec's vast network of friends and acquaintances. One evening, we went to a nightclub where we saw flamenco dancing and, on another, to a popular disco with a salsa band. I met wonderful people and had a good time dredging up my high school Spanish. But I was alone a great deal and, inevitably, my thoughts wandered to my long-ago visit with Patrick: the quiet afternoons on our terrace in the sun, the freshly made tortillas that we bought for pennies, and the roasted *pollo* from the *mercado*, the guitar music and the cobblestone streets, the passionate nights in bed. That time with Patrick had become part of me, as indelible and necessary as my childhood memories. I sat in the courtyard of a museum, and the scent from a blossoming orange tree brought back his voice. I remembered his smile, the way he could talk, with that Irish lilt in his voice, about anything, everything. I remembered how he had laughed and said, Te amo, te amo, *I love you, Wynnooka.* It was ridiculous, I told myself, after all those years. Patrick and I were middle-aged, long estranged, married to other people. But everywhere I looked I saw him.

Later that afternoon, I met Alec, and we went shopping at the Mercado de Artesanías. He wanted to buy me a heavy silver necklace that cost the earth. It was beautiful. I loved it. But I couldn't let him do it. And, God help me, all I could think of was Patrick and the turquoise beads hidden away in the little box with the cat and the clippings.

By the time we got back to Cambridge, I knew I couldn't stay with Alec any longer. It was one of the hardest decisions I ever made. I was aware of how Alec's first divorce had affected him, and how much he hated to be alone. He liked company, an audience for his jokes and his erudite musings. I thought of him traveling without a wife, staying by himself at the quaint inns we had discovered. How hard it would be for him to admit to his friends and colleagues that a second marriage had failed. And how selfish it was of me to want to leave him and our enviable life and all the kindness and affection between us, the shared memories, the interests in common. In a way, it was unimaginable not to be married to Alec. And yet something—Marietta's advice, the passing of time, the vivid memory of my old love—had made it no longer possible. I didn't love my husband. I loved a man who no doubt despised me. A man I hadn't seen in nearly twenty years and would probably never see again.

With all my heart, I wished it were otherwise. But it wasn't, it would never be, and my life was a joke.

• • •

I kept putting off my talk with Alec. I practiced saying, "Alec, I need to talk to you," and I imagined how his face would change at my tone of voice, how he would understand before I continued that I wasn't going to say anything he wanted to hear. I dreaded bringing something so sordid into our lives, which were about avoiding trouble, seizing pleasures where we could find them. There would be no pleasure in this conversation.

I did nothing until, one morning when I was putting away Alec's laundry, I came across two jewelry boxes, one plain white, the other in the distinctive dark blue of Shreve, Crump & Low. They were tucked behind a pile of clean T-shirts. I looked at them for a moment. My first impatient thought was: *No. Please. No more gifts.* Then on an impulse I opened them. Inside the white one was the silver necklace Alec had wanted to buy me in Mexico. The other contained a thin gold bracelet studded with diamonds.

I took them both over to a chair by the window. The necklace was no less lovely. I imagined Alec slipping back to the *mercado* to buy it for me. What holiday was coming up? Easter? The vernal equinox? My birthday wasn't far off. I would undoubtedly find this under my pillow or waiting on my breakfast tray.

The bracelet was more problematic. I slipped it over my wrist. The diamonds twinkled up at me benignly enough, but I felt a quick, instinctive revulsion, and took it off immediately and put it back in its box. There were two possibilities. One was that Alec had bought me two gifts. But, aside from the extravagance, the bracelet was daintier than I liked and conservative in design—Alec knew my taste well, and it wasn't for diamonds—and so the other possibility was more plausible: He had bought it for another woman.

The window looked down at our small fenced yard, still deep in snow. I sat there numb, staring out at the blue shadows, the scrawny black trees, the fence crusted with ice. What I felt wasn't the anger of a betrayed woman, or even relief that the diamond bracelet had made my task easier. My feeling surprised me: I was engulfed by regret. The bracelet was a revelation. Alec had been unhappy with me, more profoundly, urgently miserable than I had been with him—unhappy enough to turn to someone else. All the bad reasons I'd had for marrying him had backfired. I was supposed to find peace, and my life had been full of sadness and longing. I was supposed to make him happy; I had not only failed to do that, but I had underestimated him. Why, in my arrogance, had I assumed that our tepid marriage with its bland comforts could be enough for him? For anyone?

We had salmon for dinner that evening; Alec had poached it with capers—I heard him humming along with Teagarden's trombone while he cooked—and with it we were drinking a California fumé blanc that Alec was particularly fond of. It was a lovely dinner—all our meals were amazing—but I couldn't eat. I thought of the first time I told Alec good-bye, in the coffee shop in Boston, and how he had laughed when I told him it was because of a sculptor I hardly knew. Now it was because I had tried to live a life I knew was a fake. How could I explain such a thing? What could I say? I drank some wine, twisted my hands together in my lap, and, interrupting him in the middle of a sentence, I said, desperately, "Alec, I think we should get divorced."

For a few long seconds he didn't say anything. He took a bite of fish, chewed, swallowed, sipped his wine. Then he said. "How extremely odd."

I wasn't sure if he had taken in what I'd said, or if there was something wrong with the wine. "What do you mean—odd?"

"I've been wanting to say the same thing to you."

My clenched hands were trembling. "Yes, I suspected you were seeing someone."

"Really. And what about you? Is there anyone I should know about?"

"No," I said. My voice was unsteady. I got up and left the dining room, went into the living room across the hall, and stood by the fire. I was shaking, chilled to the bone. I thought I would never be warm again. After a minute or two, Alec joined me. I imagined him taking a few more bites of salmon, washing it down with wine, wondering what I knew, how I knew, being glad I had said what I said. My eyes filled with tears. He came over and stood next to me. "What's wrong?"

I faced him. "What's *wrong*? Alec, we want to divorce each other. *What's wrong*? Isn't that enough?"

"We can be civilized about it, Wynn. Can't we? It's a mutual thing, at least. Thank goodness."

"Yes, thank goodness for that." I felt hysterical laughter overtake me. "That makes it all right. That makes it just fine."

Alec took me by the shoulders. "Wynn. Please. Sit here." I wasn't crying any more, but I was still shaking, and my teeth were chattering. I sank down on the sofa, and put my cold hands to my burning cheeks. Alec said, "I'm sorry, I don't mean to be so—" He gestured, looking for a word, not finding it. "I'm sorry," he said again.

He brought a cashmere throw from the study and tucked it around me. He poured us each more wine. He took my hands and chafed them between his until they warmed. "I'm sorry, too," I said. "I'm sorry it stopped working."

We smiled sadly at each other, but there was a kind of exhilaration in Alec's face, too. I remembered that he had another life, another woman.

He sat on a chair facing me. "I did love you," he said.

"I know you did."

His gaze drifted to the fire. What was he remembering?

Something good or bad? "But you didn't love me," he said abruptly.

"I did."

"You never loved me enough, Wynn. You know that's true. You didn't love me the way I needed to be loved."

I didn't argue with him. Of course it was true. I pulled the blanket up around my chin. I was calmer, beginning to thaw out. A CD was still playing in the other room, Chet Baker singing "Look for the Silver Lining." It ended, and in the silence Alec continued. "It took me some time to figure it out," he said. "That there was something in the way. I don't know what it was. The sculptor? Somebody in England? Something else? I don't know, I don't even want to know any more. But something wasn't there between us that should have been there. Or vice versa."

I took a sip of wine. At that moment, I wanted desperately to talk about it: about my child's birth and death, about my flight to England and about Patrick—things I had never completely revealed to anyone. The terrible facts of the story pounded in my head. But this wasn't the time, and Alec wasn't the person. I wished Marietta was there, or Hannah. I wished for my father. I closed my eyes. Mostly, I wished for Patrick. The thought of him, there in Alec's elegant living room with the fire crackling and snow falling softly outside the window, was suddenly as vivid as it had been in Mexico. *Patrick*. Where was he? What did he look like? What was he doing?

"Wynn?"

I opened my eyes. "A lot of things happened to me before I ran into you again that day in Harvard Yard," I said. "Painful things that I blamed myself for. I was in a bad way."

When Alec answered, his voice was tight with irritability. "Am I supposed to sympathize with this?"

I shook my head. "I guess not." I wanted to say that this was not what I had meant to make of my life. Maybe I had intended to deprive myself of certain things, I had wanted to limit my pleasures, to renounce passionate love. But I hadn't wanted to make a hash of it, and I certainly hadn't wanted to make Alec suffer.

He looked at me a long minute. "You really wanted a child."

"And you didn't."

"It never seemed right."

"It might have helped."

He shrugged. "Maybe. Who can say? I've never heard of a marriage that was saved by having a baby. *Au contraire.*"

We were quiet again. A log shifted in the fireplace, scattering sparks. Alec picked up his glass, drank some wine, set the glass down. He sat back in his chair, his legs crossed, one elegant loafer dangling from his foot. He was wearing a pair of cashmere socks of the palest gold. He took another sip of wine. I could tell he wanted to say more.

"What is it, Alec?"

He raised his head. "There's something I want you to know. I've fallen in love with someone. A woman named Annette. I met her at a conference. She teaches at a state college near Chicago."

"I'm happy for you." I pictured a conservative woman in a suit, little gold earrings, a gold bracelet studded with tiny diamonds. "I think that's wonderful, Alec."

She would be coming to Cambridge for the summer, returning to Chicago in the fall. She had a year left of her three-year contract at the college. Then she would move here permanently. She hoped to find a position in the area. It was all distressingly reminiscent of his first marriage, but I didn't mention that.

"There's something else." He hesitated, then plunged on. "Annette has two children, a boy and a girl. Ten and twelve." His eyes softened. "And I think can handle that. I'm ready to have that in my life. Children. Family. You know?" He smiled. "I have to admit I surprise myself."

He got up to prod the logs with the poker. If he had hit me with it, he couldn't have hurt me more. I felt a surge of anger. Suddenly I had no idea who I was talking to. My husband. Some man who liked good food and bought me extravagant gifts and wore cashmere socks, who wanted to be a father to some other woman's children. I wondered if he knew how cruel his words had been. I watched him for a moment as he fussed with the fire. Then he smoothed his hair, took off his glasses and wiped them on his handkerchief. He turned around and faced me, put his glasses back on. "So that's why I want a divorce, Wynn."

"Don't you want to know why I want a divorce?"

He just looked at me. "Not really."

"I think I want to tell you anyway."

Alec sighed. "Go ahead."

"It was in Mexico."

He looked up, interested in spite of himself. "Yes? I thought it was a good trip. I thought we had a pleasant time."

"I was there once before, long ago," I said. "I was there with someone I loved deeply. And being there again showed me the difference."

I said it to be cruel, and I could see that it was. But he only smiled. "Well, I'm glad it's mutual," he said. "Of course, I managed to talk to Annette on the phone every day while we were there. Sometimes it wasn't easy, but—" His smile intensified. "Not to be corny, but love always finds a way."

• • •

I rented an apartment across the river in Boston, but until I could move in I slept in my studio at what I now thought of as Alec's house. He and I were polite, cold, avoiding each other. Alec was gone for three or four days—to Chicago, I assumed—and when he came back we got together with our lawyers. Everything was amicable—*civilized*, as Alec had said. The financial settlement was absurdly simple: There was none. I had money of my own—not riches, but enough to live on. I stayed at Alec's for a week, getting rid of old clothes, dismantling my studio, packing my things and arranging to have them stored. I called my students and told them there would be a short break. I couldn't move into the new place right away, but when I finished my chores I became uneasy in that beautiful, alien house that was no longer part of my life, and on which I had made such a shallow impression. Packing up my worldly goods, I was astonished at how little I had. It occurred to me that for all those years, except for my teaching, I had been living Alec's life. I was eager to leave and get on with my own.

It took me a few sleepless nights to figure it out, but eventually I knew where I had to go and what I had to do. Another pilgrimage, I thought. Another journey.

On my last night at Alec's I set an alarm so that I would wake up very early. It was already mid-March, but winter lingered in New England that year: Snow had fallen while I slept, and I had to shovel the driveway so I could pull my car out. Sweaty, invigorated, my careful braid hopelessly frizzed, I was on Interstate 95 with a doughnut and a cup of coffee by seven o'clock.

Driving, I was full of hope. At some point in that conversation with Alec by the fire I began to understand that I was dying of silence—of hoarding nearly twenty years, worth of pain and guilt. It was as if I'd been slowly creating a strange, twisted self-portrait, a painting so labored, so worked over, it was no longer recognizable. It had to be dragged into the light and looked at. It had to be drastically changed. It had to be started again.

The roads were clear, but all along the highway, as the sun rose in the sky, the pure, cold light glinted off the snow, turning it gold. The weather was perfect for my mood. I headed north, and when I crossed the border into Maine I found a country station on the radio and sang those corny, tragic songs at the top of my lungs, all the way to West Dunster.

## *Question Four*

# Why Did You Return?

There was a new Ramada Inn at the edge of town, on the site of what used to be a seedy motel called the Mountainview. The view was still there: From the window of my room, I could see Burbank Mountain. Once it had risen blank and forbidding against the sky; now a pattern of houses and roads wound between the pines: the work of Mark Erling's family, who had bought large tracts of land, cleared them, and sold them off to developers back in the seventies. Fitting, I thought, that the first thing I should see when I came to town was the work of the Erlings. But I smiled as I looked up at that ravaged mountain. It seemed a good omen.

I had come to West Dunster out of curiosity, nostalgia, and a certain need I couldn't quite define. I wanted to see the town where so much happened to me, and where my parents had been well and happy. If I were going to start my life over, I had to see where it began.

But I had also come in search of Mark Erling. During that last week at Alec's, as I packed books and sorted clothes and lay awake in the guest-room bed, I went over and over the story of my daughter's death and the last eighteen years of my life until all I could think about was confessing it to someone who would understand. I'd been unable to tell the people closest to me—Patrick, Rachel, Marietta, my father. But now it began to fill my waking hours, it invaded my dreams, it beat insistently in my head like an old song, and I thought if I could only say those words out loud, let the story pour out honestly and completely, then finally some of the pain would diminish.

I knew what I would say before I was sure to whom I would say it. It wasn't until I had pondered it for several days that I knew the person I had to talk to was Mark.

I had scarcely thought of him all those years, certainly had never had any wish to see him. But of all the people who knew about that baby, he was the only one who had cared about her. About *her*. That little girl. Instead of about getting it over with, going on with our lives. The only one who knew that life shouldn't go on as if nothing had happened. I remembered Mark's phone call to me the night of the Junior Prom, and understood how extraordinary it had been that he had cared enough to ask those questions, that he had shed tears for that baby. *I wish I could have seen her.* He had been an unusual seventeen-year-old, and I assumed he would be unusual still, and that I could talk to him. And that I would finally have someone to mourn with.

• • •

The first thing I did was take a drive out Route 8 to Brewster Road.

I hadn't been back to West Dunster since my parents moved south over twenty years before. But Marietta's sister Pat still lived in town, and Marietta visited her periodically. She had warned me that our old place had been drastically changed, the house covered with cheap aluminum siding, the barn made into a three-car garage. "Imagine the inside," Marietta had said, sounding pained. I knew it wouldn't be easy, and I had never wanted to before. But now things were different. I needed to see it.

I turned the corner onto Brewster Road and parked the car so I could walk by and really look at the place. The sun had faded as I drove north, and it was a bitterly cold Maine day. The air was damp, threatening snow; it cut right through my heavy jacket and wool hat. I trudged down the road stamping my feet to keep them warm, went by Marietta's old house—which seemed largely unchanged—and suddenly, sooner than I had expected, there was the house where I grew up.

I remembered what it had been like walking home from that same corner every day after the school bus let us off, and coming upon our green-and-white house nestled there in the snow, with the trim red barn out back. A thread of smoke would spiral from the chimney. Sometimes my mother would be at the door watching for me, or my father would be making his way down the path from the barn to the house. I could count on the fact that inside there would be the smell of cocoa or hot apple cider. There would be warmth, peace, everything I loved.

Now it was hard to believe it was the same house. I stood in front of the old place for a long time, shivering. The aluminum siding was brown and in bad repair, there were new, larger windows, and the front door that had always been so brightly painted was some indeterminate dark color. A ramshackle glassed-in porch had been added to one side, destroying the proportions. Out back, the barn was unpainted, peeling, seemed to be falling apart. The apple trees were gone, and so was the perfect hedge that had been my parents' pride and joy.

I was glad they weren't there to see it, but the changes bothered me less than I'd thought they would—less than they bothered Marietta. The house looked comfortable enough. Smoke still trailed from the chimney, the porch windows revealed a jumble of toys and ice skates and sleds, there were children's crayon drawings and cutout snowflakes taped to the windows. I thought of my parents' aversion to chaos and mess. Then I thought of the orderly, predictable life I had just left behind.

I went up to the house and knocked on the door. A woman answered, with her finger to her lips. "Shh. I just got the baby off to sleep." She spoke in a near whisper. "What can I do for you?"

"I'm really sorry to bother you," I said. "My name is Wynn Tynan. I used to live here years ago. I just—well, I don't really know what I wanted. Just to see the old place, I guess."

She was a dark-haired woman in jeans and a sweatshirt. "I'm Ellen Garner," she said, holding out her hand. "You'd probably like to look at the inside. Come on in."

"You're sure you don't mind? I don't want to intrude."

"No problem! Please—come in. You look half-frozen. No, don't bother to take your boots off. Really. It's okay. Just please, *please* be *very* quiet. He's got an ear infection, and it's hell trying to get him down for his nap."

I wiped my feet on the mat as well as I could and stepped inside. I took in the cheap carpeting, the big TV, a wreath of artificial flowers, a wall calendar with cutesy pictures of kittens. Ellen led me, tiptoeing, through the living room. A woodstove blasted away where our woodstove used to be. My father had made us a wood box, a work of art with a hinged top and mitered corners. Now there was an untidy pile of logs, a film of ash everywhere, burn marks on the carpet. A dog snored softly beside the stove. The table in the dining room was littered with magazines, puzzles, a half-built LEGO fort. Crooked mini-blinds that had seen better days covered the windows. In the kitchen, the sink was full of dirty dishes, and a red-cheeked baby slept in a portable crib.

"Chad," Ellen whispered. Chad made a noise in his sleep, and we held our breaths, but he didn't wake. I peeked into the room behind the kitchen that had been my little studio; it was now a playroom, strewn with dolls, parts of dolls, plastic toys, coloring books, markers. Magnetic letters on a board spelled out JENNY. There was a tiny TV in one corner, a VCR, a pile of videos. "I'm sorry you missed my girls," Ellen said. "They're in school."

"How many?"

She smiled. "Three. Ages six, eight, and nine."

An overflowing laundry basket sat at the foot of the stairs to the second floor. Ellen hesitated. "Do you want to go up?" she asked.

"No, that's okay." I could tell she really didn't want me to see it. I thought of my pristine white bedroom at the end of the hall, my parents' lofty room with its brick fireplace. I had once painted the two of them sitting side by side in bed, reading: the fire banked, my mother in her red nightgown, my father's glasses slipping down his nose, their books propped on their knees.

The old dog heaved himself to his feet and followed us as we walked back through the house. There was no longer a Franklin stove in the kitchen, and the floor was covered in blue-patterned vinyl tile. Underneath it somewhere, I knew, was the honey-colored pine planking my mother had loved so much. I had a sudden memory of her sweeping it one day and stooping down to pick up an earring that had fallen through the cracks. "The valley of lost things!" she had cried happily, and laughed.

"We've been here two years, and we love it," Ellen said. "We put in the new wall-to-wall in the living room, and we're trying to fix up the bedrooms—wallpaper, carpeting." She sighed. "It's a slow process. I'm sorry the place is such a mess. This one is a lot bigger than our last house, and I keep trying to get a handle on it, but it's kind of hopeless. Brant's working two jobs. He helps out all he can, but when he's got the time, I want him to play with the kids, not do housework."

"I don't blame you."

We paused at the front door. Ellen said, "I wish I could ask you to stay for a cup of coffee, but it's one of those days. I wouldn't mind hearing some stories about this place. Somebody told me a toymaker used to use the barn for his workshop." She smiled. "The kids love that. They think it was Santa Claus."

I chuckled. "It was my father."

"That must have been great for you kids."

"There was only me," I said. "But yes, it was great." We stood smiling at each other. Then I said, "Well, thanks for letting me track snow all through your house."

"I didn't mind one bit. Thanks for not waking the baby." She hesitated. "What do you think of the place now? Or maybe I shouldn't ask."

"It's a lot more lively. Things were pretty quiet in my day."

She rolled her eyes. "Lively. That's a polite way to put it."

"I mean it as a compliment," I said. There was no way I could convey exactly what I meant, and how much I liked her house. "It looks great, it really does."

"Well—thanks. You in town for a visit, or what?"

"I came to look up an old friend."

"Wow! That sounds like fun. I hope you have a super time. And it was awfully nice to meet you."

I realized suddenly that I was hungry, so I drove into town to Louie's Diner, where Marietta and I used to put away huge piles of French fries and talk about boys. But Louie's was gone, replaced by a Dunkin' Donuts. The ice cream place was gone, and so was the sub shop run by the Hauser twins' father; a big discount store had obliterated them both. I walked up and down the two blocks of Main

Street: Virtually everything I had known had disappeared except, in the distance, the dark slope of the nameless mountain that was crowned by the Erlings' house, the Castle. I could just catch a glimpse of its two turrets, the gray stone vividly pale against the surrounding trees. The mountain was bigger, more impressive than I remembered, maybe because the town at its feet seemed sad and diminished, a place of seedy, deserted stores and boarded-up windows. *The valley of lost things.*

I ended up having lunch at the motel, and then, in my room, I paged through the skinny local phone book. I hadn't necessarily expected to find Mark himself—had hoped, at most, to locate his parents or his brother or an old friend who could tell me how to contact him. But, incredibly, there was his name: Mark V. Erling, with an address on Mountain Road. Just below it was another listing: M. V. Erling Enterprises.

I was surprised that he had settled in his hometown and was living in his old house. I remembered the lovely, remote woman, the overbearing man in the seersucker suit, my humiliating half-hour in their frigid living room. Mark was the only Erling in the phone book, so I assumed his parents had died or moved away. It was difficult to imagine Mark, the wastrel jock, heading a company with the grandiose handle *Enterprises* attached to it. But the years had changed us all. There was Marietta, with her divorces and her film career. Marietta's old love, Keith, was a recording engineer in Australia, and her brother David, who had taught me how to kiss, had become a Franciscan monk. I'd heard that Deirdre Coyle of the wild parties was a commodities trader in Manhattan.

It was just after two in the afternoon. Mark would be at work. Before I could think about it much, I dialed the number of his company.

"Good afternoon." A woman's crisp voice. "Erling Enterprises."

"Yes. Hello. I wonder if I could speak to Mark."

"Who's calling, please?"

"This is an old friend of his from high school."

"No kidding!" The voice warmed, sounded delighted. "Hang on." Whatever Erling Enterprises was, this was still small-town Maine, and she put me through.

"Erling here."

*Erling here.* Crazy laughter bubbled up in me. "Mark?"

"Yes, this is Mark Erling." I hadn't been aware that I remembered Mark's voice. I couldn't recall his face exactly, but I could see his blond sideburns.

"Mark, it's Wynn Tynan. From Dunster High. I know it's been a long time, but—"

"Wynn. My God. Wynn Tynan. Where on earth are you?" he asked.

"I'm at the Ramada Inn. I'm going to be here for a few days, and I was wondering if we could get together."

I had rehearsed this speech along with everything else, and it came out smoothly, as if we were indeed just two old pals and I was passing through on a business trip. But my throat was tight with nervousness.

"You're in town? You're in West Dunster?"

"Yes." I sank down on the bed and stared at a painting on the wall of a French street scene. Shops. A poodle dog. BOULANGERIE. CAFÉ. "Mark," I said. "I'm here because there's something I need to talk to you about."

"There's something you need to talk to me about."

I couldn't tell if his voice was hostile or just puzzled or something else entirely. I didn't dismiss the idea that he had reached the same conclusions I had when he saw the Molly McCormick story on television. I thought it was more than likely that he despised me.

"Yes," I said. "Would you have time to meet for a drink, or a cup of coffee?"

There was a pause, longer than was polite. I was about to speak again when he said, "Wynn Tynan. Jesus." He stopped. "This is unbelievable." I didn't know what to say. I just waited. I imagined him remembering everything. "Of course. Yes," he said finally. "How about later today? I could come out there, I could meet you in the cocktail lounge at the Ramada."

He said he could be there shortly after five. He didn't say much more, only that he would be glad to see me. I was sure it was my imagination, but it sounded like he was trying to hold back tears.

• • •

I had nothing to do, and so I spent the rest of that afternoon driving. I went by my old elementary school, which had been transformed into housing for senior citizens. Then I drove into Dunster and out past the high school. Yellow buses in front. Kids in bright winter jackets, defiantly hatless in the frigid air. Not much seemed changed, except that there were some black faces. Twenty-odd years ago, there had been only one, an exchange student from Ghana. I stopped the car for a few minutes and sat with the motor running, watching the kids board their buses. I had forgotten how loud teenagers are, how the drama of adolescence demands noise. I noticed wire cages on the school windows. I wondered if they had a weapons detector, gang problems, if knives were drawn in the stairwells. It was hard to imagine. I thought about Mark Erling's famous fight with George Fisher, when George had reportedly been taken to the emergency room with a broken nose and a gash that needed stitches—how shocking that had been.

And I remembered how my pregnancy had to be lied about. Now they probably had support groups, a nursery, classes in child care, free condoms. At least, I hoped they did.

I watched until all the buses were gone, and then I drove to the outskirts of town, up and down the bare country roads. Forests of tall, straight pine trees rose up on either side, the landscape I had grown up with and that, at some level, I would always miss—the world of my mother's stark photographs. Here and there was a clearing with a house on it, snow banked beside the front walk, a snowmobile or a pickup parked in the driveway. Osmar Lake was frozen solid, stretching out vast and gray, dotted with the huts of ice fishermen. Two young men in red hats with earflaps were skating near the shore. I wished I had a camera or a sketch pad, but I had brought neither. I hadn't come to Maine as an artist. I had come as a penitent. I had come to confess.

Driving the familiar roads, my agitation left me, and I became strangely lighthearted, almost giddy—filled with an emotion I couldn't really identify. It wasn't happiness, certainly—nothing that simple. I suppose it was partly the excitement of opening a long-closed door and not knowing exactly what was behind it. And maybe it was partly the relief of the criminal who has been running and running, and who is about to turn herself in.

• • •

The Ramada's cocktail lounge was dimly lit, but I immediately spotted Mark sitting at a table. I was early; he had been even earlier. There was a half-empty glass on the table in front of him.

When he saw me he stood up. We shook hands. He took mine in both of his. "Wynn," he said. "You look wonderful."

I doubted it. I had tried to tame my hair into a braid, but the static electricity in my room had thwarted me, and I had finally just pulled it back with a barrette. Otherwise, I hadn't fussed. "I'm glad to see you, Mark," I said. I thought I had prepared myself, but the sight of Mark brought back everything, and I felt suddenly sixteen again. I knew I was blushing fiercely. "Actually, I'm a bit overwhelmed."

"I know what you mean." He pulled out the chair for me, and we sat down across from each other. Mark was much heavier but still handsome; his receding blond hair was silvery at the temples, and he had a small mustache. He wore a corduroy jacket, a checked shirt, no tie, a wedding ring. He looked like a nice, ordinary guy. I imagined an attractive wife, good kids, a pleasant life. To drag out the terrible truth of years ago struck me suddenly as cruel. Now that Mark Erling was sitting across a table from me, I didn't know if I could go through with it. And yet, of course, I knew I would, I had to.

He was staring at me, shaking his head. "This is amazing. After all these years. I pick up the phone and it's Wynn Tynan."

"I'm surprised you're still living in West Dunster."

"It's a long story. We'll get to it. We'll get to everything, but at the moment—" He grinned, picked up his glass, and drained it. "Frankly, I think I need another drink."

He signaled the waitress and ordered a whiskey on the rocks, and I said I'd have the same. When she was gone, he asked, "Where are you living now? And what the hell are you doing here in the boonies?"

"I live in Boston. I haven't been back here in years. I drove by my old house this afternoon."

"It's a lot different now out on Brewster Road."

"A little. Not really."

"Must have been strange, seeing it again."

"It was. But it was good. I'm glad I did."

"So is that why you came? To look at the old hometown?"

"Sort of." I clenched my hands together in my lap. I didn't want to be making small talk. "But I'm mostly here for another reason."

Mark gave me an odd look. "You wanted to talk to me."

"Yes."

His smile returned. "Well, I have to say that that is one incredible coincidence."

"What do you mean?"

He put his elbows on the table, folded his hands together, and stared at me for another few moments. Then he said, "I've been looking for you for the last six months."

At first I didn't take it in. It seemed impossible that he had said what I thought I'd heard. "I'm sorry—you've been *what*?"

"Looking for you. But I kept coming to dead ends. Your parents apparently moved out of town years ago. I had great hopes for that thing on the Internet that searches phone listings. I had my secretary working on it for half a day. But you weren't listed, and neither were your mom and dad. I got your father's first name out of an old West Dunster phone book, and actually called quite a few James Tynans, but they weren't the right ones. And I called some W. Tynans. Do you know how many W. Tynans there are in this country? And I tried calling a couple of the people we'd gone to school with, to see if anyone was still in touch with you. Nobody was. If you'd been trying to disappear, you couldn't have done a better job." He smiled. "Maybe you were."

"No, I—I don't know, I've been married for a long time, and the phone was in my husband's name."

He raised his eyebrows. "I wouldn't have expected that. I figured by now you'd be a pretty well-known artist. In fact, I tried some artist's listing service I dug up, but you weren't there either. Are you still painting?"

"A little—not really, I mean, not seriously, but—" The waitress brought our drinks, and I clutched mine gratefully, took a sip. I hadn't drunk whiskey since I had last seen Uncle Austin, and the taste immediately brought back a confused collage of images: the long driveway, Patrick's bare, sweaty back as he hurled rusty metal into the truck, Uncle Austin's angry grip on my arm. For a moment, I lost my bearings. What was I doing here? Why was I talking to this smiling man? I set down my glass and took a breath to clear my head. I was suddenly filled with dread, with the old gnawing guilt. Why would Mark be searching for me unless it was about Molly McCormick? And yet he wasn't acting like someone about to accuse me of a crime.

"Mark—"

"Wait. Let me just finish." He wouldn't stop smiling, but it wasn't my imagination: There was a glimmer of tears in his eyes. "All I can say is it seems like a miracle that you're sitting here across the table from me. I called my wife and told her and she couldn't believe it. It's—I don't know what. The answer to a prayer."

"I have no idea what you're talking about."

He laughed. "How could you? I don't know how to— Wait." He dug into his pocket and brought out his wallet, flipped it open to a photograph, set it before me. "There."

It was a formal shot, probably a yearbook picture, of a dark-haired young woman. I felt a stab of envy: He did have children, then. All those years I had been living with Alec, hoping and being rebuffed, Mark had been raising his family.

I studied the photograph. "She's lovely, Mark. I assume she's yours."

"Wynn."

His voice sounded so strange I had to look up at him. Yes, it was more than a glimmer; his eyes were wet, and as I watched, one tear spilled over and ran down his cheek. He wiped it away with his knuckle, a funny little-boy gesture that made me smile. "What?"

"Can't you see it?"

"See what?"

"In the picture. Wynn! I'm trying to tell you—"

I looked again. An attractive girl with short curly hair, Mark's wide gaze and direct smile. Dark sweater, string of pearls. I looked into her eyes: Was this girl supposed to tell me something? She looked sweet. She looked intelligent. She looked like Mark. "Okay." I shrugged. "Let's start again. This is obviously one of your kids."

"The only one I've got," he said. He reached across the table and put his hand over mine. "Wynn. This is what I'm trying to tell you. It's our daughter. Yours. Mine."

I stared at him. Madness. Tears stung my own eyes. "That's not possible."

He leaned back in his chair and laughed. "It's not only possible, it's God's own truth! That's why I've been looking for you. Her name is Kathleen. She wants to meet you."

• • •

After high school, Mark had become a kind of hippie. He hadn't had much interest in going to college, he said, but he had stayed in school—barely—to keep out of the army. He had done a lot of drugs, bummed around the country, hitchhiked across Europe, gone to India one summer with a girlfriend. His family hadn't approved of him, but they supported him, grudgingly, until he came home the summer after he graduated and had a major argument with his father.

"It started with the usual fight over my hair," Mark said. "I had a ponytail. And a beard. You wouldn't believe how that bothered my parents. Or maybe you would. God, those were crazy days. Anyway, this time we got off the subject of my hair, and things became more serious. The Erling Paper Mills had branched out into real estate development. You've probably seen what happened to Burbank Mountain. And that's not even the worst of it. You should drive out east of town, toward Hampton and Merrickville. That area has been changed beyond recognition. Acres of forest cut down and shoddy condominiums in their place." Mark waved a hand. "I know it's an old story. My father wasn't the only fat-cat developer who took the opportunity to make a few quick bucks at the expense of the landscape. It's happened all over this country. But this was the seventies, and I was an idealistic young pothead. And a prig to boot. I told Dad I didn't like what he was doing, and it was for damn sure I wasn't going into the business. We had terrible arguments about it, and the upshot was that they cut off my allowance, my father went into partnership with my brother, Jeff, and the whole family washed their hands of me. I didn't have any contact with them for years."

But something about the experience, Mark said, helped him focus. He resolved to do something with his life, if only to prove to himself that he could survive without his parents. He was living in California, where he'd gone to college, and he got a job with a conservation group in San Francisco. Eventually, he got interested in computers and began designing the company's software. It was the beginning of the computer revolution, he was in the right place at the right time, and he began to do well.

And then, he told me, he became obsessed. "I started thinking about that little girl," he said. "The baby you and I had together. I don't know what it was, Wynn. Getting some maturity, or having too many failed relationships, or being estranged from my family. But whatever—I knew I had to find that child." He paused, frowning. "Even before the big blowup, my mom and dad weren't the world's best parents. They were always generous with money, but I can't say there was much affection in our house. I was one of those kids who was always bringing home puppies and kittens. Not that I was allowed to keep them. But I was always looking for someone to love, something to take care of. And I was always looking for affection. I became good at it as I got older—at getting women. Keeping them was the problem. The smart ones always realized what an immature jerk I was. You were one of them. I still remember how you turned me down for the Junior Prom." He smiled faintly. "Do you remember when I called you? You gave me the name of the hospital, the name of the place that handled the adoption. You told me what the baby looked like, how much she weighed, who the obstetrician was."

"Yes," I whispered. "I remember."

"There are agencies that find children who have been given up for adoption," he said. "I hired one. It was amazing—took them less than a month. Her name was Kathleen Bryant, and she lived in Cleveland with her mother. Her father had died when she was two, in a car accident. Her mother, Annie, was a nurse. They gave me the address, the phone number, the college where Annie went for her nursing degree, the names of Kathleen's grandparents in Georgia. I swear, if I'd wanted their shoe sizes I could have had them." He paused, sipped his drink. His smile returned. "So I went to Ohio and looked them up. I got to know them. And, to make a long story short, Annie and I celebrated our twentieth wedding anniversary last summer."

I stared at him. For a moment I didn't understand. "And you—you raised this child—Kathleen—"

He nodded. "My daughter. She's been the joy of my life, Wynn."

Around us, the Ramada cocktail lounge was busy, the low murmur of voices became louder, but I was aware only of Mark's words—of what appeared to be, if I could believe it, the slow fading of a nightmare. *Kathleen,* I thought. Not poor Molly McCormick. *Kathleen Bryant. Kathleen Erling.* Who had not died. Who had lived. Who was alive.

Mark went on, "It was a funny thing with me and Annie. It wasn't just Kathleen that brought us together. I mean, at first it was—God, the kid was everything. I can't tell you what that was like, Wynn. Meeting my own child. I'll never forget it. She was almost seven. She had on this little plaid dress, and she had these big green eyes, and she looked like me, she looked like you, she—" He had to stop and wipe his eyes, but he was smiling. "Anyway. I met them. And I really admired Annie and what she'd achieved, raising this great kid as a single mother, a widow, going back to college to get her nursing degree. Eventually, we found out we had a lot in common—her family was even more screwed up than mine, it turned out. Southern Baptists from Georgia who disapproved of her marriage to a Northerner, disapproved when they adopted a child, disapproved of her having a career. They didn't like the way she was raising Kathleen, and they *for sure* didn't like me. I still had that long hair." He grinned. "They've gotten used to me over the years, though. I won't say we're best friends, but they've softened up some." Then a thought occurred to him. He frowned at me across the table. "Wynn," he said. "Did you ever have any other kids?"

"No. My husband didn't want children."

"You're divorced?"

"We're in the middle of a divorce," I said. "Partly because of that. We were married for thirteen years." My words were unreal; it seemed weeks since I had left Alec's house.

"Oh God, I'm sorry."

"It's for the best, believe me." I took another drink of whiskey. I didn't want to talk about it. I wanted him to continue. "Please. Go on."

"I considered getting in touch with you a couple of times. I thought maybe you ought to know about all this. But I had no idea where you were." He shrugged. "I suppose I could have found you, but it didn't seem urgent. I figured you had your own life. Maybe you didn't want the past horning in. And Kathleen seemed contented enough. So we just let it be."

And where was I? Poring over pictures of the wrong child. Shopping for carpets and wine with Alec. Putting clippings in a wooden box. Staring at other people's children on the street.

I put my head in my hands. It was like a daydream I might have had as a young woman—a fantasy I might have indulged in as I lay awake in London listening to roar of the lions in the zoo. Those years when I mourned and hated myself and narrowed down my life—all that time, this other world had existed, in which my daughter's happy childhood had rolled on: the doted-on daughter of loving parents. A childhood not unlike my own, probably. I remembered the dreams I had had when I was with Patrick, of having my daughter with us, of the three of us together—a family. A childhood like that.

I had to ask: "Are you—are they—this agency—are they sure this was the right child?"

"We actually have a copy of the birth certificate, with your name on it."

I felt faint: The world, turned on its head, made me dizzy. Mark reached over and put my glass into my hand. The ice cubes rattled. I swallowed whiskey, thinking of Molly McCormick's sad smile. The bitter arguments with Alec. The baby in the hospital asleep in my arms.

"Now it's Kathleen who wants to find you," Mark said. "She's twenty-six—she'll be twenty-seven next month." He caught himself. "But hell, I don't have to tell you that. Annie always told her she was adopted, of course, and when I came into the picture I told her the whole story, how young you and I were, how confused." I stared at him. Was it so simple? Was it just that I had been young and confused? "I told her a little bit about you, and she seemed satisfied with that. She wasn't particularly curious—never said much about it. Then last year, she got engaged. Nick Hayes. A great guy—we like him a lot. They're getting married in the fall." Mark started to speak, paused, studied my face for a moment. Then he said, with a tentative smile, "I think she'd like to have you for a wedding present, Wynn. If you're agreeable. She says she needs to know where she came from. Who she is. That's the way she puts it. I've done a lot of reading about adopted kids. It's been great for Kathleen to be raised by her natural father, of course, but they never get over wanting their mothers. To see where they came from. Literally. The woman who carried them for nine months and then gave birth to them. And so Annie and I figured we'd better try and find you."

Tears spilled over and ran down my cheeks. I finished my drink, and the waitress came over to our table. "Another round?" she asked impassively, as if weeping women were a dime a dozen at the Ramada cocktail lounge.

Mark ordered me another whiskey. "I was actually on the verge of hiring a detective," he said. He paused again and then, slowly, he began to laugh. I stared at him: a large, garrulous man with a big belly and a mustache. "And then I hear your voice on the phone! God. It's incredible."

"Incredible." I wiped my eyes. "That is exactly what it is. I can't—I'm not—"

He looked at me suddenly with concern. "I probably didn't handle this very well. On the way over here, I tried to think of the best way to tell it, but there didn't seem to be one."

The waitress brought our drinks. I knew I should say something else, but I couldn't, and I heard myself give a long, shuddering sigh that made people turn and look at us.

"Wynn?"

"I'm okay." I blew my nose and took a deep breath, then another. "I'm getting used to it." I kept wanting to cry—it was a distinct physical need, like hiccups or a coughing fit. I had to concentrate to keep the tears from coming. I stared at Mark's shirt, the green checks and white buttons. My life, I kept thinking. My whole life.

Mark continued his story. He was a talker—I remembered that—and I was glad of it. I needed time to gather my wits. He told me about reconciling with his mother and his brother—belatedly, at his father's funeral—and about coming back to West Dunster to live. He'd missed the forests, he said, and the snow. He started a small software business that had prospered from the first. His mother and Jeff had sold the paper mill, and when his brother moved to New Hampshire and his mother to West Palm Beach, Mark and his family had taken over the Castle.

"It's crazy," he said cheerfully. "Now that Kathleen's grown up, the two of us just rattle around in there. I suppose one of these days we'll sell it. But we love the old place, and I can't imagine who'd want to buy a white elephant like that. Maybe Kathleen and Nick will want it someday, who knows? It was a good place to raise a kid. Great for birthday parties. We used to have an Easter egg hunt every year for the kids from her school, and we threw a fabulous party out in the garden when she graduated from college."

I tried to imagine, but all I could remember was how cold the living room was on a hot summer day, and how his parents' indifference had frozen me even more.

We were quiet a moment. I felt Mark's gaze on me, and I looked up to meet his eyes. He said, "So Wynn—maybe you should tell me why you came here to track me down."

"Oh God," I said. "Where to begin."

"You don't have to—"

"No—I do. That's why I'm here. I have to tell this to someone." I drank some more whiskey. For a mad moment I couldn't remember what I had come to say. The old story was buried under this new, staggering tale. I had brought with me the photographs of Molly McCormick with the idea that I might show them to Mark, and I considered getting them out, letting them explain. But now those clippings I had wept and cursed myself for seemed unimportant: absurd.

"Take your time," Mark said.

I collected my thoughts. "There was this other child. It was years ago—1975. Summer. You may not even remember. A child was murdered by her adoptive father. Abused for years, then killed. It was on TV, in all the papers. Her name was Molly McCormick. She lived in the Midwest. She was exactly the age our daughter would have been. And there were pictures of her in the paper, in all the news magazines. She resembled me." As I talked, the story became real again. How could it stop being true? In the space of a whiskey on the rocks? I had to stop and steady myself before I went on. "That little girl," I said, "I thought she was our daughter. For all these years I've lived with this. That I gave her up—to that. To those people. I came here to talk to you about it. I never told anyone else about it, and finally I knew I had to, or go crazy."

"Are you saying that all this time you thought you were responsible for that kid's death?"

"Yes." My voice broke.

"And you never talked about it with anyone? My God, Wynn, what a mess. I wish we'd gotten in touch with you years ago."

I thought of the barren years with Alec. What would have happened if the Erlings had come into our lives? If Mark had sent me a letter at the loft on Lafayette Street telling me he had adopted our daughter?

I couldn't even think about it. And yet I knew I would think about it, constantly, compulsively.

Mark said, "You know what it sounds like to me, Wynn? If you can forgive the amateur psychology. And the presumptuousness. I mean, it's just my opinion. But it sounds like you felt so bad about giving the baby up in the first place that you tortured yourself with this other thing. I mean—you didn't check it out or anything. You just went off the deep end."

What he said startled me: It made such perfect sense. He reached across the table and gripped my hand, hard. "It's okay, Wynn. It's going to be okay now."

I stared at him. Mark Erling. For a fleeting instant, I remembered lying with him on the sand at Osmar Lake. That, and now this. Eighteen years had been kicked out from under me. I closed my eyes and let the tears run down my face.

Mark continued to hold my hand; he gave it a little shake. "Hey. Wynn. You all right?"

I opened my eyes. "I'm all right. I just feel—" I made a futile gesture.

"All of a sudden you're somebody's mother. It must be like giving birth all over again." He squeezed my hand. "Kind of different, though, this time. Isn't it?"

"Very."

We looked at each other for a moment, and then he said, "Is this okay with you? I mean—hell, I don't even know if this interests you, this reunion. If you even *want* to be in touch with Kathleen. I didn't even ask, I just assumed—"

"I do," I said quickly. "Please. Believe me, I want this more than anything, Mark. More than anything else I've ever wanted." I didn't even have to reflect: I knew that was true, it had always been true. I managed to smile at him. "But I think that what I need is to go sit down for a while someplace quiet and take this all in."

"I understand." Mark signaled the waitress and paid the check, and we stood up. "You know, Wynn," he said, shrugging into his jacket. "All these years you thought you did something wrong. But you didn't. All you did was what any sensible kid would have done. You gave up your baby for adoption. And that was the right thing to do. She was adopted by a couple of great people, the Bryants. She's had a wonderful mother, a good life. You don't need to reproach yourself for a damned thing."

Suddenly Mark put his arms around me and folded me in a bear hug. "You're part of our family now," he said when he let me go. He got out his handkerchief and blew his nose, beaming at me. "You've got to come up to the house, meet Annie. I'll call Kathleen as soon as I get home. She's living down in Portland, but maybe—what's today? Friday? Maybe she and Nick could drive up tomorrow and we could all get together for dinner."

This was unimaginable. "Yes," I said. "Yes, fine."

"And take this," Mark said. He put Kathleen's picture in my hand. "To make it real. So you won't think you dreamed the whole thing."

I stared at the photograph again. "Mark? There's no doubt about this?"

"Are you kidding? Look at her! Look at that chin, and that hair."

My curly-haired daughter. Mark's eyes. My mother's arched eyebrows and narrow nose. Absolution in a school photograph.

"Wynn." I raised my head. Mark's smile was full of affection. "She's our daughter, honey. Believe it." He leaned down and kissed me on the cheek.

• • •

The next afternoon I drove up to the Castle in the middle of a snowstorm.

I had slept heavily, and, when I woke, it was late. I went to the motel coffee shop and forced myself to eat breakfast—still feeling shaky, as if I were recovering from an illness. I kept in front of me the photograph of Kathleen—this girl who was my child. I couldn't stop looking at her face. Kathleen—not Molly, but Kathleen. I tried to get used to it, a name I never would have chosen. I recalled how I had held her in the hospital, kissed her warm pink cheek and whispered: *Remember me, remember me,* while she slept in my arms. How I had felt my self slipping away, leaving behind some other self. And now, after this other birth—Mark's little joke had been exactly on target—now, who was I? I studied her face as if she could tell me, but all I saw was a pretty young girl in pearls. The idea of meeting her in person terrified me.

As I sat over my pancakes, it began to snow—big, fluttering, wet flakes. "Doesn't look like much now, but they say we're in for it," the waitress said. "Another five or six inches at least." She grinned as she poured me more coffee. "All we need—right?"

Driving, I realized how horribly nervous I was—not about driving in the snow but about what was ahead. She could hate me. What if she burst immediately into recriminations? Or what if I looked at her and felt nothing? At the very least, the encounter might be awkward, unpleasant in ways I couldn't even imagine. I had dressed as well as I was able to in what I'd brought with me—boring black sweater, gray slacks, the unavoidable knee-high boots. My hair was forced into a precarious bun, I had no jewelry but the big silver hoops in my ears. I felt inadequate, not pretty enough for a long-lost mother; I imagined my daughter's disappointment.

I also hated going empty-handed, and wished I had something to take with me, a gift for Kathleen or something for Annie—a few family photographs, even, so I could give my daughter a piece of her history. *She wants you for a wedding present,* Mark had said. It didn't seem nearly enough.

I was glad there was the snow to think about, and the slippery driving conditions. Visibility wasn't very good; I had to drive slowly. But the winding mountain road lined with pine forests was as starkly beautiful as ever. The familiarity was a comfort. I felt a surge of well-being, and, as I got closer to Mark's place, of pure anticipation.

The Castle wasn't as ugly as I remembered it; the harsh gray stone looked blue against the whiteness, and the two absurd turrets, capped with snow, were romantic. The long driveway had been cleared but was rapidly filling up again. I parked by the garage, then made my way to the house through fresh snow up to my ankles.

The door was opened by a small, brisk woman with graying brown hair, brown eyes, and an unexpected Southern accent: Annie. I was surprised that she seemed older than Mark, but then I realized that of course she must be, she had been adopting a child while we were teenagers in high school.

She stared at me a moment—I suppose I stared back—and then she began, quickly, to talk and make me welcome, fussing over my wet coat, my cold feet. We exclaimed about the weather, both of us talking too fast. "Wouldn't you know?" she said. "We haven't had snow in weeks, and today of all days it has to do this." Then, impulsively, she hugged me and said, "Well, I sure never expected to be having dinner with my daughter's mother. Isn't it the craziest thing?"

The house was warm; a fire burned in the vast fireplace. The place hadn't changed much in the twenty-eight years since I'd been there. In the huge, long living room, I recognized the sofa I had sat on in such misery, the table where the pitcher of iced tea had sweated untouched. I looked for the painting of Mark and Jeff over the fireplace; it had been replaced with a seascape. I stood before the fire and stared stupidly at sailboats on blue water until Mark said, "Wynn? This is Kathleen." And there, coming toward me across the room, was the young woman who was my daughter.

My first thought was that she didn't look like me. In person, she managed to look a lot like my mother without resembling me much at all, except for her hair. She was as tall as I, but much more slender than I ever was. She had Mark's green eyes and high cheekbones, my mother's fine features, very pale skin that was all her own. But I knew immediately that she was my flesh and blood.

We stared at each other, and then we embraced. For a while it was all a blur, a crazy, wonderful movie that whipped by me—too much to absorb. I was introduced to Nick, who looked something like

Mark—tall and sandy haired. Annie hovered, smiling anxiously. The Erlings' fat calico cat rubbed against our legs. Mark brought in a pot of coffee, and finally we all took a mug of it and sat down in chairs around the fire. Annie passed a tray of cookies. We wiped our eyes. There was an awkward silence. Then Mark said, "Well, here we are—one big happy family." It wasn't particularly funny, but it made us laugh, and then it was suddenly almost ordinary—just an unorthodox family reunion.

I sat beside my daughter. The others drank their coffee and drifted away—Nick to shovel snow, Annie to the kitchen, Mark to make some phone calls—and Kathleen and I talked.

"I used to wonder about you." She had a soft voice, a hint of a Maine twang like Mark's, and she sat with her hands folded demurely in her lap. "I used to wonder who you had become. What you were doing. Sometimes I wished so much that I could just call you up on the phone. I wanted to know what you looked like, and how you were like me, and how you were different. I used to daydream about finding out where you were, and following you, spying on you. I never understood those feelings, because I loved my parents. I didn't ask about you, and I tried not to think about you because it seemed disloyal to Mom. But I couldn't help it sometimes."

She dropped her gaze to her hands. On the left one was a modest engagement ring. She wore a light blue sweater, pale stockings, delicate shoes. Her hair was cut short, the way my mother used to wear hers. I stared at her: This was that baby, this sweet, fragile girl. My heart overflowed.

"Didn't you ever just plain—hate me?" I had to get it over with; it was a question I needed to ask. I hadn't given her up to die, but I'd given her up nonetheless—deliberately, blindly, thrown away the opportunity to be this girl's mother. "For not keeping you?"

"You were sixteen years old," she said, with a little smile. "When I was sixteen myself, I thought about you. When I was the age you were when you had me. I tried to figure out what I would do if that happened to me. I mean, if I were pregnant and not married."

"And—?"

She shrugged. "What else could you have done?" she said. "Especially in those days."

I thought of all those depressed girls with their swollen bellies. Suzanne and her twins. "It was so hard to know. It wasn't what I wanted. I let myself think it was for the best."

She touched my hand. "Don't feel guilty. You made the only smart decision." She paused, then said, "But yeah, I did hate you sometimes. It wasn't logical, but sometimes I wanted to talk to you just so I could tell you how much I hated what you had done. One Halloween I had this terrific witch costume—big pointy hat, black cloak, and a fantastic scraggly wig made out of yarn—and I looked at myself in the mirror and saw this scary old crone and, all of a sudden, I really felt like a witch, and I cast a spell on you."

"What kind of a spell?"

"Do you really want to know?"

I tried to laugh. "Sort of."

She took a deep breath. "I hoped you would die," she said. "I hoped you would boil in oil. I hoped toads would eat you. I stood looking at myself, saying a lot of mumbo-jumbo imagining those things and terrifying myself." She grinned suddenly. "God, I was an awful brat."

"You sound just like me."

Her eyes were lit with tenderness. I could see that she was memorizing my face as I was hers, trying to find herself there. Then, hesitantly, she said, "Wynn?" We looked at each other, a little startled. "Should I call you Wynn?" she asked. "Or what?"

"Wynn will do fine."

"Wynn." She smiled and went on. "Did you ever wonder about me? Where I was, or—" She spread her hands helplessly. "Did you ever think about me at all?"

"Oh, Kathleen," and my voice wavered. "I don't know how to say this. I don't know how to tell this story. I thought I did, but I don't." I looked at the fire, the cat asleep before it, the seascape over the mantel, the plate of cookies. It all seemed blessed and beautiful, lit with radiance. The years that had passed since I last sat here no longer seemed real. Nothing made sense but this warm living room, this house and the people in it, this newfound daughter who called me by my name.

Kathleen's gentle voice said, "What? Tell me."

"I can't. It's all so—" I had to stop, start again. With this miraculous girl beside me, my long sad story was absurd. "I'll tell you someday, but I can't now."

"There's a lot to tell?"

I smiled at her. "Yes. There's a lot to tell. But take my word for it—I thought about you. It's just that now—here—seeing you like this—it all seems irrelevant."

"I don't want to press you," she said. "Tell me when you're ready."

"I will." I looked at her through a film of tears, and then I said, "You know, Kathleen—you look so much like my mother it almost breaks my heart."

"It makes me happy to know that—that I look like my mother's mother."

Kathleen smiled, too, and now for the first time I saw a bit of myself in her face—briefly, the way a headlight from a passing car illuminates an object in a dark room. I thought: *I am not alone.* I couldn't help remembering my mother's letter, the way it broke off. *I only wish. . .* That unfinished sentence had haunted me for years. Had she ever wished for something like this, I wondered—for the story to end not in anguish and loss but in this shocking quiet wonder. In this bright young face that was, somehow, my mother's face, too. I thought of another sentence in that letter, the one that had infuriated me: *I hope someday you'll forgive me, maybe when you have a daughter of your own.* And here she was. And what I felt for her overpowered me—even now, when I had just met her, before I knew her. It gave me an inkling of what my mother meant: that a loved child can make a parent irrational, crazy—that love not only doesn't guarantee wisdom, sometimes it can subvert it completely.

Impulsively, Kathleen put out her hand and touched my hair. "We have the same hair," she said, and began to laugh. "Oh my God, Wynn. You're my mother. You're really my mother."

• • •

Why did I return? This is why I returned, Kathleen. To have my life restored to me. To roll back the years and be given this gift: the chance to start over. You returned from the dead, Kathleen. And, God knows, so did I.

• • •

The snow continued to fall, the fire burned in the grate, and we spent the afternoon together, my daughter and I. She wanted to know about my childhood, my life, my paintings. She was especially curious about her grandparents; all she knew was that my father made toys, and they had lived in the little house on Brewster Road. Telling her about my mother and my father, about Anna Rosa, about my childhood there in West Dunster, was an unexpected pleasure: Who else could I ever say these things to? The years disappeared, and with them the anger I'd been hoarding. My childhood returned, redeemed somehow: It hadn't been a childhood that led up to an act of careless irresponsibility with horrifying consequences. This girl, this lovely Kathleen, was part of those years. She was what they had produced. What could I do with my old resentments? They had no place in this new world.

Kathleen had Mark's easy gregariousness; she liked to talk. She told me about Nick, who wrote press releases for an environmental group in Portland, and about her work—she had a degree in journalism, and covered local politics for the Portland newspaper, a job she loved. Just looking at her, studying her face while she talked, filled me with joy. I kept discovering new things, like a certain expression in her eyes, halfway between a smile and a frown, that reminded me of my father. I watched her smooth her skirt over her knees, straighten her ring so that the diamond winked in the light. I wondered if she had also inherited my mother's passion for order. And I wondered what she ate for breakfast, what books she read, what made her laugh. I thought: Someday I will know all this. Someday I'll take it all for granted. I'll buy her Christmas presents, I'll think: *Kathleen will like this, Kathleen loves this color.*

After a while, she dug out photograph albums full of pictures of herself growing up, and her life unrolled like the coming attractions of a movie I would never see: Kathleen on Annie's lap, being carried piggyback by Mark, blowing out birthday candles. Kathleen on roller skates, on her bike, mugging with her girlfriends, posing with someone's dog. There was a picture of her in the evil witch costume. And with Reggie the cat when he was a kitten. Kathleen dressed as a flapper for a school play, then awkwardly regal in deep blue at some dance with a boy named Eric. Kathleen in Georgia visiting her Aunt Merle and in Palm Beach with Mark's elderly, still beautiful mother: Gramby, she called her. Kathleen's college graduation, the party out in the garden. Kathleen a bridesmaid in some cousin's wedding. Kathleen and Nick in hiking clothes. And here were the two of them again on Thanksgiving with Annie and Mark at Mark's brother Jeff's house in New Hampshire, there were Jeff and his wife, Sally, and their daughter Tess, and their son, Damon, and Damon's girlfriend Maureen, and Nick's brother Kyle, and Boomer the dog. . . .

The photographs bowled me over: a record of the large, complicated world my daughter had inhabited during the years I was mourning her. I examined that world as avidly as I used to pore over the clippings about Molly McCormick. Kathleen explained the photos to me, patiently reeling off names and dates and circumstances, and I listened to the tale of each cousin, each skinned knee, each dog and cat and hamster as if the information would save my life. You're part of our family, Mark had said. These words touched me more than perhaps anything. I had had no family for so long. There had just been Alec. My parents had been dead for years, and so had his. His sister lived in Michigan; we never saw her. We hadn't even had a pet, because of the rugs. And here I was with people who had been looking for me, who wanted me to be a part of their lives. I tried to imagine my own face in these photographs, the extra mother at the Thanksgiving feast, at the wedding to come. Part of the family. Whatever that would mean.

Nick came in for a minute, scattering snow, his cheeks bright red, then disappeared again to watch a football game. Mark entered from time to time with a weather bulletin: The roads were bad, the plows couldn't keep up with it. And how were we doing? Did we need anything? Annie brought fresh coffee and little sandwiches, patting my shoulder in passing, stooping to kiss Kathleen lightly on the forehead. I was puzzled by Annie and the warm casualness with which she seemed to accept my presence. I tried to imagine how she must feel, and could only conclude that she was nothing like me. I doubted I would consider the intrusion of my daughter's mother such an uncomplicated pleasure. But then I was certainly no role model for motherhood.

The five of us had a late dinner in the dining room: beef stew, a salad, the table set with exquisite china and crystal that looked like it dated back to Mark's parents' time, and another fire roaring in another huge fireplace. Mark sat at the head of the table, Annie on his right, me on his left—his two consorts, I thought, though I was the only one who seemed to find the situation strange. The Erlings' calm acceptance of what had happened continued to astonish me, but it seemed genuine. When Mark opened champagne, poured it, and raised his glass to say, "Welcome, Wynn, from all of us—from the heart," everyone clinked glasses, and I burst into tears. Kathleen passed me a tissue, and Nick made a joke about the excessive number of mothers-in-law he was facing. Annie laughed and said we'd have to figure out a way to share the work of interfering, she was glad it wouldn't be a full-time job.

There was more joking, and we put away a lot of champagne. It was not very good champagne: I imagined Alec taking a few sips, then, with exquisite politeness, declining any more. But I drank it willingly enough, and happily got slightly drunk. The conversation at dinner was about football, a Portland politician's mishandling of campaign funds, a fluffy sweater of Nick's that had become a family joke. After my third glass of champagne, I began to feel I had died and been reborn as a member of the Erling clan, and I entered into a long conversation with Mark and Annie about local zoning and development.

By the time we had finished coffee and dessert—apple crisp, an old family recipe from Gramby's cook—it was obvious that I would have to stay the night, the weather was much too foul to consider driving back to my motel.

They put me in a tidy guest bedroom with its own bath, a big four-poster bed, a down comforter. It was the kind of house that always contained spare toothbrushes, and Annie lent me a flannel nightgown. I didn't expect to sleep, but once I got into bed exhaustion took me over. For years I had done my best to keep my feelings at bay. Now I barely had time to get used to one jolt before another one came along. I had just enough energy left to be amused at myself, and then I fell deeply asleep to the sound of the snow and the wind.

I awoke early, in the middle of a confused dream that took place on the steps of my London row house and involved Alec and the diamond bracelet I found in his drawer. My watch said 5:15. I listened to the absolute stillness. The storm was over. The house was very warm. I didn't want to return to my dreams, and I lay there for a long time, wide awake, replaying the events of the day before, until in the gap between the curtains I could see the beginning of a cold dawn.

Then I got up, pulled my sweater over my nightgown, and went downstairs to the living room. A pale morning light illuminated it, and seeing that room again I realized it was a completely different place than it had been in Mark's parents' day. The proportions were the same, and some of the furniture, but Mark and Annie had added comfort and life, an indefinable aura of contentment. I was thankful that Kathleen had grown up here, that life had been so good to her.

I had a sudden need to see her face. The photograph albums were where we had left them, and I opened one at random. There she was, sitting demurely on a wicker porch chair. Her hair was in braids, her smile was uncertain.

I heard a noise behind me: Annie. She wore a plaid bathrobe and furry red slippers. "That was taken shortly before Mark and I were married," she said. "That was one confused child. All of a sudden her father comes out of the woodwork. Happy, but definitely confused." She smiled. "Have you been awake long?"

"A couple of hours. Couldn't sleep."

"Me either. I'm going to make coffee. Want a cup?"

We went into the kitchen, and I took a seat at the table. Out the window, the tentative morning brightness showed a terrace banked with snow, and beyond it a long stretch of garden with snow-covered trellises and a half-buried gazebo. Far in the distance, over the valley that was West Dunster, Burbank Mountain loomed black in the cold light. Neither of us spoke while Annie ground beans and made coffee. I watched her: a naturally small, wiry woman who was thickening through the middle as she aged. It was easy to see her as a nurse, a reassuring presence, cheerful no matter how devastating the diagnosis.

She set a mug in front of me—yellow with a smiley face on it—and sat down across the table with a sigh. "So."

"The sleepless mothers." The coffee was bitter and scalding, but I was still slightly fuzzy from the champagne, and it tasted wonderful. I looked around me, feeling dazed and happy, taking in the kitchen's homely details as if I were a visitor in some exotic country: baskets on a shelf, a pile of cookbooks, a bowl on the floor that said CAT. "It's nice here," I said, inadequately.

"You're doing incredibly well," Annie said. "For a woman who's just had her life turned upside down."

"Or right-side up." I took another sip. "I haven't thanked you yet, Annie, so I want to do it now."

"Thanked me? What on earth for?"

"For letting me into your life like this."

"Oh, that. Nonsense. This has been wonderful for us."

The window became suddenly lighter, and we both looked out. The low sun had reached around the garage and lit the terrace. Below us, the mist was clearing from the rooftops of West Dunster. The snow sparkled where the light reached it, and the sky beyond Burbank Mountain was blue streaked with rose. It would be a beautiful day. Then Annie said, "Well, maybe I should revise that. I do want to be honest."

My stomach turned over. I had no idea what to expect. "Please," I said, and it was probably hard to tell from my tone if the word meant polite acquiescence or was a plea for mercy. I had a sudden urge to go back to bed and start over.

But Annie was absorbed in what she was trying to explain. She said, "The real, actual truth is that when Kathleen first said she wanted to find her birth mother, I was very upset. Frankly, I was scared to death."

"I thought that was my department." I tried to speak lightly. *Just let me not cry any more,* I prayed to someone. "What were you afraid of?"

She glanced up in surprise. "Of losing her, of course. An adoptive mother always feels kind of insecure. She's never the real thing. I was terrified."

"I guess I can imagine that." It was true. If there was one thing I could imagine, it was losing a child.

"I don't know if I can explain what it meant to me, when Bill and I adopted Kathleen," Annie said. She stirred her coffee slowly, frowning, weighing her words. "When I was growing up in Georgia a million years ago, I always imagined I would have a daughter of my own someday. I don't know why that was—I mean, why a daughter instead of a son, and why just one. Lord knows, I came from a family of six." She laughed. "Well, maybe that explains why I craved a peaceful kind of household with just one pretty little girl in it. Then of course I found out I wasn't going to be having any children at all, not even that one. I have a congenital abnormality in my uterus. I knew from the time I was a teenager that I was barren. That was hard, I'll tell you. That was real hard." Annie stared out the window a moment, nodding her head. "But then we were able to adopt Kathleen. That sweet curly-haired baby. Exactly the daughter I had wished for."

It was oddly unnerving to realize that all that had gone on without me—another country existing next to my own. I had driven home from Boston with my mother. My stitches had healed, the hair grew in where I had been shaved, my figure gradually returned to normal, I went back to school, and all that time, somewhere in Ohio, this person had fed bottles to my baby, sung to her, taught her to say Mama and Dada. I think in that moment, sitting there across the table from Annie Erling, in the midst of my gratitude that it was this kind, cheerful, pleasant woman who had been Kathleen's mother, I felt more cheated, more bereft, than I ever had before.

Annie continued. "Then she decided she wanted you—that other mother. At first I felt like she had run over me with a truck. I really fought the idea. But Mark and I talked about it." She grinned suddenly. "Someone who only knew him in high school might not believe it, but my husband is a very sensible guy. Very smart. And the more we talked about it, the better I felt about the whole thing. It began to seem *wrong* not to know you, and I knew it would always bother Kathleen. I decided it was better to face it—to bring you into our family if we could. After all, if it weren't for you, I wouldn't have had Kathleen in the first place. And I decided that if you took her away from me—a lot or a little—well, I'd just have to live with it."

I tried to think of whom she reminded me, and I realized it was Mark: Mark as a teenager on the phone, begging me for information, saying how he regretted he hadn't seen the baby, letting himself—a seventeen-year-old boy, a jock, a heartbreaker—weep openly, without shame. How did anyone get to be so honest, so unafraid?

Annie was surveying me fondly, as if I were an old college chum. "You look overwhelmed, Wynn. Not that I blame you."

"You terrify me," I managed to say.

She paused with her coffee mug halfway to her lips. "Me?"

"How can you just do this? How can you be so nice about it? I don't know how to react."

She let out a bark of laughter. "I'm not *that* nice. I had plenty of evil moments, believe me. But in the end I only wanted my daughter to be happy. I was just like you, Wynn. That's why you gave her up to be adopted, because you figured she'd be happier."

"I hope that's true, Annie," I said. "I hope I wasn't just being selfish."

She stared at me. "Wynn, you were a *child*!" She reached over and squeezed my arm. "Honey, you've been blaming yourself and thinking you should have kept that baby and raised her and—well, you've got to get over it. You did absolutely the best thing for her, and everybody knows it. And I'll tell you something else. I think it's fate, Wynn, I think it's *meant to be* that you turned up right here in West Dunster, looking for Mark. He told me the story, by the way—about that poor child who was murdered. God, what an awful thing." Then she smiled again, awkwardly. "You know, as long as we're being honest, I have to say what a relief it is that you're—well, *you*. Because the other thing I thought was: This woman is going to be some kind of force in my daughter's life. What if I don't like her? I mean, aside from the fact that she's—what? Six years younger than I am. Probably disgustingly glamorous. And she was involved with my husband all those years ago."

Moonlight on the lake, sand in my clothes. "I wouldn't call it *involved*, Annie—"

She waved her hand. "Whatever. It was a zillion years ago. But what really bothered me was what if she was someone who would—I don't know—hound us for money. Or someone who would try to turn our daughter against us. Or just someone I'd rather Kathleen didn't know. Someone—you know—*unsuitable*, as my mother-in-law would probably say." She paused and sipped coffee. "You find out a lot about yourself in times of crisis. Those weren't pretty thoughts, and I'm not proud of them."

Annie's candor gave me courage to say what I felt should be said. "I'm not very good at talking about things sometimes. Difficult things." I thought again of my mother's letter, her reluctance to say aloud the things that were in it. "But I'm trying to get over that," I said.

"Well, I hope we can talk freely to each other, Wynn. I mean, I've told you what a snob and a coward I've been." Annie bent down to pet Reggie, who had wandered into the kitchen. "And I know that if I were in your place I'd feel very odd."

"When I see those old photographs," I said, and then I stopped, not quite knowing how to go on.

"You feel like shit," Annie said bluntly. She lifted Reggie to her lap, where he sat and stared at me. "How could you not be jealous of us—right? Our happy little nuclear family. You'd have to be a saint."

I felt my face flush. "Looking at the pictures, seeing what I've missed—I have to envy you all those years. She's had this vast family, all these experiences. And she's had you. I'll never be anyone's mother—not even Kathleen's, really. You're her mother. You're the one she calls Mom. No matter how close she and I might become, I'll always be Wynn."

Annie shook her head. "I think it's much more complicated than that. There really isn't any word for what you are to her. You gave birth to her, after all. And she does feel that you're her mother, in a way that's hard to explain. She told me that last night, before she went up to bed. She feels a real bond, a real connection. She says it was there from the minute she first saw you. It wasn't like meeting a stranger, she said. It was as if, somehow, she had always known you."

"Yes, I felt that, too," I whispered. I was pierced with happiness at her words, but behind the pleasure remained the thin, bitchy little thread of envy. They had talked about me. In the end, my presence was something that brought them even closer, this ideal mother and loving daughter.

Annie said, "So I guess I have to say I'm a bit jealous of you, too,

Wynn. For just walking in on this. Getting it all for nothing. Being the answer to my daughter's goddamned prayers."

We looked at each other for a long moment. Then, slowly, we began to smile, and all the bad feeling went out of me. "Look at us, Annie," I said. "Two nice respectable ladies having coffee at the kitchen table and hating and resenting each other like crazy."

Annie's laughter broke out. "We need a how-to book or a support group or something. I'll tell you what." She held out her hand across the table. "I'll forgive you if you'll forgive me."

We shook hands, smiling into each other's eyes. Then, embarrassed, we both looked down at Reggie, who had jumped to the floor and was washing his whiskers at our feet. Annie chuckled. "It's all so weird," she said. "Isn't it? Who would believe this crazy story? The whole bizarre thing is a kind of ventilator, really."

I thought I had misunderstood her Southern accent. "Did you say *ventilator*?"

"Yeah. Kathleen used to say that. She was such a funny kid. When she was six or seven, she fell in love with certain words. *Ventilator. Optimist* and *pessimist. Massacre.* She used to call really good dinners *massacres*, and she used to alternate between being an optimist and a pessimist. Thought it was hilarious. And whenever anything unexpected and wonderful and sort of—I don't know—*far-out* happened, she'd call it a *ventilator*. Like when Reggie was the only calico in a litter of coal-black kittens. That was definitely a ventilator. Kids are strange little critters. Anyway, I think that's what we have to call this." Annie looked at me. Her eyes were bright. "This great adventure we're having, Wynn. This amazing thing that's happened to us all."

• • •

It was an Erling ritual to eat a huge meal on Sunday morning, and so we gathered around the kitchen table for omelettes and sausages and fruit and toast and a coffee cake Annie had made the day before. Then Kathleen and Nick had to get back to Portland.

"I'll call you," Kathleen said to me at the door. We clung to each other. "And I'll write. And Nick and I will come to Boston to see you. Or maybe you could come up to Portland."

We made plans, wrote down addresses and phone numbers. "This has been the most amazing weekend of my life," Kathleen said. She looked into my eyes. "Thank you for finding us. Thank you for *having* me, Wynn."

I had to search my pockets for a tissue. "One of these days I'm going to stop crying, I really am." We embraced again, and Nick hugged me, too, and then they got into their little blue car and pulled away down the driveway, waving. Watching my daughter's bright face framed in the car window, I had a thought that staggered me. For most of my life, I had been wishing that none of it had happened: Deirdre's stupid party, the half hour on the beach with Mark, the bleak months at the Edna Quinlan Home.

Now I felt only gratitude. Now I could wish none of it undone.

• • •

That would have been enough to last me forever, the meeting with my daughter and her family when I knew myself to be not only blessed but also absolved.

But there was more.

I drove back to Boston on a day glittering with sun and checked into a hotel near Harvard Square. Over the next few days, I called the movers and arranged to have my things delivered, I went to the new apartment, took measurements, made a list, and went shopping for small necessities.

These simple tasks soothed me, and I sorely needed soothing. Huge chunks of my life had been chipped away, and the events of the last week had rushed in to fill the empty spaces. The business of divorce, the visit to West Dunster, the shock first of Mark, then of Kathleen. I felt like someone who had been left in a prison to starve, and who, suddenly released, eats too much, too fast. Or like an unaccustomed drunk who needed to walk it off, to spend some energy in a quiet way in order to restore myself to the person I had been. Or some version of the person I had been.

I called Marietta and told her what had happened, and she said, "This is the best thing I've ever heard in my entire life. My God, what a movie plot! Promise I can have the rights." Then she laughed her cackling laugh and said, "Hey—didn't I tell you that you should leave Alec and become a mother? And that's exactly what you did!"

When I called Hannah she wept. "Oh Wynn, it's like those wonderful scenes in Shakespeare where the child abandoned on the mountaintop is alive after all, rescued by shepherds or something!"

"This one was rescued by a software entrepreneur," I said, laughing.

"But why didn't you ever tell us about this before?" she asked me. And I had no answer.

I dug out some old family photos and mailed them to Kathleen—my parents in front of the house on Brewster Road, in Florida on their boat, the picture of Anna Rosa in the thirties in a fox-collared coat, one of my grandfather behind the counter of the store, ancient pictures of my mother's parents who died before I was born. Kathleen sent me some of her bylined pieces for the Portland paper—lively accounts of the dedication of a homeless shelter, a case of election fraud, a councilman accused of bribery. I talked on the phone to Annie, who kept me posted on plans for the wedding, coming up in August. Yes, she said, I must definitely take part. These days, anything was possible, the world was full of weird family situations, and who cared, anyway?

I moved into my new apartment on a sunny Saturday, a characterless modern place on Commonwealth Avenue. It was only two blocks, oddly, from Haskell Graphics, the firm that had made greeting cards from my mother's photographs for so many years. The apartment was not ideal, but I had been in a hurry. At least it had good light, and a room I could use as a studio. I hadn't completed a painting in over a decade but, perhaps irrationally, I knew I had to have a studio, and not only for teaching in. The first thing I did was to set up the painting table I had used since I was in school. I hung my old smock on a hook. I found the easel and got out my brushes, the box of paints, my ancient turpentine jar. Then I tacked to the wall some sketches I had made in the Rickerts' garden, of Jay weeding the bean patch and Hannah, in one of her long dresses, sitting in an old metal chair with a cat on her lap.

I stared at the sketches for a long time, seeing their possibilities, feeling a rush of excitement. My painting had changed when I lost my daughter, changed again during my years in New York, and then the ability to paint had deserted me entirely. What would it be like now to pick up a brush and apply paint to canvas? What would be the effect of this miraculous reprieve? I looked forward to finding out—to digging down and discovering what was there, to struggling up from the bottom again and teaching myself as I taught my students. Patiently, with kindness. But I wasn't quite ready. For the moment, it was enough to anticipate it.

On a shelf in my studio, I lined up some of my father's old toys, and I ran my hand over the smooth maple, thinking that some day I would give them to Kathleen and Nick for their children. The trucks and buses, the cars with their little red wheels. And my old high-sided bed. The crazy quilt. A pine doll's cradle stenciled with a pattern of birds, my green bookcase. I had assumed those things would die with me. Now I had a daughter. Not dead but living. It was one of the times when I was numb with joy, and I sat there with the old wooden toys as an animal might sit, a cat or a cow, content in the sunshine.

I also did something I hadn't done in years: I unpacked some of my mother's photographs and hung them on a wall. I'd lost my hostility toward her. It had evaporated the way a bad dream does when you wake up, and looking at her photographs—those spare and rigorous shots of black fences against white snow, the stillness of sunlight on a garden bench, a hawk soaring above a bank of clouds—my grief over my mother's death returned to me untainted by anger.

I began to think about her often, realizing how imperfect my knowledge of her was. She wasn't a woman who had let herself be known. *Life is complex enough,* she had written in her letter, and I wondered why she had felt that, where it came from in her own childhood, and why she'd felt compelled to devote so much time trying to reduce life to something simple and controllable. That was her peculiar mission. It was clear from her photographs, our perfectly run house and manicured garden, even her short, crisp hairdo. *An artist can't work in chaos,* was of course her chief maxim. And I remembered her coming into the room where I painted and quoting Yeats in mock horror, "Mere anarchy is loosed upon the world!"—and I knew it was time for me to wash the paint off my hands and pick up the books and papers that littered the floor. *Order from disorder* was how she described housework: I'd heard her say that more than once, down on her knees scrubbing the kitchen floor or ironing tablecloths on a broiling August day, her face shiny with sweat. And saying it cheerfully. It made her happy to rein in all the tag ends of her life. It satisfied her.

Thinking of all this, I saw how difficult I must have been for my mother. She loved me above anything, and I was always a mess—never more so than when I begged for that baby.

I wished she were still alive so I could take her by the shoulders, shake her, look her into her eyes and tell her to lighten up, chill out. And hug her. And quote to her Patrick's manifesto from Tolstoy, that the artist's task is not to solve problems, but to show us how to love life in all its disorderly mystery. And we could talk about it, openly and honestly. We could learn from each other.

All this only intensified my grief that she was gone. I had become a mother, and it had made me, I felt, a better, more understanding daughter. Too late, of course. And yet this affectionate, impatient regret, all I had left, was better than the bitterness that had gripped me for so long, and I cherished it.

I had a vague, sudden memory of a photograph of hers. It had been a big hit with Haskell, I recalled, part of a series of animal photos that had sold spectacularly well, but it was one that I'd never paid much attention to, never framed and hung on the wall. Now, though, it was something I had to have. I spent part of an afternoon searching through storage boxes, and finally dug it out. She had printed a date on the back: 3/20/1969. A few weeks before Kathleen's birth. The photograph was taken the spring I was pregnant, while I was at Edna Quinlan. I had to smile. Maybe life was neater than I'd thought.

It was an extraordinary image, taken on a bright spring day, of a doe and a very young fawn in a clearing in the woods. I imagined my mother sitting, perfectly still, on the little portable stool she carried, waiting. The deer come into view, unaware, upwind from her. They stop, and the sunlight falls on them between the budding trees. They're only twenty-five or thirty feet away. The doe's flanks ripple with muscle, the fur on the fawn's back is still rough, puppyish. The fawn stays close to the doe's side, always touching her. My mother hesitates until the moment is right, and then she releases the shutter. The deer disappear instantly, bounding out of sight at the tiny sound, but the image remains: the fawn raising its head to its mother, the doe bending down to nuzzle it, the two of them oblivious to everything except what they are, a mother and her child.

• • •

Looking back at that spring when I found Kathleen, it seems to me that every day was sunny. That can't have been true, but still I think it was a particularly mild season. The snow that was banked along the roads melted swiftly, the daffodils in the parks bloomed ahead of schedule. Tulips appeared on the front lawn of my apartment building, and I knew that across the river at Alec's the deep purple ones I had planted would be in flower. But I was without regret; I felt completely detached from that life.

What struck me when I went out for my daily walk was how different the city had become. For years I had walked in Boston and in Cambridge—as a clumsy pregnant girl navigating the icy streets, as an art student consumed with love and ambition, as a melancholy wife doing her perpetual errands. Now everything was subtly changed. The pewter-colored river, the trolley tracks, the clutter of shops and cafés, the broad avenue I lived on, the trees in new green leaf—I saw all this as I never had before, through the eyes of a single, middle-aged woman with a grown daughter. I felt both older and strangely youthful. One of the things I took pleasure in was buying presents for Kathleen—small, silly things: a book of cat cartoons, a bunch of paper roses, a straw hat the same green as her eyes. Some of these things I would probably never give her, but buying them made her more real to me, and saying to a bored clerk, "It's for my daughter," made me want to laugh with the strange, unaccustomed satisfaction of it.

For her birthday, Kathleen and Nick drove down to Boston, and I cooked dinner for them—my father's fried chicken, my grandmother's potato salad, my mother's lemon pie. In May, they went hiking in the White Mountains; they sent me a postcard: "Mud!" it said, and was signed, "Love." I learned that Kathleen had sung alto in her college chorus; that her handwriting was a daintier version of my mother's clear script; that she got sick on shellfish, loathed pumpkin pie, adored Indian food; that she longed to travel to Greece, liked the ballet, was afraid of water and bad at math.

Those spring days seemed to me the beginning of a truly good life—one that was vivid and rich and delicious, that bore hardly any resemblance to my time with Alec—the life I had denied myself for most of my adult years. Since I left Patrick, I had never lived anywhere that wasn't lonely in some way: Now it really did appear that the loneliness was over, the gaping black hole was filled. There were mornings when I woke in my new apartment and had trouble placing the feeling that came over me. I would lie there puzzled while the spring light washed over me from the window, and then I would sit up with a start and burst out laughing: It's happiness at last, you ninny. *Happiness.*

And then, one aimless evening in May, flipping channels, I paused at a PBS program I sometimes watched when I couldn't sleep—*Midnight with Jack Skelly*—and saw the tail-end of an interview with Patrick Foss.

*Patrick.* I heard his voice before I looked and confirmed who it was. I would have known his voice anywhere, the elongated vowels, the quick deep laugh, the Irish lilt at the end of a sentence. . . .

I left my chair and dropped to my knees in front of the set. *Patrick.* I was almost afraid of what I might see. He was older, of course. And he was a bit stouter: Like Mark, he had gone from raw leanness to a comfortable substantiality. I had known him as a boy; he had become a grown-up, with lines around his eyes, gray in his hair, new gauntness in his cheeks. He didn't look like the suave man in the tux, but he didn't look like my old rough Patrick, either.

"To me, oddly enough, it's an event that's already over," he said.

"How do you mean, exactly?" the interviewer asked him, peering over his spectacles. They were sitting in two armchairs, and Jack Skelly was sprawled comfortably, ankle resting on knee, holding (absurdly) a pen which he jabbed into the air when he wanted to make a point. By contrast, Patrick, hunched on the edge of his chair, looked tense and ill-at-ease—a look I remembered well. It was the way he looked when he wanted to be somewhere else, when he was bored. He never seemed arrogant or patronizing or impatient in those situations, just unhappy, like a puppy at the vet. Watching him, I knew he had agreed to the interview under duress, and that he wanted only for it to be over.

"After all," Skelly went on with a little laugh. "The exhibit hasn't even opened yet."

"No—yes—but what I mean is—" Patrick's speech was halting. He spread his hands: *his hands,* with their long fingers, the big, flat nails, the bony wrists. "For me, that work is over. You know, it's inevitable with sculpture like mine, objects that take so long to construct. That the work being—being shown doesn't really interest me any more. Not—uh—not really." He paused, staring down at his hands as if in apology, or deep embarrassment. "Some of it was done so long ago—years—years ago. The only thing that interests me is what I'm working on now."

"Which is—?"

I could see him close down, as if a door was suddenly shut. He had never liked to talk about a work in progress—he considered it a jinx. "A new—" He cleared his throat. "A new piece," he said reluctantly.

Skelly jabbed his pen into the air. "More copper and steel?"

Patrick sighed. "Yes," he said, and I had the feeling he wasn't telling the truth, that he had in fact branched out into some entirely new material, he was working in plastic, or knitting wool, or old phone books cast in bronze, but he'd be damned if he'd tell Jack Skelly what he wouldn't even tell his friends.

"Well, we're all glad to know you're still working—still producing after a career of—what?—almost twenty years as one of the art world's leading lights."

Patrick winced, and Skelly beamed at him, waiting for a response but getting only a weak smile. He went on blandly. "So—I want to wish you the best of luck, Patrick. My wife and I plan to be at the opening, and—" His smile broadened. "I know you certainly will be, to receive the good wishes of your many friends and admirers. Thanks for being with us." Skelly turned to the camera. "We've been talking here with Patrick Foss, about the new exhibit of his work at the well-known Taggart Gallery in New York City, opening—" He ducked his head, raised his eyebrows, and gave a sly smile, as if he were about to impart a profoundly arcane piece of information. "Tomorrow."

In the few moments before the program's logo and theme music came on, the camera cut back to Patrick's face. He was looking in the direction of Jack Skelly, who was apparently engaging in the obligatory post-interview chatter, but for a moment, a brief second, Patrick looked straight at the camera and into my eyes. In that tiny interval I saw him—really saw him. *Patrick.* His face bore the unmistakable marks of some deep-rooted suffering, and in that moment it was as if everything was written there: his solitude, his dogged pursuit, his impeccable integrity, the simple struggle to keep going. My heart reached out to him, and I was filled with shame: It seemed as if I had betrayed him all over again with my sunny new existence, the carefree happiness that had entered my life. For these few months, I had almost forgotten him.

Then his face was gone, the program changed, and I realized I was kneeling before the television as if it were an altar, my hands twisted together so tightly I was in pain.

I felt like some medieval saint who has seen a vision. How *real* he was on the tiny television screen, how vulnerable and weary and alone he had seemed. And, to me, how beautiful—how noble—how beloved. But I knew I was no saint. Watching him, looking at his hands, his mouth, the broad set of his shoulders—so well-known to me, so well loved—I had wanted to take him in my arms, to knot my fingers into his hair and pull him down to me, to kiss him long and sweetly.

Oh God, it had been so long, so many years, so much had happened to both of us. In spite of my box of clippings, Santo's photo, Uncle Austin's angry revelations—all my obsessive long-distance stalking of him over eighteen years—I was aware that I knew nothing about Patrick. Nothing real. I had never dared to go to New York to see his work. When Alec had to be there, I always made some excuse to stay in Cambridge. Now, wrapped up in Kathleen, I hadn't even known about this show of his new work. What bizarre workings of fortune had compelled me to turn on the television at that moment? And what had I missed? Before I tuned in, had Skelly gotten him to talk about his wife, his children?

It was a Thursday evening, past midnight. I turned off the set and got ready for bed. But sleep wouldn't come. When I closed my eyes, I saw only Patrick. When I opened them, his face stayed with me: his dear, gaunt face, his lined cheeks, his burning eyes, the black hair hanging over his wide brow. God—*his ears!* How well I remembered his ears, small and neatly shaped, with soft lobes. And the way his eyelashes had fluttered against my cheek when I lay in his arms. The hollows where his collarbones were. His smooth, freckled back. His long toes. The blue veins knotted on the soft undersides of his forearms.

I got out of bed and found the box of clippings: There he was, all I had of him. And yet the tangible reality of him had left me at some point in that long expanse of years. He had been an idea—an *ideal.* Or—on the nights when I lay beside Alec, sleepless, hot with the terrible need of what I had lost—Patrick had been a feverish dream. Now his reality had been restored to me: He was a person, a man, a living soul who spoke words, who squirmed in his chair, who furrowed his brow and wrung his hands together with anxiety. He looked so much like the Patrick I knew, and yet of course he was someone else entirely. And he belonged to someone else: I hadn't forgotten that. This Patrick Foss was a stranger to me, I told myself.

But some stubborn voice insisted that that was nonsense, and that was the voice I listened to.

I was able to sleep only when, around three in the morning, I allowed into my mind the thought that had been buzzing like a bee on its fringes, the thought I had flapped away but that wouldn't leave, that was inevitable, that could not be denied: I would take the train to New York and go to Patrick's opening.

I said it aloud, impatiently, as if someone had been arguing with me: "Yes, all right! I'll go." Then I was able to turn out the light and lie quietly, letting the air coming in the window cool my skin and quiet my brain. Yes, I would see him—see him with his wife, no doubt. But it didn't matter. I would see him, I would ask his forgiveness, and a door would close that needed to close. Let it go: So many other doors had opened. He would be the last stop on my pilgrimage. I would see him, and then I would get on with my new life.

# *Question Five*

# Who Are You Now?

The train traveled through the sunny afternoon—Providence, New London, New Haven, Stamford. I did my best not to think too much—not to rehearse what I might say to him or predict what he might say to me. But I couldn't keep my mind on my newspaper or on the towns and warehouses and distant glimpses of water that rushed by outside my window. I had slept badly the night before, but now, when I closed my eyes to try to nap, all I saw was Patrick.

I had dressed with care in a simple black dress, low heels, hoops in my ears. At the last moment I clasped around my neck the beads Patrick had bought me in Mexico—the choker of small blue turquoises threaded at intervals on a silver wire. I wondered if he would remember it. I wouldn't blame him if he ripped it off my neck and trampled on it.

Somewhere around Greenwich, I began to calm down. I decided that what would happen when we met almost didn't matter. The important thing was that I see him. It would be like visiting my old house in West Dunster: Travel to the valley of lost things, see what was there, let it go. I knew I could do that. I had done without it for so long, it wouldn't be hard. And I had a new life, I had Kathleen. I would be seeing her in Portland for Nick's birthday party in a few weeks. I consoled myself with this. No matter what, I had my daughter. Still, when I closed my eyes and saw Patrick's face, I longed for him.

The train pulled into Penn Station at 5:07 sharp. I made my way through the crowds and out to the street, where I found a taxi. I sank into the backseat and concentrated on looking at New York. I hadn't been there in so long: the beautiful, grungy, frantic, jeweled city, more magical than ever in the late afternoon sun.

The taxi went west and sped down Ninth Avenue, then cut over again to take Seventh into SoHo. I paid the driver and got out. It was a beautiful afternoon, and walking would be quicker than driving the few congested blocks to the Taggart.

I hadn't been in SoHo since I fled to London. It glittered. The streets I remembered as quiet, even desolate, were lined with shops and thronged with people. And yet so much was the same. The cobblestones were still there, and the massive old iron buildings, and the blue sky at the end of West Broadway framing the looming towers of the World Trade Center. I recognized a gallery we used to go to, a bar I knew. The deli where we used to buy the newspaper was still on the corner, and Patrick had once kissed me as we crossed the street, just there.

My knees threatened to buckle. I had to duck into a doorway and lean against the wall of a building. *Patrick.* I would see him in a few minutes, and I was fooling myself if I thought it wasn't important. The reunion with Kathleen had been a very different thing: she had wanted me to find her. I was well aware that I might be the last person Patrick wanted to see on this occasion. That his only memories of me were hateful ones. He had loved me, and I had walked out on him leaving a few words scrawled on an envelope.

It was that, of course, that haunted me. That I had made him suffer. That I had worried him, stunned him, possibly humiliated him. I had suffered, too. But what had Patrick been punished for? For the first time—really, it sounds amazing, it sounds almost unbelievable, but for the first time—it struck me that I'd been wrong to do what I did. Not only impulsive, or immature, or racked by a misplaced grief, but deeply, indefensibly, selfishly wrong. *Things matter, actions have consequences.* Marietta had known that. Why hadn't I?

I stood in the doorway of a store that sold Hawaiian shirts, shaken by a moral dilemma almost two decades old. I had punished myself by leaving Patrick, the source of all my happiness. But was my punishment worth his pain—pain he had done nothing to deserve? And hadn't leaving Patrick in that way been even less forgivable than giving up my child? I wasn't sixteen when I walked out on him; I was a grown woman.

I had been crazy to come to New York. You can't go home again. You can start over, but you can't go back. What's done is done. And hadn't I already been through enough to last several lifetimes? I didn't need to do this. I had my daughter, my life in Boston, my redemption. Why put myself through it?

I stood there for many minutes, with my forehead pressed to the cool stone of the entry. The crowds bustled by, going in and out of the funky shops, the cafés and galleries, the arty little bars where happy hour was commencing. No one noticed me in the vast, pungent stew that makes up the city, where only something truly extraordinary arouses anyone's interest. A man wearing a sequined dress and high heels, his long muscular legs in bright green tights, turned heads, and so did a crewcut blonde walking a brace of poodles. A middle-aged woman undergoing some kind of invisible trauma in the doorway of a shop scarcely rated a glance. Thank heaven.

Gradually I became calmer, but it was the calmness of desolation, of despair. Yes, I would continue on to the Taggart. I had come all this way, and I had to see him. It would be the opposite of the reunion with Kathleen. That had been all joy. This would be—what? My mind couldn't encompass what it would be. But it would be different.

I took out my sunglasses and put them on; maybe he wouldn't notice me, or even recognize me. I didn't know if I could go so far as to speak to him. Maybe that was asking too much of myself. But I wanted to see his work. And—I realized this with a greedy anticipation—I had to be in the same room with him; I had to be near him.

I walked down West Broadway to Prince and then the two blocks to Greene Street. The Taggart had been one of SoHo's first major galleries—a clean, soaring space for large sculptures. Henry Taggart had been considering Patrick's work when I left New York, and shortly after that I had started seeing reviews of his shows there in the art journals. I was glad Patrick had been faithful to him.

On the large plate-glass windows, PATRICK FOSS: METAL ON METAL was spelled out in graceful black type. Inside, the place was jammed. A buzz of conversation wafted out from the open door, punctuated by the occasional loud laugh. Because of the way the walls and partitions were arranged, I couldn't see the sculpture, and I didn't see Patrick. I spotted a couple of people I remembered. Henry Taggart's wife, Suzanne, glamorously elegant, with an austere face-lift. Jim Blair, gray-haired and stooped, who had showed several people I knew at his uptown gallery. Althea Allen, a neighbor of ours on Lafayette Street, all pipe-stem arms and legs, still girlish in a miniskirt. I wondered if Santo would be there, or any of our other old friends. The room was full of beautiful women; which of them was Patrick's wife?

I made myself go through the doorway. The noise immediately increased. A young, black-clad man with complicated nose and eyebrow piercings poured me a glass of champagne. I sipped thankfully and took a stuffed mushroom from a tray, then some smoked salmon. I began to feel better. It was just an art opening, after all, and no one paid me the slightest attention. Patrick was nowhere to be seen. I began to think that he might not appear, that the shy, uneasy man I had seen on television didn't *do* things like this—and maybe that would be best of all. I would see his work—where I knew the real, true Patrick always resided—but I would not have to face him and his anger, or his scorn, or his indifference. I took a second glass of champagne from a passing tray, ate some more salmon, and looked at the sculpture.

There were perhaps a dozen pieces. Metal on metal. Massive bars of cold rolled steel had been bent, twisted, wrenched into tortured shapes, then welded to sheets of beaten and burnished copper. Most of the works were huge, heavy, earthbound, but somehow delicate too, with spaces where the light could filter through. Even in my dark glasses, I could see that they were also very sensual, with surfaces I longed to touch.

I paused in front of a piece called *Copper on Steel III* and studied it. If I could afford to buy one of these works, this would be it. The steel was sinuous and alive against the copper, which was cut into rough shapes that shimmered with the marks of a hundred hammer blows. The metal was hard, unyielding, inorganic stuff, but the piece managed to evoke natural forms: giant leaves, fungi, some mysterious, fugitive animal. Every minute decision that had gone into it showed me Patrick's hand and his unerring eye. I could imagine him in his goggles, see the sparks from his torch. I could hear the familiar clang of his hammer. I remembered the quote from Tolstoy tacked to the wall back in our Boston days: *An artist's mission must not be to produce a solution to a problem, but to compel us to love life in all its countless and inexhaustible manifestations.*

I suddenly wanted this piece of sculpture more than anything in the world. I had an absurd image of movers trying to maneuver it up the stairs and through the door of my apartment. I began calculating in my head whether I could possibly afford to buy it before I realized with a shock that it wasn't the sculpture I wanted; it was Patrick. Surrounded by his work, I knew I was crazy to think I would ever get over him. I never would stop wanting him, regretting everything, wishing for the impossible.

I had to get out of there. I finished my champagne, and turned away from *Copper on Steel III*, and that was when I saw him.

He had been in the back office, the room where deals are made, and he emerged with Henry Taggart and an elderly couple. Henry clapped him on the back and said something that made them all laugh.

My heart stopped and then, rapidly, started up again, raced, knocked hard against my chest. I could hear my pulse in my ears, and I thought I might faint. He was wearing a dark green linen shirt and a gray silk tie. He looked handsome and confident—not awkward and mumbling as he had on television. It was obvious that his new work was being well received, that he had already sold several pieces. I wondered where his wife was. Maybe they'd divorced. But then there would be a girlfriend—wouldn't there? Of course there was a girlfriend, a lover, maybe many lovers. One of the chic and beautiful women in the room was his, surely. . . .

I could only think about getting out of there unseen, and yet I couldn't move. I looked at Patrick, how pleased he seemed, how happy. If he saw me, his face would change: I would see there all the revulsion and resentment that had been simmering for eighteen years. Eighteen years and eleven months. Eighteen years and eleven months and two days. I closed my eyes, opened them again. He was staring at me.

I stared back. There was nothing else I could do: It was Patrick. A long moment passed. I don't know what happened to Henry Taggart or to the wealthy art patrons or to the waiter who had been about to pass with a tray of caviar on toast. I saw only Patrick. And after who knows how many seconds had passed, I reached up, as if in a dream, and removed my sunglasses.

Immediately, incredibly, he smiled. His face lit up. He made his way to my side. He stood near me. He said, "Wynn. It's you."

I touched his arm, the linen sleeve of his shirt. My sunglasses fell to the floor. We embraced. It's hard to describe this moment. Even now, my eyes blur with tears, remembering it. His arms tight around me, the slight roughness of his cheek against my forehead, the scent of his skin—the years were eclipsed. It was as if I had last seen him that morning.

He held me; that was all. I said into his shoulder, "Forgive me." He didn't answer, he only said my name again, and I realized that he was in tears. I knew people were watching us. This, for sure, was something one noticed: a prominent artist at the opening of a new show, in a prolonged and weepy embrace with some nameless woman.

We pulled away, finally, and looked at each other. "You came back," he said.

"Yes. I came back."

There was an awful pause. "Better late than never," he said, and now I heard bitterness in his voice.

I didn't know what to reply. I was desperately conscious of the crowd around us, the need to keep things bland, normal. This was Patrick's big day: He didn't need me to mess it up. He just stood looking at me, his face unfathomable, and I finally said something about seeing him on television.

"Oh God, that awful interview," he said, recovering. "I'm told I came across like an ape."

"I had to see your show."

"What do you think?"

"Your welding has come a long way."

That made him laugh. "Is that all?"

"You know it's wonderful," I said. "It's been a joy just to walk around and look at your work." I felt tears threaten again. "I've missed it."

"Jesus, Wynn, it's so crazy to see you. You're the last person I expected to walk in that door."

Looking into his eyes—that amazing, familiar golden brown, as golden as ever—I gathered my courage. "Patrick," I said. "I came here to see you, too. To explain. I want to tell you everything."

"All right. My God, yes," he said. "I want to hear it. I want to hear it all." He laughed. "It's been—what? So many years. And it seems like a year, or months. You look wonderful." He touched my neck. "Those beads—"

Henry Taggart came up to us. "Is that Wynn Tynan?" he said. "Good to see you! It's been a long time."

I shook his hand, and then Suzanne came over and hugged me, and—oh, I don't know—other people. They came up to us and said things, shook my hand, shook Patrick's hand. Patrick kept his arm around me; he was obviously distracted, preoccupied. Finally he said, "Look, Henry, Wynn and I have to get out of here, we have to talk," and Henry exploded, he said, "Are you out of your mind? The Lambertis just came in, and the Van Arsdales! They want to see you, Patrick. Please. Whatever it is, put it on hold for a while. Here's Elaine now. Come on over here with me. And hug her, for Christ's sake."

Patrick looked at me. We smiled at each other. He fished a handkerchief out of his pocket and gently dabbed at my eyes. He blew his nose with a loud *honk*. Then he took me around the room with him, and hugged Elaine Van Arsdale and shook hands with her husband, Gaylord. He introduced me, but I remembered them: They were the Brookline doctors who had started buying his work when we were still in art school. He walked them around the room and talked to them about the sculptures. Then he did the same thing with the Lambertis, a young, chic, wealthy, and jet-lagged couple who had flown in from Rome and who spoke little English but who loved his work, were enchanted by *Copper on Steel III*, and arranged to buy it on the spot. I took a look at the price list: The sum was staggering.

Patrick did his duty. He worked the room, introducing me as his old friend Wynn Tynan, the painter. People looked blank, said *Oh yes*, smiled politely. The Van Arsdales said the name sounded familiar. The Lambertis couldn't care less who I was. They wanted Patrick. They wanted to talk to him, look into his face, stroke his sleeve. "We want this one for the *giardino*, Patrick. For the rose garden. Against the stone wall." Patrick said that sounded *molto bene*, the work was designed to be displayed—*come se dice* "outside"? *Fuori?*—and the Lambertis nodded and laughed and hugged him again. The Van Arsdales had already claimed another copper-and-steel piece. And an English actor I recognized who collected Patrick's work wanted another, one of the huge ones. The Guggenheim had bought something, and a committee from the Spoleto Festival was in town to talk about a commission. Henry rubbed his hands together gleefully and made jokes and kept slapping Patrick on the back. I couldn't wait to get Patrick to myself, but, incredibly, I was having a great deal of fun. Everyone was. It was a circus, and Patrick was the ringmaster, and the air was thick with money and champagne and affection and success and, best of all, a real appreciation for Patrick's art. The Lambertis stood in front of their acquisition talking rapidly to each other in Italian, unable to stop smiling. The Van Arsdales were serious and awestruck. And finally, after another hour or so, Patrick and I were released.

Henry embraced us both. "It's wonderful, wonderful," he said, his voice choked, as if he knew all about us. But of course it was the opening he was talking about. Eight of the dozen sculptures had already sold. The money involved fascinated me. I couldn't help calculating Henry's commission; even considering his lifestyle, it was a tidy sum. And the show would be there for a month. It was a given that everything would find a buyer.

Patrick and I went to a crowded bar around the corner on Prince Street. As we walked, I could feel his ebullience fading; he didn't speak, and seemed tired. He gave the headwaiter a twenty to let us have a quiet booth near the back. We sat opposite each other, just looking. He glanced at the wine list and ordered champagne. Then neither of us was able to say a word. The waiter flourished the label, popped the cork, poured, stuck the bottle into a bucket of ice and disappeared.

Finally, Patrick spoke. "It wrecked me, Wynn, when you left," he said. "I have to be honest. I hated you."

He hated me. I sat immobile, looking down into the beige bubbles in my glass, thinking of Kathleen in her witch costume, looking in the mirror and wishing me dead. "Of course," I managed to whisper. Then I didn't trust my voice.

"I'd gotten out of the habit of unhappiness, thanks to you," he said. "I didn't deal with it well. I hated you for a long time." He paused. "And then I stopped." I looked up at him. He shook his head. "Don't say anything yet. Let me tell you. I've wanted to tell you this for years."

He said that after I left he virtually stopped working. He began sleeping ten, twelve hours a night, and when he woke up he drank. He became reclusive, bad tempered, a trial to his friends. He nearly lost his welding job because he showed up half-drunk one day and didn't show up at all the next. One night when he was drinking he went through the loft searching out everything that suggested I had ever lived there—a book I'd left behind, a few sketches, a barrette he found in the bathroom, a pair of tights, an old T-shirt—and burned them all in the bathtub. It was a miracle he didn't set the whole place on fire, he said. Another time he picked up a woman in a bar who looked something like me, brought her back to his place, and instead of making love to her, he got blind drunk and hit her; she hit him back before she walked out—slapped him, hard, across the face, cutting his lip with her ring—and he ended up sobbing and retching and bleeding into the toilet. He started doing a little cocaine, then a lot, and he thought about heroin.

As he talked, he became increasingly agitated, and I could see how painful it was for him to recall those horrors. I said, "Patrick, I—" and he slammed his palm down suddenly on the table, spilling champagne. "Let me *finish*, God damn it!" The people in the next booth turned to look at us. Patrick leaned back against the booth, his eyes squeezed shut, rubbing his forehead with his hand. I sat there frozen, thinking of Uncle Austin. After a moment, he said, "I'm sorry."

"So am I," I whispered.

He paused again, then took a sip of champagne and went on. He said he'd begun walking over the Williamsburg Bridge to Brooklyn at night when the bars closed; he'd wander the dark streets by the river, then walk back. He knew the bridge was dangerous, and he didn't care: *Let them kill me,* he thought, but no one ever bothered him. Sometimes he would stare down into the black water, wondering why he didn't just leap into it, telling himself that next time he would. Or he would buy a gun and blow his head off.

"I was amazed at how badly I coped. I wasn't the type." His smile was grim, inward. "You know me. Single-minded workaholic seething with ambition. I didn't know I had that other guy in me, that crazed depresso unhinged by grief."

He didn't speak for a moment. He glanced over at the bar where a small, jolly crowd let out a cheer at something happening on TV, and I scrutinized his face: the new furrows in his cheeks, the wrinkles fanning out around his eyes, the threads of gray in his black hair. Yes, he had been marked by the years and what they'd done to him. He turned back to me, and his luminous eyes were suddenly tired, as if what he'd been forced to remember had worn him out. "Or maybe I did," he said. "Maybe that was the guy I was always afraid of. Do you remember how I used to talk about not trusting happiness? Maybe it's because I suspected what I was capable of and I didn't want to find out."

I tried to imagine Patrick snorting cocaine, drinking himself nearly to death, thinking about blowing his brains out. It was difficult. In his way, he had been as focused and controlled as my mother; as far as I could recall, he had never even smoked a joint. At most, he might have a couple of beers. I had always been aware that the abandoned boy Uncle Austin had told me about still lived somewhere inside him. *He had this little bicycle, and he would ride it into the road. . . .* Now I knew just how near the surface that child was.

"How did it end?" I asked him, as I'd asked his uncle.

"Art saved me." He smiled again, faintly. "In the fall, I sold one of my sculptures, and the guy who bought it—our landlord, remember him? Tom Wiest?—he commissioned another one, for the garden of his country place. I couldn't let him down, he'd always been good to me. He had three or four of my smaller things. But now he wanted a big one—a really major piece. And so I began to work again."

He finished the sculpture on time, the first of his pieces inspired by natural forms, he said. Wiest paid him a lot of money for it. And in the late winter, Patrick took off for Mexico, traveling on foot and by bus through the dusty towns in the central plateau where he and I had gone so many years before on our way to Querétaro. *Cortazar, Dolores Hidalgo, San Luis de la Paz, Río Verde*: Hearing his voice pronounce the names of those places, it all came back to me, the lost golden days when we were young—and my last visit to Mexico, where I sat in a courtyard and knew I had to leave Alec.

"It was like a reverse pilgrimage, Wynn. I was trying to exorcise you." He brought almost nothing with him, he said—only a sketch pad and some clothes. He still spoke virtually no Spanish, though by the time he left he had picked up a good deal of it. He quit drinking cold turkey, and he didn't do any drugs. He walked until he was exhausted. He sat in the sun. He was completely alone there for two months, and during that time, he said, he came to terms with my leaving, and with his feelings for me.

He was unable to say exactly how this happened, only that the experience of isolation in Mexico was profound. He had never lived so intensely inside his own head, and it had made him see things he hadn't seen before. He was sure I had been going through a kind of hell that last week before I left, but he had no idea what it was, and he knew I wouldn't tell him until I was ready. He had never suspected that I wouldn't tell him at all.

He said that the words of my note had imprinted themselves on his brain: *I'm leaving you because I have to. Please don't ask me why.* The rhythm of those words became part of his consciousness, he said. It was with him before he fell asleep each night, it entered his dreams, it was there waiting when he woke. And gradually he began to grasp the reality of what I had said. *I'm leaving you because I have to.* He couldn't comprehend the statement, but he could sense the desperation behind it.

"I knew that what I had to do was get you out of my mind," he said. "So I could keep working. There were two things in this world that really mattered to me, Wynn. My sculpture, and you. One was taken from me, so I dedicated myself to the other one. But it took me a while to stop expecting you to come back to me and explain. For a long time I had little fantasies about the doorbell ringing, you being there. And I thought about trying to look you up—I almost called your father one night when I was drinking, I even dialed his number, and then I couldn't do it. I hung up the phone. *Don't track me down,* was what you'd really meant in that note. And so I didn't. I couldn't. You didn't want me. I didn't know why, I didn't know what was going on, but—I wasn't going to beg you." A shadow passed over his face. "I was drunk. When I was sober, I knew it couldn't be as simple as that. But I just didn't know what to do. So in the end I didn't do anything."

We sat in silence for a minute. I took a sip of champagne. I was afraid to speak. Finally, he sighed and went on. "I was married for a while," he said. "Not even two years. It was a whim. I realized one day I was lonely and I was sick of it, and so I married an art dealer, someone I met at an opening. A very nice woman. She deserved better. She's married to someone else now—not an artist. But we parted friends—sort of." He shrugged. "It was a long time ago."

I wanted to tell him that I knew about his marriage, but he said, "Wait. I'm almost done. I want to say one more thing, Wynn, and I'm not sure how to. The odd thing was that even when I finally got it into my head that I would never see you again, even when I got married to Sonia, I knew—well, I don't know what I knew." He frowned. "It's hard to put into words, and if I had told this to anyone they would have said I was a fool, but in some weird kind of way I trusted you. I trusted what had been between us. Somewhere at the back of my mind. Something wouldn't let you go. I think I always knew you would come back and tell me what happened." He looked at me again. A hesitant smile spread across his face, slowly, narrowing his eyes, deepening the lines around his mouth. "And here you are. Jesus, Wynn. Here you are."

It was as if something broke inside me, something that had been held taut all these years. I had always assumed Patrick hated me—that, like Uncle Austin, he would never forgive me. That was, in a way, what I wanted—what I deserved. And yet, of course, I hadn't tried to make him hate me, I could never have written *I don't love you any more* on my note. Instead, I had written the truth. Still, I had never expected him to keep on caring for me, to trust me. It was like the day Mark told me Kathleen was alive: It was exactly like that. History was revised, darkness was made light, the world was turned right-side up again. Something that had been left on a mountaintop to die had come back to life.

"Wynn," he said softly. "Talk to me. Tell me about it." He reached out tentatively, touched my hand. "Please. Tell me why you did that terrible thing to us."

I told him then, about Mark Erling and the Edna Quinlan Home for Girls and Molly McCormick, about my years of shame, about England and St. Clement's. About my box of clippings and the visit to his uncle. About Kathleen. It was a complicated, freakish little story, but it was easier, now, to tell it. After all the years of concealing it, of hugging it to myself like a secret thorn—my private torture, my hair shirt—the story poured out as it had with Mark, in a rush. But sitting in the back booth of that bar on Prince Street explaining it to Patrick, babbling half-incoherently about my long agony and its ending, I think that for the first time I really comprehended what a malfunctioning human being I had been when I was young, and how giving up my child had unhinged me. I had done this not only to myself and Kathleen, but also to Patrick, this good, innocent, vulnerable man. I had inflicted a wound that nearly killed him. How could he forgive me?

I underestimated Patrick. When I described seeing Mark in Maine, and then the meeting with Kathleen, he reached across the table to grip my hand. "My God, Wynn," he said. "Life is so goddamn wonderful and strange." Then he gave me a curious look. "But why on earth did you never tell me all this?"

Other people had asked me this, but with Patrick I had an answer.

"I was afraid you would despise me if you knew what I'd done."

"*Despise you.* Jesus, Wynn." He shook his head. "What kind of monster did you take me for? Was I really such an arrogant bastard? You should have told me everything."

"What we had was so perfect, Patrick. I couldn't risk it."

"If you couldn't tell me this, then what we had wasn't perfect. It was unreal. It was a dream."

We sat and looked at each other, and I knew there was truth in what he said. "We were so young," I said. "We were so in love. I couldn't stand the thought that you might condemn me."

"You never gave me a chance."

"I think it was just that I hated myself so much." The memory of those last days in New York, when I lived in a cold fog of pain, nearly choked me. "I don't know if I can ever make it clear to anyone else how I felt, how sure I was, how terrified. How worthless my whole life seemed. Now everything looks so *lucid*, Patrick. But then—I was crazy."

"You were," he said. "That's exactly right." He squeezed my hand. "All these years, Wynn," he said, and shook his head. "It was very hard for me. Thank God I had my work. I've worked like a beast, like a madman. That was one of the reasons my marriage failed. But otherwise, I don't know how I could have gotten through my life."

Eventually he asked me about my life in Boston, my marriage. I told him my divorce would be final in September, and he looked down at my hands, touched my wedding-ring finger where there was still a mark. "You were married a long time."

"Yes. It was a long mistake." I told him about the trip to Mexico, and the moment in the courtyard. I touched the beads at my neck. "He wasn't happy either. He was seeing someone else by then. So when we got home from Mexico, I told him I wanted a divorce."

"Why then?"

"Because it took me that long to figure out that I had only married him because I couldn't have you."

"Wynn."

I looked down at our clasped hands. I said, "Patrick, I'm so glad to see you. You can't imagine."

We stayed there until the place closed. Patrick said he drank a little now, on special occasions, but neither of us had really drunk much of the champagne. We walked down the familiar stony streets to the building on Mercer, near Grand, where Patrick had a studio on the ground floor and an apartment at the top. We took a freight elevator up six floors. His place was large, stark, nearly empty, with a view east over the rooftops of Chinatown and Little Italy on one side, west to the darkly gleaming Hudson on the other. His dogs, Dougal and Spark, black Labradors, came to greet us, and sniffed my shoes suspiciously before they decided to lick my hand.

Patrick fed the dogs, and we took them out and around the block, and then we went back upstairs and stood before the huge bank of windows in his living room, looking out at the river. Behind us, in the kitchen, the dogs noisily slurped water from their bowls.

"I've had women, you know," Patrick said, after a moment. "These years that I've been alone. I haven't been celibate."

"I wouldn't have expected you to."

"I tried to fall in love with some of them. I had good times, I got to know some great people, but I did not succeed. I couldn't do it. And I didn't really want to, I think. Didn't want to put myself through it again. I had my dogs, my friends. I always had my work. Sometimes it seemed like enough."

There was a silence. I could hear one of the dogs grunt as he lay down somewhere. Then, outside, a car alarm whooped once. I heard my own pulse beating in my head. The room was lit only by the faint city glow from the windows. In that dimness, Patrick's lean face was beautiful, his gaze was intense, his golden eyes were full of heat. He drew me close to him.

"Will you stay with me tonight?"

My heart turned over. "If you want me."

"I want you."

"How can you want me?"

"Let me worry about that. I want you. I've always wanted you."

I said, "I thought I could let this go, Patrick. I thought I could come to New York and see you and that would be enough. I have so much in my life. I told myself I didn't need you in it, too. But that's not the way I feel now."

"How do you feel now?"

"I want to get it all back. What we had together. Do you think that can happen?"

It took him a minute to answer. I could feel his breath in my hair. I waited, remembering how the story of his despair had poured out almost against his will, and how his anger had flared up. We had talked for hours, and yet I think we both knew there were things unsaid, maybe things that could never be said.

Finally, he answered, "I don't know. Maybe it's not worth getting back. But maybe we'll find something better." He kissed me then, gently, and said, "This is the easy part, Wynn. Tonight. Afterward, who knows? At least, we can try. We can get to know each other again."

I ran my palm along the familiar planes of his cheek, his jaw, and touched his lips with my fingers. "I never stopped loving you, Patrick. Not for a moment. For what that's worth."

"It's worth something."

"I wish I could go back. Just rewind the tape and make it all different."

"You've got to let it go," he said. "Give it up, love. You were young and foolish, you were badly wounded, and you hurt me, too. But it was a long time ago. Thank God you've got your daughter back. You've been given a second chance. We both have. My God, Wynn. This is an amazing thing—this is an amazing day." He put his arms around me. I could feel his smile against my cheek. "Boofinka, wheemara, Wynnooka?"

I buried my face in his shoulder. "Feek," I said softly. "Humprammi."

We began to laugh, and suddenly everything was very simple, we were nineteen again, we were crazy for each other, and we collapsed onto the bed and began kissing, tearing at each other's clothes. We stayed awake making love until dawn, and then when the sky turned pink and the sun began to illuminate the rooftops and the water tanks and the river, we fell asleep, with Dougal and Spark snoring on the floor beside the bed.

• • •

Kathleen and Nick were married that summer. For a wedding present—in addition to a large check—I gave them a framed print of my mother's photograph of the doe and her fawn. The wedding was held in the Erlings' garden on a perfect day, warm and dry—the kind of day I remembered when I thought of the Maine summers of my childhood. The garden was dense with flowers, filled with friends and the two families' huge trove of relatives: It astonished me that anyone could know so many people.

Annie had told nearly everyone the story of how they found me, and I was treated like a cross between a beloved long-lost relative and a possibly scandalous curiosity. But people were very kind, even Annie's elderly parents, whom she had warned me might be slow to warm up. Mark's mother was too frail to make the trip from Florida; I was sorry, but a little relieved, too. I don't know what she would have thought of my role in the ceremony. An improvised aisle was made down a garden path, and Annie and I accompanied Kathleen, each of us holding an arm, to the gazebo where Mark and Nick stood with the attendants, grinning at the three of us. Two of Kathleen's friends sang a glorious excerpt from a Bach cantata. It was the most joyful wedding I have ever attended—except maybe for my own.

I continued to see Patrick. The Friday afternoon train from Boston to New York became a way of life. I wish I could say that love immediately conquered all, and that we fell right back into our old relationship, but that's not the way it went. Some of those weekends were hell. All I wanted, ever, was for us to be together again, but Patrick wasn't so sure. He had been alone a long time, he'd spent years doggedly forgetting me, doing his best to keep me out of his life. It wasn't easy for him to let me in again.

We discussed it endlessly, we argued, he gave me absurd little loyalty tests, I became sullen, he became angry, his anger terrified me. Separately and together, we wept. Once I slammed out of his apartment and sat in Penn Station in the middle of the night waiting for the early morning train back home. We didn't speak for a week, and when we did he said it was all too hard, relationships were more trouble than they were worth, love wasn't enough. I said he was being cruel, punishing me, being as judgmental and inflexible as he'd been eighteen years ago. *You drove me away,* I accused him. *You're a madwoman,* he said. The next morning he was on my doorstep with an armful of yellow roses.

One weekend we borrowed someone's summer place on Long Island, and I spent three days reading thrillers on the deck while Patrick took long walks and watched the Yankees and the Red Sox on TV—both of us too sick of the subject, sick of our troubles, to talk at all. Another time, Patrick called me in Boston minutes before I left for the train and said don't come, please, he needed a weekend off, he couldn't face it, he had to have a rest.

And of course he was still an obsessive workaholic, worse than ever, and I knew I had to learn all over again that his involvement in his work wasn't a rejection of me.

To complicate things, I had begun to paint again, too. The long-planned painting of Hannah and Jay in the garden was a failure, but I started it again, working on a larger canvas, making it harder for myself, forcing myself to deal with the problems of scale and composition as if I were a teacher devising devilish assignments. The second painting was better. I showed it to Patrick one weekend when he drove up Boston, and he said, "There's something here that used to be missing." He looked at a long time, and when he said, finally, "I think this is really good, Wynn," I realized he had never actually said those words to me before. He had encouraged me, said he believed in my ability, urged me to keep working, but he had never praised one of my paintings. His words meant everything to me. I began to paint furiously, and maybe half the work I did during that time was pleasing to me. I started to think that maybe I was a painter after all, that life was returning to a part of me that had been numb. When I was working, I could hear my mother's voice: *You're a painter, Wynn.* She must have said that on a hundred different occasions, and for the first time I felt that she was right: That was exactly what I was. Painting, I began to like myself.

But of course, on weekends when I went to New York I had to leave what I was doing, and Patrick had to do the same when he came to see me, and this didn't make either one of us happy.

Then there was Uncle Austin. We had agreed not to tell him the whole, long complicated story, but Patrick had called him and said I had returned, we had resolved our old misunderstanding, we were trying to make a go of things again.

We drove up to see him; it was horrible. Uncle Austin's anger was as fresh as it had been fifteen years before. He wouldn't look me in the eye, and his scorn was almost palpable, something he seemed to take a fierce pleasure in. I could tell that Patrick's obvious affection for me was incomprehensible to him and that it lost Patrick some of his uncle's respect. The three of us ate pizza and drank beer together, but nothing changed: Uncle Austin still had no use for me. None of us talked much, and Patrick and I left after dinner, driving back to the city in a glum silence.

I didn't ever want to go back, but Patrick said we had to. "It's important to me," he said. "And it's important to you, too, Wynn. Admit it, you're fond of the old bird." He pulled me into his arms, kissed me, smiling. "And he loves you, too, somewhere down there buried under everything else. You know he does. Come on—we're going to win him over if it kills us all."

Patrick's persistence paid off. On our next visit, things were a little easier, and the third time we drove up to see him, Uncle Austin had made a pot of pork and beans and bought an ice-cream cake from the supermarket. He told us stories during dinner, just as he used to, about his crazy relatives back in Ireland: his cousin Mary's husband, Tim, had gone into hock to buy a ridiculous red sports car, Mary's daughter's boyfriend the out-of-work actor had taken a job as a stripper in a gay bar, cousin Arthur had been thrown out of the pub three times in one week. At first, he addressed everything to Patrick, doing his best to ignore me, but we all ended up laughing a lot, and Uncle Austin invited us to stay overnight up in Patrick's old room where I lay in Patrick's arms after his uncle went to bed. "We've worn him down," he murmured to me. "It's going be okay."

The next day, before we left, I sat with Uncle Austin for a while on the front porch while Patrick took the dogs out for a run. I told him how glad I was to see him, how sorry I was that we had all been estranged for so long, how I had missed him, missed Patrick, how I hoped we could all be friends again.

Uncle Austin didn't say anything for a long moment. He looked older now, more frail; his hair was still thick and wavy, but he had arthritis in his knees and his eyes were clouded. When he looked at me there was wariness where there used to be a twinkle. Finally he said, "This is hard for me, Wynn."

"I know."

"I'm an old man, and it ain't easy to change your mind when you're my age."

He got up, painfully, and stood by the porch railing, his back to me, looking out over the field where, in the distance, we could see Spark running full speed, barking, with Patrick and Dougal behind him. Uncle Austin watched them cross the field, and then he said, "Don't ever do that again. Don't take up with him if you're going to let him down. Don't make me start hating you again."

"I won't," I said in a small voice. "I love him, Uncle Austin."

"Love." He turned back to watch Patrick with the dogs. "You loved him then, too, didn't you?"

I cried all the way home.

• • •

Thank God for sex, Patrick and I used to say: Our lovemaking was always good, but at times it was also a peacemaker, a way to communicate, a consolation, a bribe, an incentive, a sleeping pill, a reward.

And we loved each other: That was what was always clear, even in the midst of our worst turmoil, our stupid quarrels and justifiable anxieties. What we'd felt in our twenties was even stronger in our forties; it was just infinitely more complicated, and sometimes we almost forgot it.

There was a day—one we'll both always remember—when he and I were feeling wrecked after a long, harrowing discussion about trust and commitment and the difficulties of merging our lives. It was a warm Sunday in late summer. We had gone out for lunch but barely touched our food, both of us I think feeling tired and a little hopeless. There were still hours until my train, and I sat across from him, half reading the paper, half trying to think of an excuse to leave early.

Then Patrick said, "Remember your old bicycle, that I fixed that first time we went to Maine?"

"My old rattletrap Schwinn?" I laughed. "Sure. I got that bike for my tenth birthday, and I loved it as much as I loved my cats."

"How long since you've been on a bike?"

I thought about it. "Since just about then, Patrick. Come to think of it, maybe when I rode it down the driveway after you fixed the brakes was the last time."

"Me, too." He jumped up and said, "It's been too long. Let's rent bikes and go for a ride."

He paid the check and we walked over to Lafayette Street to a bike shop located in the building next door to our old loft. I looked up at the fourth-floor windows, remembering a hundred things. "Patrick." I pointed, but he refused to look. "That's not a place I have much nostalgia for, Wynn," he said, and went into the shop to see about the rentals.

I stood in the street, stricken, and when he came out with two bicycles his face was stony.

But we both cheered up when we got going. Even in the city traffic, it felt good to be riding a bike. We turned down Spring Street, heading for the path along the river, and when we stopped at a red light at Wooster, Patrick pulled up beside me and we smiled at each other.

"Isn't this great?"

"I feel like a kid."

"You look like a kid. You look like you did that weekend in Maine," he said, and leaned over to kiss me.

We rode south on the path along the Hudson in the midst of a cheerful crowd of Rollerbladers, bicyclists, walkers, people wheeling babies in strollers. There were sailboats on the water, and a red-and-white sightseeing boat in the distance. New Jersey glittered, baking in the sun. We went to Battery Park and around the tip of Manhattan to the Brooklyn Bridge. We rode over it to Brooklyn Heights and stopped on Montague Street to buy pretzels and cold drinks from a cart. Then we walked our bikes over to the Promenade and flopped down on a bench.

We sat there in silence, holding hands. I was tired and sore, but the ride had sweated all the bitterness out of me. It was just beginning to get dark, a sunset starting over the World Trade Center, the sky turning rosy. I didn't know exactly what time it was, whether I had missed my train or not. I didn't care. I was so glad to be with Patrick, nothing else mattered. I leaned my head on his shoulder.

"Wynn," he said.

"Mmm." I was half-asleep.

"I've been thinking. These weekends are killing me. Me commuting up there, you coming down here, everything revolving around the train, or what the traffic is like on I-95. It's not a healthy way to live—I don't think I can take it any more."

I raised my head and looked at him, my heart pounding. "What does that mean?" I dreaded hearing his answer, but I was ready for it. I was ready to fight. I had no intention of letting him go again. But, to put it bluntly, he owed me one. I knew that if he wanted to be gone, there was no way I could hold him. "What are you saying?"

"I'm saying I don't want you to leave me."

"I'm not going to leave you, Patrick."

"I mean ever. I mean Sunday nights, Monday mornings." He put his arms around me. "I guess I'm saying let's get married. Let's quit talking about everything and just do it. Now. Soon."

We were married six weeks later on his rooftop terrace. Patrick wore a dashing white suit, I wore a silk dress that matched my turquoise beads. A goldsmith friend of Patrick's made rings for us. The Italian restaurant on our corner catered. It began to rain right after the ceremony, and we had to grab everything and dash inside, but it didn't matter. There weren't many of us, but nearly everyone we loved was there—Kathleen and Nick, Mark and Annie, Henry and Suzanne, Patrick's old pals Clem and Richie from art school with their wives, his good friend Wayne who has been his assistant for all these years, Santo and Doug, a few friends of mine from Boston. Our old pals Gwen and Andrew came from San Francisco. Uncle Austin traveled down on the train, almost unrecognizable in a suit and looking reluctantly pleased. Marietta flew in with her husband, Gregory, the winemaker, on his private plane. Hannah and Jay drove up from the Cape bringing flowers from their garden.

Kathleen stood beside me as I had stood beside her, and when the ceremony was over, first I kissed my husband, and then I kissed my daughter.

Only Rachel and Will couldn't come, but after the wedding Patrick and I flew to London for a week; it was Patrick's first real vacation since his long-ago trip to Mexico. We stayed with them and their children for a few days at their house in Chelsea, off the King's Road. It seemed fitting to have a honeymoon in the city where I had fled to escape my sorrows. We visited St. Clement's, and Patrick's gallery on Blenheim Crescent, and the pub where I learned to play darts—how charmed all my old haunts seemed now, suffused with happiness—and we went to the zoo and saw the lions, but they refused to roar while we were there.

"You're an amazing woman," Patrick said. "You have even tamed the wild beasts."

We stood there on the grass with our bag of popcorn, kissing like teenagers.

• • •

We live together, Patrick and I, in what I think of as passionate contentment. It has been hard-won. We still have rough times, when the old resentments and failures of trust return; I never, ever take what we have for granted. I find myself stunned sometimes by the simple happiness of a normal life. But, just as I'm learning, at last, to paint in a way that satisfies me, I think I'm also learning what happiness is made of. It's not crazy euphoria, and it's not an impossible ideal, and it's not self-sacrifice. It's just this, the days passing, work being done, quiet affection that grows and becomes a habit. It's a framed photograph on a wall, it's a particular shade of ochre, it's a dog asleep under a table, a hunk of rusted metal, a box of old toys addressed to Portland, Maine. It's lying in my husband's arms at the end of a full day—tired, hopeful, alive.

Sometimes I have a need for my daughter that can't be satisfied with phone calls or letters or visits. Patrick and I talk sometimes about moving to Maine, maybe in a year or so. We'd keep an apartment here in the city, but pack up most of our goods, our work, Dougal and Spark, our double lifetimes of memories, and head for those cold mountains and pine forests, maybe up near Sebago Lake, where Mark says we can probably find a few acres, and Patrick can build the giant factory of a studio that he craves, and Kathleen and I can make up for the lost years.

• • •

One of the first things I did when I returned to New York was to lug my portable easel to Cornelia Street in the Village, to my grandmother's old building. The candle shop was gone, replaced by a Moroccan restaurant. Anna Rosa's windows were curtained in white, and the name on the doorbell was now BRADDOCK. As I stood there, a red tourist bus came down the street, and I could hear the loudspeaker giving the history of the neighborhood, something about Cornelia Street in the twenties, the jazz club on the corner.

I set up my easel. Except for the details, the building was unchanged. I had no trouble remembering it as it had been forty years ago, when my father had lifted me up so I could ring the bell. "It's us, Anna Rosa!" I would cry, and she would call "*Us?* Who on earth is *us*? A pack of wild dogs?" and buzz us in. I smiled, recalling a winter day long ago, one of our Christmas visits, when my parents and I had been out somewhere, at a museum, most likely, or ice-skating at Rockefeller Center, and we were returning to my grandmother's place at dusk. The street was magical then, the street-lights golden, Christmas carols piped from some store or other, my parents on either side of me holding my hands. I remember my mother looking up at my grandmother's windows and then bending down to hug me, holding me tight, kissing my cheek. "Remember this, sweetie," she said. "Don't forget one single thing. This is the way life should be. Remember it forever."

Her words came back to me while I painted. The years fell away, and the rest of the street, the passersby and the cars, the sirens and car alarms, the noise of the traffic over on Sixth Avenue, the people who stopped to ask me questions. I painted all day; toward evening I stepped back from my easel and looked at what I had done. And there it was: my grandmother's apartment building in all its homely glory, the light falling as I remembered it, the melancholy beauty of the scene intact. There were no people in the painting, but somehow they were all present: my grandmother with her arms outstretched, my father's tall presence beside me, and my mother with her face alight, telling me to remember it all, remember everything, keep it forever.

• • •

And so who am I now?

I am Wynn Tynan, the wife of Patrick Foss. I'm the mother of Kathleen Erling Hayes, and—soon—grandmother of the baby she and Nick are expecting. I still teach, and I hope I always will—at the moment, I work a couple of days a week at a school in the Village, teaching painting to children with behavioral problems. I live with my husband on Mercer Street, and I work at my paintings in a corner of his mammoth studio downstairs on the first floor. We're not a logical pair of artists to share a space: a sculptor who works noisily, on a grand scale, often with a team of assistants, welding enormous chunks of metal together, making pieces that have to be lifted on cranes and taken out on a truck—and a rather demure oil painter whose largest work has been, perhaps, two feet by three.

When the dust and the din drive me crazy, I retreat upstairs or take the dogs out for a walk. But Patrick doesn't like to be away from me, even while we work, and I love it that I can look up from my canvas and see my husband across the room. I was right, he's no longer working in copper and steel, now he's combining steel with wood, welding the pieces of metal together, then incorporating smooth wooden shapes to create large, complex forms that suggest monolithic figures, gods or apes, or whatever the beholder wishes them to be. *An artist's mission is to compel us to love life in all its countless and inexhaustible manifestations.* That is what he still believes, and that's what his work says to anyone who looks at it.

Who am I? It's the last, the most important question, the one with the best answer, and now that I've written it all down, it has come clearer—just as you said it would, Kathleen. I'm a woman who took a wrong turn, then another—an endless highway of them, God knows—and who, miraculously, found her way back home. I'm a woman who has taught herself how to ask questions, and to answer them as honestly as she can, and to forgive herself when she gets them wrong, and to forgive the past when it threatens to take over. I had to learn all that, but I think most of all I had to teach myself to separate love from grief, and to believe that, while it's true that sorrow can reveal to us who we are, sometimes happiness can, too.

# Epilogue

Molly Erling Hayes
Born April 3, 1999
This story is for your mother—
and for you, Molly,
with love.

www.ingramcontent.com/pod-product-compliance
Ingram Content Group UK Ltd.
Pitfield, Milton Keynes, MK11 3LW, UK
UKHW022303280225
455674UK00001B/152